CONFESSIONS IN WHISPERS

Chimia Y. Hill-Burton

This is a work of fiction. Names, characters, businesses, places, events, and incidents are either the products of the author's imagination or used in a fictitious manner. Any resemblance to actual persons, living or dead, or actual events is purely coincidental.

Copyright © 2012 and 2020 by CHIMIA Y. Hill-Burton
All rights reserved. This book or any portion thereof may not be reproduced or used in any manner whatsoever
without the express written permission of the publisher except for the use of brief quotations in a book review.
Printed in the United States of America
First Printing, 2015
ISBN-13:
978-1500313722

ISBN-10:
1500313726

Acknowledgements

All my life ever since I was a child, I have loved to write. From poems, figurative writings, short stories to novels, my passion for writing flourished over the years. I felt my words could speak to the souls and hearts of the world. Through my stories I would express the love, pain, struggle, courage, and spirit of the human heart. This novel is humbly dedicated to all the special people in my life, who have always inspired, encouraged, and illuminated my creative talent and passion for writing.

Love Always

Chimia Hill-Burton

Table of Contents

The Miles Sisters	1
Opposites of	45
Sanity	76
Secrets of an Adopted Son	126
The Color of Red	178
Switching Shadows	212
The Devoted Daughter	239
Tangible Justice	270
Within Dreams	299
Torturous Addiction	357

Chimia P. Hill-Burton

Confession 1

The Miles Sisters

It was a windy night when the police came to the door and announced that my father had died that night. I was sixteen years old, and my little sister was fourteen. My name is Trina Miles, and it was the night my father died. It changed my life. The police did not explain how he died but I already knew. My little sister Erica and I had been trained for years on talking to the police. You see my father had always told us that a day or night would come when he would be gone, and the police would ask us a whole lot of questions.

The night my father died he was out doing "special work." Erica and I knew that night after night that daddy would go out in search of his perfect wife, Vivian. She was a woman he had seen in his dreams; he had sexual fantasies about her and would leave the house searching for her or her prototype. She

Confessions in Whispers

was-about five-foot and weighed about hundred-fifty-seven lbs.; she had black shoulder length hair. Daddy would always say she knew what to say to him to make him feel better and how to touch him.

   The police officers from Carol Heights Police Department came to our house to collect Erica and I, then took us to the police station. We were separated into two rooms, and it took about an hour because Erica said she did not want to leave me. I had to explain that I was not going to be gone long. It took about an hour to insure her that I would be back. In the conference room I sat in an office chair closest to the door, looking around I could see a dim light swallowing the whole room.

   The room was of medium size and there was one window that only let in light but would not let any escape. I looked in front of me and there was a rectangular desk with a microphone on it and a yellow legal pad. I crossed my arms and thought about my sister in the other room. I could see her face; she would be folding her arms and rolling her neck at the officers as they tried to ask her questions about daddy. She would cry next because she was scared and whine that she wanted to see me.

As I got lost in thought about my sister Erica, the detective came in, she was a nice-looking white lady with short brown hair whisked back from her forehead. She wore a grayish suit with black medium high heels. She broke my concentration when she pulled out the fold out chair and said casually "That's my seat." I just looked at her, smiled, and said, "I got here first."

She introduced herself, "I am Detective Sharon Mons; you can call me Sharon if you want, ok?"

I sat up in my chair., "Ok Sharon, what in the hell do you want?"

She had a vanilla folder under one arm, took a seat in front of me and opened the folder. It contained pictures of younger girls about my age and some slightly older than me.

"Trina, do you have any idea who these girls are?"

I looked at the photos and shrugged my shoulders. "No, I do not know who they are? Who are they?"

Confessions in Whispers

Detective Mons looked at me and said in a stern voice, "These are pictures of young women and girls who were raped by your father."

I pretended to be shocked as I shoved the photos back at her exclaiming, "NO! That's a lie, my daddy would never do anything like that!"

Detective Mons reached over the table and attempted to calm me down. "It's ok Trina, I know that you did not know what your father was doing, but I needed to let you know because I am going to explain what happened to him."

I looked at her in a fake concerned way and said in a half laughing and half crying voice. "Ok. I will listen."

Detective Mons then started to tell me the story of my father Andrew Vincent Miles.

She said that a long time ago some young women and girls went missing for seven days at a time; some were alive when they were found and others were not so lucky, one was a bright light skin girl by the name of Angela Heart. She was sixteen when she was kidnapped from her high school in late November.

She was very pretty and smart. I was told that my daddy kept her for seven days in a basement of some sort and she was never released after being brutally raped, they found her body lying on the front porch of her parents' home with her neck slashed opened.

I asked the detective, "How do you know it was my father who did this?"

Detective Mons continued that Angela was pregnant later that year and the coroner believed that it was her rapist's child. Sharon said that Angela had seen a man at her window a few times and gave a description on the man and it fit my daddy to a T. Sharon also said it was her first case as a Detective, and that she had spoken to Angela before she suddenly disappeared.

I rolled my eyes and sighed, "Are you sure it was my dad?"

Detective Mons stared at me. "Yes, Trina, we are sure. Tonight, he was stalking a young seventeen-year-old in a neighborhood about twenty miles from your house. The young girl was Alisha Scott, she called the police when she realized there was a black male standing at her window staring at her."

Yeah, that sounded like dad alright, the lady's man.

"Then what happened?" I asked.

Detective Mons continued reading a report that the police found a black male standing at six foot two inches, about one hundred eighty-seven lbs. with brown eyes and dark brown hair, walking into a strip club.

He was slightly drunk at the bar when the police asked him to step outside and talk with them. The man did as he was told, the police asked him what he was doing on Terry St, the same street that Alisha Scott lived on. He said that he was taking a walk. The police asked the man his name and the man replied that his name was Andrew Miles and presented the police officers with a photo ID.

The police asked Mr. Miles what he was doing on Terry St, Mr. Miles got upset and said he was going home. The officer asked where his car was, and Mr. Miles pointed at a black Ford Camry. The officers advised Mr. Miles that he should not drive if he was still intoxicated. Mr. Miles said that he only had a few and that he was fine.

The officer asked Mr. Miles if he would submit to a breath test. Mr. Miles nodded and said, "Sure, I can do that if that will make you feel better."

The officer gave Mr. Miles that breath test and Mr. Miles passed. The officer was about to let Mr. Miles go when a man shouting for the police came running down the street with his daughter, Alisha Scott. As Alisha came closer, she screamed, "That's him, daddy! That's the man that was staring at me through my window!"

The officer went to draw his gun at Mr. Miles only to realize that Mr. Miles had already jumped in his car and was trying to speed off. The officers there jumped into their vehicles and attempted to block Mr. Miles, but Mr. Miles rammed through and continued Terry Street.

The officers chased Mr. Miles for about ten miles until they rammed his car into a near ditch. They asked Mr. Miles to step out of the car and put his hands up. Mr. Miles shot at the officers and the officers shot back shooting Mr. Miles in the chest and killing him instantly.

I just sat there numb to those facts that were being given to me about my daddy. I tried to calm myself, tried to pace my answers but my anger was getting the best of me, I was not taking this bullshit I was hearing about my father. I was about to give this bitch a piece of my mind when I heard Erica screaming.

I jumped up from the chair screaming, "I want to see my sister!"

Detective Mons looked at me and touched my shoulder. "Calm down Trina, she is ok."

I yanked my shoulder from her grasp, turned, looked into her light brown eyes.,

"Keep your hands off of me, let me see my sister," I said. Detective Mons sighed heavily., "Fine."

She led me down the hall to a room where I could see my sister, Erica having a fit, which is pretty immature for a fourteen-year-old, but Erica was not that normal anyway.

She caught a glimpse of me and ran for the door as the male officer tried to grab her. I opened the door and yelled at him, "YOU BETTER NOT TOUCH HER!"

The male officer showed me his arm which had a pretty bad bite on it and shouted, "That little bitch bit me."

I looked at him and said, "That bitch that you are referring to is my little sister and she hates to be touched."

Detective Mons turned to the male officer and said, "Lake, what happened?"

Officer Lake explained that he was talking to Erica, and she saw the pictures and started to laugh. She pointed at a girl named Angela Heart, and pounded on the picture.

Detective Mons turned and looked at me and asked, "Does she know Angela?"

I could have kicked Erica's ass right there and then! She was always the bold one.

I turned to Detective Mons, "No, she doesn't, she has a medical condition she has different emotions to everyone else, and she laughs at things that are inappropriate."

Confessions in Whispers

Detective Mons seemed to be trying to figure me out, but I knew by the sigh and a head shake from her she would never be able to.

We were now wards of the court and sent to a group home thirty miles from our house. Erica hated it there; I could say it was not a picnic for me either. We lived in a moderate middle-class house with about four other kids who were taken from their homes because of an abuse or their behavior. Our group home elders were Jackie and Mark Dustson.

A white couple with one child of their own, eighteen-years-old, an average teenager with a huge attitude problem. His mother, Jackie would always put him in charge of us when she went to the store, or out of town.

The other kids that were there were Julie Patterson, she was a thirteen-year-old white girl, who had been taken from her mother who was a drug addict, and who had a history of temper tantrums and had been sexually abused by her mother's dealer since she was nine years old. She was incredibly open to sex and would sleep with anyone who asked her.

Next, was a seventeen-year-old black boy named Drew, I can never remember his last name because he changes it ever few days. No one at the house knew his real name, all I can say is that he had a terrible temper and was always waiting for his mother to come and get him. Some fantasy that he kept giving himself; rumor has it that his mother left because her new boyfriend did not want any children.

The third was a fourteen-year-old white boy whose name was Nel. Nel was just a lost soul. I guess he is normal but not normal he believes that the world is nothing more than a rollercoaster ride waiting to end. He was a weed head, he thought like he was thirty-four years old, always preparing for his ultimate future as a millionaire.

And last in this group home of madness was a sixteen-year-old black girl name Ayers. She is not lost or found in my eyes. She was an overly depressed person who hated the world because she felt alone. This was only due to the fact that she

Confessions in Whispers

had been in foster care since she was five-year-old, and her mother did not want her.

Everyone in the house looked at Erica and I, you could say we were the odd ones, compared to their lives, my life and my sister's life was a fairy tale.

Erica and I were separated into different rooms in the beginning but after two fights with her roommate Julie, Mrs. Dustson found it better she shares a room with me. Life at the group home was no picnic, too many damn kids being shipped in and out like FedEx packages.

Then there was the secret sexual affair between Ayers and the Dustson's son Dylan. I realized it one night when I could not sleep thinking about daddy. I was walking in the house as I normally did when I heard a stifled noise coming from the laundry room. I peeked inside and there they were, going at it like rabbits. I closed the door and walked back to my room. The little secret affair went on until Ayres became pregnant.

The Dustson's did not condone unwed mothers in their house and threatened to kick Ayres out until Dylan came clean that it was his baby. The look on the Dustson's face was priceless; they kicked Ayres and Dylan out that night which I thought was kinda harsh due to the fact they were about to be grandparents.

Erica and I lived at the Dustson's house for about a year; within that year Erica being Erica, started up on her fun and games. She claimed she was bored with a normal life. I could not blame her though it had been a while since we had any fun and so around springtime, Erica found a friend in the neighborhood named Holly.

She was a pretty twelve-year- old girl with lovely brown hair and precious eyes. Erica felt it was time to have some real fun, so she became friends with Holly, and they would always go and play in Holly's basement and the game was always the same – kidnapped.

Erica would pretend to kidnap Holly and tie her up and abuse her. The abuse started out small. Erica always did like to take her time when it came to having fun, and she had always been the bold one. Once, Erica tied Holly to a chair and burned

Confessions in Whispers

her with a lighter, not very visible but the pain was enough for little Holly, and she would whimper and cry that it hurt and that they should stop. I would always advise my little sister that we were not at home anymore and that her "victim" might tell on her one day.

Erica would just cock her head to the side smile and always say, "If she does, I will just have to kill her."

Well, that day would come on a cold fall night. I was in my room doing my homework wishing daddy were here when Erica ran into the room looking like she had seen a ghost.

"What's wrong?" I asked.

Erica closed the door behind her and said very calmly, "I killed her."

I raised an eyebrow, rolled my eyes, and said, "How?" Erica would then tell me in detail about her first kill.

She said that she asked Holly to play in the woods that afternoon with her. Erica explained that one day when she was really bored, she went out into the woods by herself and found this wood cabin that looked abandoned. She thought that it would be a perfect place to play and torture someone.

I became upset and said, "You know what daddy said about going off on your own, I do not ever want to hear that you went somewhere like that without me coming with you, do you understand!"

Erica pouted and said, "It was going to be a surprise for you, but she wouldn't wait for me to come and get you, I'm sorry."

I couldn't stay mad at Erica, she was going to let me in on the fun, but she was right; victims just don't wait so I motioned for her to continue.

I realized as Erica went on with her story that Holly adored my sister and said yes naturally to go and play with her. They went into the woods till they came to the cabin that had been abandoned. Inside Holly got scared and asked to go back home, but Erica would not let her.

She started to tell a story about one of dad's victims who had been hungry and cold for days. I listened very carefully to what my little sister had to say, and she smiled at her accomplishment. She

Confessions in Whispers

continued saying that Holly started to scream for help but by now it was too late. She tried to explain to Holly that she only had to wait for me to arrive, and then they could play, but Holly kept screaming and begging to leave.

This irritated Erica. She said I had to get her to stop screaming before someone really heard her, so she stripped Holly naked and tied her to a pole in the house. Erica said she couldn't do any of the thing's daddy had done but felt that this self-righteous bitch needed to be taught a lesson. She beat Holly with a large stick knocking "Little Miss Goody Two Shoes" unconscious.

She said she thought about the bitch who had ratted out daddy and said that this bitch would pay for the police taking our father from us. She took out of her back pocket some white gloves, she smiled at me, and said "Daddy always said be careful with evidence."

I smiled at that joyful memory. Erica grabbed Holly by her hair and started to slam her head against the pole. Thump Thump, she banged Holly's head until she could see the blood coming out of the back on her head, then she said she got excited and hit Holly's head harder and harder until she saw color leave Holly's face. Erica said she liked Holly, but the bitch would never listen, and would have made a horrible wife.

After Erica had finished telling me the story I asked, "Who are you going to blame this on, my bold little sister?"

She smiled and said, "On a man of course, there was an article in a newspaper two days ago about a child molester that was molesting and killing little girls in the area. I simply called Holly on the phone and asked her to come play with me, her mother will be worried that the child molester had gotten her."

I thought about it and said, "Nice, but did you molest Holly?"

Erica's smile was huge and with bright white teeth showing she said, "Yes, I did."

It was like clockwork, the police came over to the house and informed us that little Holly had been kidnapped, raped and murdered. Everyone was genuinely shocked, but Erica and I pretended to

Confessions in Whispers

be. My sister the little actress cried in Holly's mother's arms that her dear friend was gone. Everything was going well till I saw Detective Mons, "Hello girls."

I rolled my eyes at the bitch and Erica walked away with Holly's mother.

Detective Mons asked me did I know the little girl and I told her, "My sister did, they were friends as you can see?"

Detective Mons looked over at my sister who was still putting on a star performance. She tried to ask my sister some questions, but Erica was not talking to the police; she was "Too heartbroken to talk about it."

I went to console Erica when I saw Mrs. Dustson approach Detective Mons, I pretended not to overhear their conversation but was surprised at the news that was being given.

It seemed that Mrs. Dustson was walking by Erica and my room the other night and she overheard Erica mention a murder about a young girl. She told Detective Mons that she only heard that the girl had been locked up and that was it. She also informed her that she feared for the other girls' lives because she felt there was something not quite right about Erica and me. She wanted us removed from her house and if Detective Mons could help her.

I thought to myself that BITCH, how dare she eaves drop on us and then ask the bullshit Detective to help her remove us. I grabbed my sister by the arm gently and held her close, as I whispered in her ear, and to keep on with her performance. I told her how Mrs. Dustson wanted us out and that we should give her a present before we go. Erica looks to Mrs. Dustson and gave her an evil smile before crying in my arms again. Mrs. Dustson did not have time to react but stared at my face which had a smile on it, as she tried to get the Detective's attention.

I lowered my head into my little sister's soft hair. Detective Mons stayed until about nine o'clock that night trying to get Erica to talk to her, but my sister just cried out she did not want to talk about it anymore. Detective Mons then turned to me asking

Confessions in Whispers

me questions about the information she had received that afternoon from Mrs. Dustson.

I looked at the Detective and said, "I have no idea what that woman is talking about, she has been pissed at every black girl ever since her son Dylan left with Ayres, a black girl who lived her and became pregnant by her son."

Detective Mons asked me about that Ayers, and I told her that "Dylan and Ayers had been fucking for a long time right under Mr. and Mrs. Dustson's noses."

Detective Mons scratched her head trying to think if she should believe my story about Dylan and Ayers. She then asked Julie and Nel about Dylan and Ayers, and they confirmed my story. Detective Mons then went back to Mrs. Dustson and asked about the affair that had gone on between her son Dylan and Ayres. Mrs. Duston complained that we were trouble and she wanted us out of the house. Detective Mons informed her that it was up to the family courts to decide replacements for Erica and I and that she would have to file the proper paperwork to remove us.

Mrs. Dustson said she would do that first thing in the morning. Later that night I heard that Mr. Dustson never came home. His cell phone was still at the house and the keys to his car were missing.

The next morning there was a knock on the door, it was the police and with them Detective Mons. She explained to Mrs. Dustson that her husband had been found dead late last night in his car. Mrs. Dustson's screamed and woke the whole house. Everyone but Erica and me, we had been awake packing to leave.

We all came downstairs when Mrs. Dustson saw Erica and me, and she screamed, "What did you do to him?! I know it was you two! What did you do to my husband?!"

She came running at us and tried to get her hands on us, but the police grabbed her. Detective Mons looked at us, we looked at her, and shrugged our shoulders.

Detective Mons asked me, "Trina, where were you last night?" I looked over at Drew and winked at him. Detective Mons just looked at Drew who smiled at her.

Confessions in Whispers

She shook her head, and then asked, "Erica, where were you last night?"

Erica smiled and locked hands with Nel and Julie. Looking frustrated she asked all of us if we had seen Mr. Dustson at all last night?

Drew spoke and said that he saw Mr. Dustson leave late, that there was a young woman in the car, she had shoulder length hair. Mrs. Dustson became terribly upset and ran back into the room screaming, "You liars! All of you! "My husband never cheated on me; he would never do that!"

Drew looked at Mrs. Dustson and said, "You are wrong, he did cheat on you with Ayres, before Dylan told him that he was in love with her."

Mrs. Dustson sank to the floor crying and sobbing, she looked up and saw Erica looking into her eyes, and then she saw the smile slide across her face and a wink from her left eye.

"YOU LITTLE BITCH!" screamed Mrs. Dustson as she grabbed Erica by the hair.

Erica cried out and I ran over to Mrs. Dustson before the police could reach her and slapped her clear across the face.

"You let go of my sister you racist bitch!"

Mrs. Dustson hit the floor and the police ran over to check on her, she had a cut on the side of her face. Detective Mons ordered that everyone calm down and then ordered that the Children Services be called to remove all the children from Mrs. Dustson's home. Everyone was ordered to go upstairs and pack their things; Erica and I already had our things packed but went upstairs anyway. Once we were in our room, I dropped the piece of glass I had in my hand in the trash can, and then wrapped it up and threw it out of the window.

We were all removed from the house; Erica and I were sent to the police station to talk to Detective Mons about Mr. Dustson.

This time we were not separated, Sharon came in and looked at the both of us stating, "I know there is something funny going on here with you two and I AM going to find out what it is!"

Erica lay her head on my shoulder, and I just stared at Sharon and said, "Do you think we liked living there, with a bunch of rejects who never had parents! I hated it!"

Confessions in Whispers

Detective Mons sat down and asked, "Is that why you did it?"

I looked at her and said, "Did what? Oh, you think I killed Mr. Dustson. Did you not take the hint, I was with Drew that night and we fucked?"

She said, "What about you Erica? What were you doing?"

Erica raised her head and said, "Fuck you! I was playing with Julie and Nel, we played checkers and cards all night."

Sharon became really mad and shouted, "You two think you are pretty smart huh, you each have airtight alibis. Everyone covered for you, but you are going to slip and when you do, I am going to put you away for so long you will meet your daddy before you get out!"

I ran blood hot and jumped in Sharon's face and said, "You have NO idea who our father was!"

Erica added, "Don't you dare talk about our dad that way, he was a great man!"

Sharon looked at the expressions on our faces and shook her head, "You have no idea, what kind of a man your father was, he raped young women and girls your age, he kept them in a basement for seven days. He got them pregnant, and then he killed them. That's what you call a Great Man?"

She walked over to the window, looked out, and said in a low voice, "Girls, he hurt people, he hurt innocent girls. Now I know you two may have not known about his actions, he may have been a great dad to you, but he was not a great dad to the rest of the world. He hurt, beat, raped, and abused these girls! Can't you see that?"

Sharon came back and opened her briefcase, taking some pictures out. She threw them on the desk.

"LOOK! Look at what your father the GREAT MAN did!"

Erica picked up one photo and I whispered for her to put it down.

Sharon asked, "What? What is it about this picture that is SOOO funny, Erica! Do you know her?"

Erica looked at her and said, "No, I just think that she is pretty, is all."

Sharon turned to me.

Confessions in Whispers

"No, we did not know what he did, but does that give you the right to discount the father he was to us! He was our dad, we loved him, and I just feel it's unfair for you to keep trying to bash that memory we have of him," I defended my dad and began to cry which made Erica cry as well.

Sharon seemed defeated. "I am sorry girls, I should have been more sensitive, you are right; you didn't know, and it was wrong of me not let you have the memory of your father the way you saw him, a perfect man."

Detective Mons called for the child services to take us away.

*

We were placed in foster care; the courts had discussed separating Erica and me but once the judge saw our reactions, he found it best that we should remain with each other. Our new foster parents were Darrien and Tiffany Meadows.

So, Erica and I now had foster parents. Darrien and Tiffany were a black couple who lived quite nicely in the suburbs. Erica and I liked our new life, it was free from Detective Mons and all the bullshit that surrounded our father. Erica began to calm down and actually made friends, starting to really try and live a normal teenage life. By this time, I was seventeen years old, and Erica was fifteen. Everything seems to fit into place now, I was happy with my high school Green Tree High, I had a cute boyfriend Lee, and everything was good. I was making great grades and really thinking things were turning around for me and Erica. Then, when I least expected, fate came around and danced in our lives again.

   I was a junior now and there was a new girl in our class, Alisha Scott. She was a pretty, light skinned girl with black shoulder length hair; she was the correct height and size and seemed genuinely nice.

   I tried not to stare but could not resist seeing in front of me the bitch that had cost my father his life, she was just his type, and she was the prototype of Vivian. She sat right next to me, and I introduced myself, "Hi, I am Trina Miles, and you are?"

Confessions in Whispers

She turned and said, "I am Alisha Scott, I just moved here."

Alisha and I became friends, how ironic the same girl who had cost me my dad, I become friends with. We hung out together, ate at each other's houses and everything, even our boyfriends were friends, it was a cute little set up. But everyone was not happy about our friendship.

Erica was pissed off about it. She would always remind me that this is the girl that had cost dad his life and was I really going to let her get away with that shit. I explained to Erica that this was all just part of my plan to get back at her. Erica smiled and agreed that she should be handled very carefully, after all, dad had wanted her for our new mother.

Thinking about it, the night we kidnapped Alisha, Erica was right. Dad had picked her for our new mother and if she would have just got with the program, we could have been best of friends. Instead, she ratted daddy out and caused him to die, so now it was her turn. Erica had become quite the little lady and could pull any man she chose.

She chose Alisha's boyfriend Matt. Matt was a light skinned black boy with nice eyes and a killer body, he loved younger girls, rumor had it, so Erica was just his type. She caught him washing his car and talked him into having sex with her at our house.

I set up the video camera in the guest room, and they walked in. I got to it. I taped them in great detail, and then dropped the tape at Alisha's house. She saw it, cried, and called me on the phone. She went on and on about not trusting men after the encounter with a stalker staring at her from her window.

My blood boiled as she gave me the events of my father's death, she said she didn't want them to kill him; just wanted them to make him stop scaring her was all. I almost felt sorry for her.... almost, she had still caused me and Erica our father and no amount of apologizing was going to bring him back, she had to be taught a lesson.

I told her I was taking a day trip over to our dad's warehouse. She asked if she could come along with me. I said yes. I went to pick her up and had my sister jump in with us, and we drove to our dad's warehouse.

The warehouse was an old building that daddy owned, and this was where he housed his girls.

Alisha asked, "What are we doing here?"

I looked at her and said, "I remembered I had something here I had hidden a long time ago and I wanted to get it,"

Alisha shrugged her shoulders and followed Erica and I down the steps into a basement.

Once in the basement Erica saw something that made her laugh. I turned to look, and it was a picture of Angela Heart in a frame on the dresser with a bunch of other pictures.

I looked at the picture and said kindly, "Your mother was a beautiful girl, wasn't she, Erica?"

Erica smiled and said, "Yes, she was, if she had just lived long enough to see how much I looked just like her, huh?"

Alisha looked a little confused. "I thought your mom's name was Tiffany?"

I turned and looked at Alisha and said, "No, her mother's name was Angela Heart, she was a sixteen-year-old girl my father had raped and kept here for seven days, she got pregnant by my daddy, and then she climbed out of here and ran away."

As I explained, Alisha pretty face looked like she was going to faint.

I continued, "Daddy would not just let her go; she was his, his perfect little wife. So, he found her and kidnapped her again, kept her until she had Erica and then he made her raise Erica until she was about eight, then she died."

Alisha swallowed hard, backed into a wall, and asked, "How did she die?"

Erica smiled and stepped in with, "She killed herself with a razor, she said to my daddy she rather be dead than his wife and she killed herself, the bitch!"

Alisha looked around and saw a bed made nicely with a glass of fresh water on the side as if things had been prepared, and then a scary thought entered her mind.

Alisha shouted, "You are going to keep me here, aren't you!"

Confessions in Whispers

I smiled and said, "Yeah, it's called karma, Alisha, when you fuck up someone's life and it comes back to bite you in the ass!"

Alisha started to cry, "What in the hell did I ever do to you?!"

Erica went over to a bench and picked up a picture and handed to her. Alisha took the picture, took one look, and dropped it.

Erica bent down, picked up the picture, turned it towards her, and said in an evil sneer, "You took our daddy from us!"

Alisha looked at me and said, "Trina, I did not know! He scared me; he was at my window staring at me. I had no idea the police were going to shoot him, I swear!"

I said, "You know my mother was one of my father's victims? Her name was Vivian Johnson. She was a beautiful seventeen-year-old black girl, five foot, weighed one hundred fifty-seven lbs. with beautiful shoulder length hair, she loved my father even after the rape and so my birth was even more special to him.

"She unfortunately died when I was eight years old. She had breast cancer. Dad went crazy and returned her to her home, to her family who never knew what happened to her, or about me.

"Dad was lonely and though he had me, he always felt I needed a mother to take care of me as well. So, night after night, he would go out and look for her, his Vivian. In search, he found pretty light skinned Angela Heart, she was sixteen, but she could make a good mother he thought so he kidnapped her, brought her here.

"I helped take care of her while she was pregnant and when she escaped, I helped find her. I believed that daddy deserved to be happy no matter what, so he returned her here and she had my baby sister Erica, but she did not want Erica, or me, or daddy, and she killed herself, she was selfish."

Alisha looked at me and said, "Trina, this is not right, your father did bad things in order to...."

Erica cut her off, "In order to save us! He wanted us to have the best mother and father anyone could have!"

Confessions in Whispers

Alisha sat down on the bed, and I continued, "After Angela's dad continued his searches, most of the girls ended up dead here because they would not co-operate, and dad by this time had started drinking heavily, he would get depressed and upset easily.

"Some of the girls would make it out alive and others never did. Erica and I learned how to kill someone quick, easy, and with less mess. Daddy taught us everything from how to talk to the police and how to get rid of bodies. It was up to us to clean up the really messy scenes like blood, urine, and what not. We were used to it. But then dad fell into deep depression to the point that killing the girl was no good to him, it did not help with his pain."

Erica said, "I know, he was torn up inside."

I then looked at Alisha and said, "You won't be down here long, I say a couple of days tops. We needed closure for our loss, so this is the best way to get that." Erica stated, "I am going to stay with you until then, okay? We are going to have a great time."

Alisha looked at the both of us like we were mad and said, "I am sorry for you guys, but I am not staying here. The police wanted to know about you two, so they set you up; they are outside right now, I'm wired."

Erica looked at Alisha, walked over to her, and ripped open her shirt, yep there it was- a wire. Erica turned to me and said,

"Oh well, so we don't have any place to call home anymore."

She turned, and then pulled out a pipe from behind her and knocked Alisha unconscious. Then she turned to me and said, "Let's go Trina, this bitch ratted us out just like dad. She is glad we do not kill her."

I nodded yeah, as I did, I could hear the police approaching. I jumped up and closed the hatch to the basement and locked it. Erica and I escaped through our secret tunnel. Once outside, we got into a black Camry and drove off.

It would take over nine years for the police to find me, but they did. I was working at a computer

Confessions in Whispers

firm when they came in and arrested me. During those nine years, Erica and I knew well to not to bring any attention to ourselves. Daddy had taught us well. We lived in different hotels around the surrounding areas of daddy's grave. It was easy to lie, cheat, murder our way around those little towns.

Erica could have all the fun she liked. Kidnap a young teenage girl and try to force her to be our new mother, if she refused, kill her without a single thought. Erica and I changed our names too. Erica went under her mother's name, Angela Miles, and I went under my mother's name, Vivian Miles. It all worked out for a while, until Erica got sick.

At first, I had no clue what was wrong with her, but after I took her to the doctor, we found it was cancer. I stayed by my sister's side as long as I could. A year later, I had to bury my sweet sister Erica; she had died of cervical cancer.

I cried my eyes out when she passed, I remember her saying she wanted to be buried next to daddy. I cried alone at the funeral for Erica. It hit me then that Erica and I had always been alone, we had no friends or family to go to and now that I didn't have her, the pain in my mind would never end.

After Erica's death, I became absorbed in my work. When I was arrested, I sat back trying to think of how in the hell did they find me.

*

I was brought into a room with grayish walls and two-fold-out chairs. I sat in the one closest to the door again, then she came in, Detective Sharon Mons, she looked proud of herself.

"Trina Miles, I never thought I would ever catch you but here you are."

I sighed to myself then asked, "How did you find me, Detective?"

Detective Mons smiled as she paced in front of the table and explained, "It wasn't easy, you and your sister almost got away scot free. I ran your names into the computer system and found nothing. I didn't give up; I knew there was something that I must be missing. So, I looked up your mother's name - it was a long shot, but it worked, and that's how I found you."

Confessions in Whispers

I clapped my hands at her, she was actually a surprisingly good detective. She had found me; I never thought she would have made that connection but hey, good shot.

She smiled as me, and then continued with, "I had to find some evidence to have you brought in, so I reviewed what you had told Alisha when you tried to kidnap her. I then remembered the picture Erica couldn't stop laughing at."

I rolled my eyes impatiently saying, "Yea, Yea, what's the charge?"

She sat down and said, "Kidnapping, or do you not remember kidnapping Alisha Scott and taking her to the place where your daddy took his girls, huh?"

I laughed, "She was not there long, she even lived, so what's the big deal huh?"

Sharon looked at me and said, "You are going away for a long time, that's what the big deal is."

I said, "It won't stick, she is not going to testify, she felt sorry for us then, and she still does. You have no case."

Sharon showed me a picture and I just stared at it, shrugging my shoulders. "What, it's Jackie's husband, Mark."

Sharon confirmed it, "You said something so interesting when you were talking to Alisha the night you kidnapped her, you said that your mother was one of your dad's victims who loved him."

I rolled my eyes and shrugged my shoulders again saying,

"Yeah, so what?"

Sharon looked at me with a sly smile as she said, "The night Mark Dustson went missing, you said you were having sex with Drew, right?"

I looked at her like she was crazy and rolled my eyes. "Drew was years ago, what does he have to do with anything?"

Sharon continued, "Well, we found Mark's body in his car twenty miles from his house, he had been drinking, and there was a broken bottle in the car. You cut Jackie Dustson with a piece of that bottle when she grabbed your sister, Erica's hair. I found that piece of the bottle after you left but I could not put the pieces together till later you were the one in the car with Mark Dustson."

By this time, I was tired, tired of running. I no longer had any family, and I was alone. I knew that I would go to prison now. So, if I was going, I might as well tell the whole story.

I looked up at Sharon Mons and said, "I am tired of holding this in; I am going to tell you everything."

Sharon turned on the tape recorder and I began with after Erica was eight.

"After Angela killed herself, I swore I would help daddy through his pain so when I got old enough, about fifteen years old, I saw my father drunk in his room. I walked in. I was wearing one of my mother's old nightgowns and I had made myself to look like her.

I climbed into bed and slept with him. I took away his pain and every time he felt lost and depressed, he would drink, and I would come in his room as his Vivian, always knowing what to say and how to touch him. I continued the whole act until Erica found out it was me.

She threatened to tell dad, if I did it anymore, but I told her that this was for his own good and if he could not find the perfect wife, I would be the perfect wife for him. I stopped helping daddy and he fell into deep depression, and then he saw her, Alisha Scott; she was the right height, weight and everything.

He stalked her for some time, and that was when he went to make his move and was killed. After Holly's death, Mrs. Dustson did not want us there anymore. She even spoke to you about getting rid of us, remember? So, I wanted to get rid of someone she loved so she would know how it felt to be alone. I brought Vivian back out.

Mr. Dustson liked little girls, so it was easy to get him drunk, and have sex with him. I was going to strangle him, but he choked instead on his gum. He broke the bottle in the car, and I took a piece with me as a token. I had it in my hand when I slapped Mrs. Dustson for grabbing my sister.

I threw it away when we were packing to leave. So now that's everything. I did not kill Mark Dustson, he killed himself."

Confessions in Whispers

Sharon turned off the recorder and said, "Damn! You did not kill him, he choked on gum!"

I sighed, "Yes, I would have killed him, but he choked on his gum. I got out of the car, walked back to the house and slept with Drew."

They released me due to the fact they had no evidence to keep me there.

I returned to my job and my boring life and when I got home, I walked into my house to see my beautiful wife cooking.

She looked at me and said, "That didn't take long, love."

I walked over to her, kissed her, and said, "Nope, not at all, I knew exactly what to say and great performance by the way, my dear."

She smiled at me as I went down into the basement, looking at the white crib and my newborn daughter, a pretty little black girl I had kidnapped last week at the park. The baby smiled at me, and I named her Erica Sharon Miles. As I picked up our new bundle of joy and hugged her, and then walked back upstairs calling to my wife and spoke.

"Hey Alisha, do you think Sharon is too white as a middle name for a black child?"

Alisha stopped what she was doing., "No, baby, its fine, your sister Erica would be so happy that you named her niece after her."

I smiled thinking of my baby sister who was buried next to my father. I then looked at my daughter Erica, and said, "Do you think we will have any more trouble out of Detective Sharon Mons, since we do have this baby together?"

Alisha kissed my cheek. "She will not be missed as her mother was a drug addict anyway, right?"

I nodded. I looked at it as a good servant thing, and she was going to die in her mother's care anyway, why not take her and give her a proper home.

"Hmm, I wish dad was alive to see his granddaughter."

Alisha walked over to me and said, "Trina, I know he can." Alisha kissed me and I asked, "Do

Confessions in Whispers

you ever regret that you lied to the police and married me."

Alisha hugged me tight from behind. "If it weren't for your dad, I would have never learned what it feels like to be this happy and we would not have our new addition, our daughter Erica Sharon Miles."

Alisha kissed my ear, and whispered, "She needs a brother."

I looked at her thinking that's my baby, she always knows what to say and how to touch me, she also knows I hate living a boring normal life. So, I was going to be back on the hunt for my wife's perfect son. She wanted the perfect family, and I would stop at nothing to give it to her.

I left the house later that night.

Alisha walked me to the door and asked, "Baby, where are you going at this hour?"

I said, "To find you the perfect son, baby."

She smiled at me and shook her head, and then kissed me goodbye.

I said, "What can I say, like father, like daughter."

Confession 2

Opposites of Obsession

For as long as I can remember I have loved photography. I can honestly say ever since I was younger, I have been captivated by the art of the human body and expression. When I was in high school, I won a contest for a picture I took of my grandmother. She had expressive eyes, even in her old age I could still see the regal beauty of her youth.

I captured it in the photo I took of her dressed up for her eightieth birthday. From then on, people would always want me to take their pictures, and classmates, teachers etc. Before I knew it, I had won a scholarship at a photography school in New York called Le' Shoot School of Photography.

The famous school only showcased the portfolios of famous photographers. The classes were simple;

Confessions in Whispers

the teachers were cool, laid back and professional. All arrows pointed to me becoming a professional photographer. Everything seemed to be perfect right...wrong! I was bored out of my fucking mind.

No matter what grade I received for my work, I didn't feel that it made a true statement. Nothing was exciting to me, I mean who gives a fuck that I can shoot a sexy broad nude, and where is the real art in that? I have been shooting nudes since high school. No, I am looking for something more, where is my real muse? Where is the one that would truly mold me into a great artist? How funny that I would find the answer on a New York subway train one late night, riding home.

*

I had just come from a photo shoot for some wanna be rap artist. I did this to make extra money on the side, always open to making more money, I always say. I was dead tired when I got on the train heading to Brooklyn. I took a seat next to the entrance to another sub car that had a sign that said, "OUT OF ORDER".

I took out my headphones and placed them in my ears. I was just about to turn on my MP3 player when I heard a noise. I paused a moment to listen, trying to figure out where the muffled sound was coming from. I strained my ears trying to listen closely, even though it wasn't that loud.

I then realized it was coming from my right, inside the broken sub car next to me. I turned trying to look inside, but it was dark. I could only see inside every few minutes when the interior lights flashed off and on. When the lights flashed, I saw a man and woman.

I rolled my eyes, ignoring it at first. Then, when the lights flashed again, I saw clearly; it was a Caucasian man on top of a Latino woman! He had her on her back in the seat with her legs in the air.

"Well now that's an exotic pose." I could hear my heart pumping fast, I was excited. I took out my camera and waited for the flash of light again. This time I took a few shots. I was going to take more when my stop was called. I got off the train.

When I got home, I went into my developing room to see the shots I had taken. I was drying the photos

Confessions in Whispers

I took on the subway when I glanced up at one of them. I gasped as I snatched it down, looking at a rape scene.

The Caucasian man was holding her down and raping her while he held a knife against her neck! I was stunned as I looked at the photo. Even though I had clearly taken a photo that was evidence of a crime, I couldn't look away.

I was turned on by the body language of the shot. The light almost made the shot look unreal; the lighting took over the scene as the angle the man had her in was highly erotic. I smiled at my work; I had taken a photo full of excitement, energy, passion, and horror all at the same time.

I walked around my apartment for hours staring at it. It was clearly my best work. I then came to a morbid conclusion. I wanted to do it again, but how? I wanted to take another picture. I shook my head at the idea, I couldn't take another shot like this, it wasn't right. I needed to turn this picture in to the police! I tossed the photo into my bag. I will turn it in tomorrow on the way to school I thought, as I went to sleep.

The next morning as I located my things for school, I took another glance at the rape scene photograph. I shrugged my shoulders as I threw it back into my bag, grabbing my keys, MP3 player, digital camera, film, and cell phone.

I left the apartment and started walking toward the subway. I was walking down the street when I saw him. I stared for a minute, not quite sure if it was him. He was walking down the street with his hands in his pockets. I then had a decision to make, should I follow him or just go to school. I chose to follow him. I crossed the street, following three people behind him.

He continued to walk, then stopped suddenly. He walked down an alley, I followed him. He suddenly turned around and I ducked into a doorway. I peeked out to see if he can see me, no, he was still walking. I continued to follow him. I slowed down when I saw him stop. He was staring at something; I sneaked up a little closer, and then looked up.

He was staring at a woman; she was a Caucasian female in her early twenties. He stared up at her attentively. I was intrigued as I pulled out my camera taking shots of his expression. I realized that he had found his next victim.

No school for me today, I was going to see what he was going to do next. I ducked behind a trash can as I watched him walk back out to the street.

I followed him to an apartment about ten blocks down the street from mine. I never realized that a man like this lived so close, but by face value I couldn't believe he was a rapist. He was an average Caucasian male and he looked like a businessman.

He didn't look like a hardened criminal or a rapist for that matter. He looked like a regular law-abiding citizen. He didn't seem crazy or angry for that matter. So, I wondered why he wanted to do such an evil act.

I sat across the street at a café waiting for him to come out. I had been sitting there are a long time, it was getting dark.

I looked down at my watch, it was past eight o'clock. "Damn I could have been in class for this shit!"

I started to collect my stuff to get ready to go home, when I looked up in time to see my man leaving his apartment. I grabbed my stuff and started following him again. He cut through a park, walked a few paces, and then leaned against a tree behind some bushes. I hid back behind some trees, watching closely.

What was he waiting for? Was all I was thinking as I watched him. I was bored so I decided to take a few shots of him. As I was shooting away, I saw a woman jogging down the path we were on. I kept my camera on the woman, and then realized this was the same woman from this morning!

He must stalk them first, before he actually attacks them. She jogged along a little further, and then he snatched her throwing her into the bushes.

"Shit, I can't see." So, I repositioned myself so I could see better. I had to be careful not to ruin it for him. I finally found a good place to shoot and pulled out my camera again. I looked through the lens to see him tying her to a tree trunk. I took a few shots; this was too good.

He then took his knife and let it dance around her body a while, and then suddenly cut open her jogging top. He revealed her suntanned breast; he caressed her with the knife. I had to give it to him, he took his time.

Almost as if he knew that no one would see or didn't care about getting caught. He forcefully kissed her, biting at her skin, leaving marks as he went on. By his rough laugh, he was enjoying himself, and so was I. The shots started to come one after the other as I became fascinated by his technique. He finally took her in a rough embrace. I was in awe as I listened to her scream her head off.

I looked around but no one heard them. How in the hell is he getting away with this?!

He repositioned her to the ground, tying her hands behind her back, pulling her hair, slapping her ass and constantly threatening her with his knife. I took a few more shots before he exploded on her face! Her expression was classic as I shot away. Once it was all over, he released her.

She must have been in too much pain to move because she didn't, she just sat there stunned, and shocked at what had just occurred. He dressed casually, and then strolled off on down the jogging path. I took a few more shots of him walking down the path. I waited a few minutes for her to move, scream, something, but she just sat there.

    I rolled my eyes and headed home. I was flushed; I had just witnessed a crime! I had goose bumps all over as I thought of all the trouble, I could get into for this. As I walked into the house, I immediately went to my computer and downloaded my shots. I stared at the computer in awe as I saw my artwork come to life. I loved the colors, the expressions, and the pain of the victim. I shook my head as I looked at my best work ever!

*

    I printed out the photos, examining the frame of the shots, and then I started to think of what I could do better next time. As I stared at the picture of him walking away, I nod agreeing as I say to myself, "This picture is going on my living room wall!"

    I then reprint the photo in black and white, it makes it more dramatic. I was impressed with my work as I locked it away in a locker in my closet. I

Confessions in Whispers

could not keep these out in the open, hell no, someone might see them, and then I would really be in trouble. Besides, this was my special private collection. I even downloaded the rest of the shots to a flash drive, labeled it and put in the locker as well. As I closed the closet, I smiled to myself. I was almost turned on by the images I had just seen. I couldn't help myself. It had been a long time since an image had such an impact on me. I longed for so long to have a muse that would mold me into something great and in one night I believed I had found him.

I started thinking. I leaned forward on my couch and stared at the blank place above my entertainment center, "Aww yes, this where the picture of him would go for sure, I loved the black and white and it would go well with my furniture."

I also thought about this whole situation, I knew by now that this little hobby of mine, that I was enjoying so very much, could very well cost me my career, but by now as I stared at the picture of him in black and white, I didn't honestly care. I laughed to myself as I listened to all of the various messages, I had from females wanting dates, or shoot set ups, my homeboys and of course my teachers asking why I wasn't in class today. I shrugged my shoulders and went to fix me something to eat. I would go to class tomorrow I thought as I got my food, and then sitting down to watch some T.V. I was eating away, flipping through channels when I caught a breaking story on the news.

I sat up to listen to the reporter as she said "Tonight Governor Samuel Highpick's daughter, Traci Highpick, was sexually assaulted late this evening by an unidentified white male in a park where Traci took her daily jogs. Police have no suspects in custody as this time but urges if anyone has any information to please call the number below."

They then showed a photo of Traci's face... "OH SHIT!" I blinked, and then jumped up running to my closet, unlocking the locker, pulling out the photos. As I stood up to examine the photos, I gasped saying, "Oh my god, it was the Governor's daughter!"

I dropped the photos on the floor. I was in complete shock as I sat on the floor thinking, "I have evidence to her rape! What in the hell am I going to do?"

I wondered who the other woman from the train was. I stood up and looked on the computer for recent crimes in the area.

Sure, enough I found "Carlotta Vega, the wife of Senator Marco Vega was sexually assaulted on a subway by an unidentified white male. No suspects have been apprehended just yet, but a current investigation is being conducted. I shook my head in disbelief, this was unreal! He was raping high-profile women, but how was he getting this close to them? Shouldn't they all have bodyguards and shit?

I then thought about the photos I had taken of them. This made me an accomplice to the crimes because I took a picture of the crime. I was just as sick as he was, I wanted to shoot pictures of them in pain. I tried to calm myself, but it was so hard. I was overly impressed by the level of women he decided to rape. I had to have more shots, I wasn't going to school tomorrow either I decided, and I was going out with my favorite rapist! I had to see who his next victim was going to be.

The next morning, I got up early and went through my cameras to see which one would be best in light and dark. I found one, threw it in my bag and ran out the door. I planted myself at the café again, ordered some coffee and waited. I waited for about thirty minutes. I sighed, rubbing my face saying to myself, "Damnit! I must have missed him." I was about to finish my coffee and head to school when I heard a familiar voice. I listened attentively and realized he was right behind me! I swallowed whispering, "Oh, shit!"

I couldn't move so I decided to listen to his conversation. He was talking to another man; the other guy had a Latino accent, and I heard him say, "Hey, good job on those two jobs I gave you, the clients are very happy."

Confessions in Whispers

I heard my guy say, "Yeah, I am glad I must admit. I had a hell of a lot of fun with them myself."

The Latino guy chuckled as he said, "Okay, since I know you are a man who likes money…"

My guy interrupted with, "I'm just saying who the hell doesn't?"

I listened to them share a laugh. Then the Latino guy said, "I have another job for you, Judge Terry Cellars; your target is his daughter Ky'Aria Cellars. She is starting some trouble and needs to be dealt with appropriately. She is some kind of a part-time model. She will be at the Le' Shoot Photography School today. She should get out by six-thirty pm; she has an appointment with some hot shot photographer kid name Quinton Styles."

I damn near choked on my coffee hearing my name! I bumped into the chair behind me, and then realized it was his! As I turned to apologize, I looked right in the eyes of my rapist! He looked at me; I then said, "My bad man, damn coffee was too hot."

He nodded agreeing with me saying, "Yeah, it's like that all the damn time here, make sure to ask for mild next time, better temperature."

"Thanks, man," I said. I then got up and left.

I was walking away when I realized I had actually had a conversation with C.R. I decided right then I would name him the Celebrity Rapist.

I then ran to the subway station. I had completely fucking forgot all about Ky'Aria's photo shoot! I made it to school on time for my second class. The whole time I was in class all I could think about was the photo shoot! I couldn't believe the C.R.'s next victim was one of my models. Hell, I know how morbid it sounded but hell I was honored! How did the Latino guy know my name, but didn't know my face when he saw me? That's what was bugging me the most! I knew now that I had to be careful with this one. For all I knew someone could be watching me watch C.R.!

Around four-thirty pm I was in my studio setting up everything for my shoot for Ky'Aria, I was too excited as I wanted everything to be perfect. I

Confessions in Whispers

wanted some good shots of her normal shots to compare to her more dramatic shots later.

As I was setting the lighting for the shoot, she walked in with her bodyguard. I was on a ladder, as I watched her talking to some guy. I looked at the guy and saw it was the Latino dude from the café!

I ducked. "OH shit, he was her bodyguard! That's how he knew her schedule."

I overheard him say to her he wouldn't be able to come back to pick her up and could she take the subway home. I then listened her say, "Sure, it's not like anything is going to happen to me, Clark! I will be fine."

I shook my head, little than she knew she wouldn't be alright. He left and she came around the curtain smiling. She was a beautiful woman. Slightly tall, milk chocolate tone, and had a sexy short haircut that showed of her lovely high cheek bones. Her coke-bottle shaped body was nice as well. I had to say C.R. was going to have fun with her.

*

I set her up in some poses and took a few innocent shots of her face and body. I was becoming overly excited mostly because I knew what great shots I would have later for my private collection. I was almost turned on, as flashes of images of her being raped came to mind. I tried to shake the images as I stared at her innocent face, but it was becoming hard.

I was in high anticipation to see her scream, yell, and cry. The beauty of it all was too much for me so I told her to take a break.

I went into the bathroom to clear my head. I looked in the mirror and I said, "What is wrong with you, Quint! You would have never thought about shit like that before you saw him, get it together man. Don't let her see you like this; she might suspect something, then what? You don't have the balls to shut her up!"

I knew I had to get myself together, showtime was just around the corner, don't blow it! I collected myself and continued with the shoot like normal.

*

Confessions in Whispers

Around five-thirty pm I started to end. I thanked Ky'Aria for coming again and told her that her photos would be ready next week for her.

She smiled and kissed me on the cheek. "Thanks Quinton, you know I love posing for you the best!"

I laughed at the irony of it all. She then went to get dressed. I was collecting my things to get ready to leave when she came out. I paused, she was dressed casually in some sweatpants, a zip up sweat jacket with a tank top.

I then watched her pull off her wig! She shook down her long hair then tied it in a ponytail. I blinked. I didn't know that was a wig she was wearing. I understood though she didn't want people recognizing her.

I grabbed my stuff and walked out with her. We reached the subway together, even got on the same train, but we didn't sit together. I sat on the sub car next to her and watched her. I waited till she got off and then started to follow her. I made sure to stand back a good distance so I could keep an eye out for C.R. She walked along a pretty crowded space. Then I caught a glimpse of C.R.

I found him watching Ky'Aria. She walked into a clothing store. C.R. repositioned himself two stores down. I moved to the same street and stayed two stores behind C.R. We both waited, I took some shots of C.R. He was amazing, he was just so damn calm and cool. I was shaking like a leaf with excitement!

Ky'Aria finally came out of the store and walked towards C.R.! I watched him investigate the alley next to the store he was standing by. As Ky'Aria was about to pass him, he grabbed her by the waist and pulled her into the alley. I waited a few minutes before walking in. He had her in the very back. I positioned myself about two feet away from them.

I watched attentively as C.R. went to work. Ripping her clothes off, it seemed he loved to tear and cut through fabric. Those shots were amazing; his facial expressions and hers were classic.

As I shot the pictures, I pretended I was shooting for a movie. The images were so unreal that they could have been for a movie! C.R. did something a little different; he had her suck him off.

Confessions in Whispers

I raised an eyebrow thinking, "Wow, ok, a new technique, but I wasn't sure about that one. She could bite his shit off!" C.R. gagged her with his dick. The shots were amazing with her tear-stained face, his snaring expressions.... Priceless! Then the main event; he positioned her laying her over a trash can! I almost jumped out of my skin.

That shot was perfect, until I saw the blood running down her legs. C.R. didn't even notice as he was banging away, and she was crying for help. I realized that this woman was still a virgin! My finger was virtually moving by itself that's how fast the shots were being taken.

Once he was done, he wiped himself off with her T-shirt, got dressed and left. I ducked into the shadows as he passed me. I looked at Ky'Aria, she was on her knees crying. I shook my head; I felt a little sorry for her. I snapped the last picture, got my things together and left.

As I walked out of the alley and went right, I rested my back on the wall thinking, "Just this once, I will be nice and help her out."

I looked for a phone booth. When I located one, I called the police. I told the operator that I heard some screaming in an alley, then gave them a fake name and address of where they could find her. I then raced home to look at my work!

When I got home, I didn't even bother locking my door as I ran over to my computer, that's how excited I was. I downloaded the pictures, damn! They were fabulous, I compared them to the shots I had taken earlier, and they didn't hold a candle to them. I leaned back in my computer chair and shouted, "YES! Quinton, you have out done yourself again!"

I realized I was too loud, got up and locked my door. I printed my collection, saved them to another flash drive and locked them away. I yawned. I was beat! C.R. had taken a lot out of me with that shoot.

*

The next morning, I woke up feeling like a real artist! I played some music to get me in the mood to handle my day. I would go to school today and look for C.R. later. I was getting dressed for school, watching the news when an alert came across the screen.

"Today, police found the body of an African American woman. After investigators examined her, they concluded that it was the body of Ky'Aria Cellars, Supreme Court Judge Terry J. Cellars daughter.

"Police claim that Ky'Aria was sexually assaulted, then shot four times. There are no suspects currently, but the police urge that if anyone has any information to please contact them immediately. There is a ten-thousand-dollar reward for any information received."

I couldn't believe it! I had called the police while she was still in the alley; how fucking long did they take?! I sat down on the couch to think. C.R. and I left at around ten-thirty pm. I caught the eleven-p.m. train home.

So, someone killed Ky'Aria in thirty fucking minutes! That meant someone followed us there too! It just didn't make sense.

*

I went to school as the other photography students decided to do a collage of photos of her. She had been a model for at least ten of the other students besides me. I agreed to submit some photos from her last shoot which was just yesterday! Fuck man! I couldn't really concentrate in class at all. I needed answers. I then really felt sorry for Ky'Aria for real now.

She lost her virginity in a brutal way, and then was killed. It wasn't fair at all, and I needed to know what the fuck was going on. After school I went to look for C.R. To my surprise he almost found me!

I walked out of the station to find him and Ky'Aria's bodyguard in a heated debate. I heard C.R. say as they walked, "Clark! What the fuck happened last night?! How in the hell did she end up fucking dead?!"

Clark tried to calm C.R. down but he wasn't hearing it. He yelled, "I did you, Cellars, Vega and Highpick a favor, I raped those women to help win pity in their campaigns so they could all be reelected, and she turns up dead?! I fucked her; my sperm is probably all over her fucking clothes!"

Clark interrupted saying, "Look, you're cool; everything is taken care of, okay. Here's your money, now just lie low for a while till I get this thing to blow over." C.R. nodded as they parted ways.

*

For the next couple of weeks, I got nothing! I was losing my mind! I hated this shit, because in one night this shit became real! Before it was fantasy, I was in a blurred world of erotic photography. It was exciting, bold, artistic, and beautiful, but with the news of the death of one of my models it was losing its glamour. In one fucking night of amazing shooting this shit became real! Now C.R. had to go into hiding and that shit sucked! I understood completely but it still sucked. For the first week I just went around like normal, but by the second week I was fiending for a photo.

On the third week I went out night after night trying to find a replacement for C.R., but nobody cut it! I found this man, he was black. I guess he was supposed to be a pimp, or some shit and I caught him smacking one of his hoes, but the shots I took looked fake, no real emotion or fucking feel at all! FUCK MAN!

I almost knocked on his door saying, "Fuck this shit man! Let's go and find you a fresh, cute, innocent woman to have some fun with and let me shoot it!"

I was losing my mind, I knew this shit was wrong, I should be more compassionate about the victims he hurt, but the art was so beautiful it made the rape worth it! I needed a new outlet; I decided to go back to shooting nudes and wanna be rappers. I had to drown myself in this bullshit to keep my mind from snapping in two from not having any decent picture!

*

A month went by without any new real photos. I decided that I would stop trying to find real victims and stage some of my own! It worked. I loved the images I was producing, but something was missing. Then I understood that C.R was missing. I thought to myself as I finished up shoot.

Confessions in Whispers

"Maybe I can ask him if he would like to pose for some photos."

I thought it over as I went home. I had basically got back to my old routine of my life. I sat on my couch turning on the T.V. to the news to hear,

"After a month of searching, police arrested Clay Ruston today in connection to the murder of Ky'Aria Cellars. Evidence found at the suspect's home included a nine mm gun, which police say is the murder weapon. Photographs were also found of Ky'Aria indicating that Ruston had stalked the victim before he sexually assaulted and killed her."

I tripped out to find that C.R.'s initials were actually C.R.

I was at a loss for words! They had the wrong guy! C.R. didn't kill Ky'Aria, he raped her, but he didn't kill her! I couldn't just let him take the wrap for that shit, but how was I going to prove he didn't do it without getting caught up in this shit myself? I needed to think for real. They were going to put C.R. in jail for a crime he didn't even commit! Then I remembered Ky'Aria's bodyguard! He knew everything; he even set up this bullshit! I went to the internet to look up the rape cases of the women I had recently shot. I looked at a few pictures of them and realized something remarkably interesting.

Clark was all their bodyguards! In every picture, I could see Clark in the background. Then I remembered the conversation C.R and Clark had before he laid low. He mentioned that he did them all a favor. So, I looked up the backgrounds of Cellars, Highpick and Vega, and I found some interesting shit. All these men had issues that could really hurt all their campaigns.

Governor Samuel Highpick was being investigated by the F.B.I for money laundering and his daughter was dating one of the agents. Senator Marco Vega was being charged with child abuse of his nine-year-old son Delmacro Vega and look who turned him in, his wife Carlotta Vega.

I shook my head as I saw that Ky'Aria was an open lesbian and was fighting against a court case her father Judge Terry Cellars was in charge of.

"Oh my God C.R. what the fuck did you get yourself into?" All these men were using the rapes

Confessions in Whispers

to soften their own cases! That shit was just cruel. I now realized that Judge Cellars had his own daughter killed to close the case in court! He is going to use her funeral as a media stunt! Fuck that shit; I am not going to let that shit happen. Now I need to find Clark, but I didn't know who to ask about him. So, I went to school to ask around about Ky'Aria's bodyguard, claiming I needed the address to send her last photos to her family.

One of the female photographers name Rachel said, "Oh yea Clark! I did a photo shoot for him of his beautiful daughter, Taylor, last year at their house on Park and third."

I thanked her for the information, and left school early, and caught the train over there. I made sure I had a tape recorder with me as well as my camera. I placed myself near a tree across the street from his house and just watched. I suddenly saw Clark come out with a briefcase in his hand.

I followed him to the ocean pier about a block and half from his house. It was crowded as people were headed to the carnival near the pier. I followed Clark to the east side of the pier. He was waiting for someone, it seemed. I got up close, setting up my camera, pretending to be a vendor snapping photos for the event. I put the recorder in my pocket as I snapped away at random people. I suddenly saw a black BMW pull up and a black man in a suit get out of the car. It was the Judge! I then walked over in their direction and started to record their conversation. I snapped some quick shots of them standing together before shooting some kids playing.

As I listened, I heard the Judge say, "Good work, Clark, you got rid of that lesbian bitch of a daughter of mine. She would have ruined the whole damn campaign."

Clark smiled as he handed the judge the briefcase and the judge handed him a brown envelope. "Yes sir, Ruston didn't even know what hit him. I set up the house, then had him rape her."

I moved so I could get a good shot of them both, and then left. As I jogged through the crowd, I said to myself, "Got' em." I went home to make a copy of the photos and the recording. Then made a copy of the rape scene of Ky'Aria, I then mailed it to the police.

A few days later C.R. was released, they gave him served time for Ky'Aria's rape. Clark and Judge Cellars were arrested for the murder of his daughter. I burned all the photos I had; I had enough of that real-life shit!

Two weeks after his release I ran into C.R. I asked him if he wanted a job.

He laughed at me asking me, "What kind of job kid?"

I smiled and asked him to come to my house. He agreed to come to hear me out. C.R. came to my house later that night. I told him I believed he would do well as a model for my BDSM magazine. He looked at me confused. "How do you know that kid?"

I pointed at the large black and white picture on my living room wall. He gasped looking at the picture of him walking away from the rape of Traci Highpick.

He turned to me saying, "It was you! You're the one who proved my innocence!"

I nodded stating, "After all that real drama, I decided instead of photographing the real stuff I would do the opposite. BDSM is still my obsession thanks to you, that's why I am offering you the job, man."

He started laughing, "Cool, but why me?"

I shook my head, "Hey, I named you C.R. before I knew those were your real initials and you are the one who got me into this lifestyle. I have to have my muse in my photos to make them art."

He laughed again. "C.R. huh, what did it stand for?"

I shrugged, "Celebrity Rapist."

He cracked up. "Okay, so what's the name of this magazine?"

I smiled big. "Dark Obsessions."

C.R. smiled as he stared at the picture of him again. We both agreed that little did people know our obsession had just begun.

Confession 3

Sanity

I let out a loud yawn, stretched my arms above my head, and sighed. I got out of bed and went into the bathroom to run my bath. When I came back, there he was, standing in the doorway staring at me as usual. I rolled my eyes, and yelled at him, "Stop doing that, would you!"

My husband walked over to me and wrapped me in his slightly built arms. "You still fall for that every time."

I nudged him as he threw me on to the bed. I started to struggle, but he had me pinned down. He grabbed a hold of my night gown from the bottom and began to slide it up my thigh. I was lost in his eyes as his hands glided up my body.

He smiled softly at me and began to speak. I placed a finger on his smooth lips, which he took in his mouth.

I glanced over at the clock; it said seven-forty-five a.m. I turned my head, looking up at my husband. "Alright Ellis, you know we do not have time for all of this."

Ellis looks at the clock, then back down at me with a devilish smile. He grabs me by the waist, spinning me around. "Oh well, so much for foreplay, bend your ass over."

I love it when he plays rough. I begin to whine in a baby voice, "Oh Mr. Officer, don't search me, I don't have anything on me."

As I raise my ass in the air, Ellis grabs my hair yanking me up to him from behind as he snarls in my ear, "Did I ask you if you had anything bitch, ass up face down!" Ellis slams my head down into the pillow.

I love it when he plays rough. Soon he was inside me grinding me to death. I was lost in the act; Ellis soon came so deep within me. I jolted from the sensation, my legs shaking as my orgasm took over.

We both fell onto the bed. Ellis kissed my neck and back whispering in my ear softly, "I love you, Neka, but your water is going to run over, baby."

I smiled as I looked back to kiss him. I kiss Ellis as his words set in my mind. I blinked, then gasped. I pushed Ellis off of me, running into the bathroom to turn off the water. I caught it just in time. I wiped my forehead as I walked back out of the bathroom.

Ellis shook his head. I rolled my eyes. "You always want to play when I have to get ready for work."

Ellis sat up on the side of the bed, motioning for me to come to him with his arms stretched open. I couldn't resist his charm if I tried. I jumped into his arms. Ellis laughed at me as he held me. "Neka, you know I work late at night, and by the time I get home, it's morning."

I knew all too well about my husband's hectic work schedule, he is a police officer after all. Ellis

Nicholas Jermson was one of the finest police officers I had ever met. He was up for a promotion as Sergeant. I kissed his lips again as I jumped out of bed. "What do you want for breakfast, baby?"

Turning towards me, Ellis shrugged his shoulders. "Surprise me, Baby." I shook my head. He was always saying that. I placed a finger to my cheek and tried to think. "What shall I cook my favorite man?"

I snapped my fingers as a menu came to me. I would cook some grits, French toast, and bacon. I walked out of the room and headed down the stairs to the kitchen. I was cooking away when the phone rang. I answered in a cheerful voice, "Hello, Jermson residence."

*

I listened to my momma Shavon Murphy laughing, "Well, you are in a good mood today, Neka."

I said, "Momma, I am always in a good mood when Ellis comes home from work."

I heard a pause on the phone, then a quiet sigh as my momma said, "Neka, baby, are you going to take care of that business for me soon." I felt a lump in my throat; I didn't want to have this conversation now. I felt like crying, but held back tears as I said, "Momma, do we have to discuss this now, you know how I feel about talking about this." I heard my mom sigh, then say, "Nekalia Dymond Murphy, you are going to have to pay for this funeral one way or the other. You better start getting your act together young lady." I didn't want to hear about it anymore. I slammed the phone down, turned off the stove and started to cry. The tears came thick and fast., I placed my hands over my eyes and tried to stop them. I didn't want to deal with this now! Not right now.

I then felt arms wrap around me and I jumped a little, looking behind me. Ellis leaned down to kiss me. "What's wrong, baby?"

I leaned back in his arms. "Momma wants me to make the payment on her funeral now. Ellis, I did not want to discuss that this morning, for months now she has been hounding me about these funeral payments and I am just not ready to let go yet."

Ellis hugged me tighter, kissing my cheek, then my ear as he whispered, "You don't have to deal with this now baby, let's eat, you are going to be late for work."

I kissed him on the cheek, he was right; I didn't have to deal with this now. We ate breakfast, I got dressed and when I came out of the bathroom, Ellis was lying in bed with the remote in hand.

"Come here Neka."

I walked over and crawled towards him. He gathered me in his arms.

"You have a great day at work, okay, baby."

I kissed him, then hopped off the bed, and headed to work.

As I drove, I began to wonder.

"Neka, girl you will have to face this one day, she was not going to be around forever. You might as well have everything in order for her, you are her only child." I sighed as I drove into the parking lot of the Raymond Plaza Hotel.

I work as the head manager of the hotel. I walked into the lobby and greeted Patrice Walsh, the hotel

Confessions in Whispers

receptionist. Patrice was a Caucasian female, and of average height and build, she was quite intelligent, smiled a lot and was one of my dearest friends. As I walked towards the counter, she said, "Well, good morning, boss lady."

I rolled my eyes at her she knows good and damn well she doesn't have to call me that. I laughed her off leaning on the counter.

"So, where is Max the hound, today Trice?"

Flipping back her auburn hair, she laughed at she pointed to my left corner.

"There is that no-good blood hound right over there, Neka, and do not get me started on what he did to me today!"

I looked back there with a raised eyebrow.

"Neka, he came in today. He told me John isn't going to be in because his son is getting married. So, he said, Patrice, while Mr. Towers is away, I am in charge, so how about a little kiss for your boss. Then turns his cheek towards me thinking I was actually going to kiss it!"

I laughed. That was Max alright; he thought he was a real lady's man. I remembered when I first got the position as a manager, Ellis had to come up here and straighten him out about slapping me on the butt. Max DeMussy was an arrogant prick who thought he could lie, cheat, and screw his way to the top.

I continued to listen to Patrice for a while, and then interrupted her because I needed to get my office to look over some paperwork. I had to take off a few months because I was dealing with the whole situation with my mom and all.

I was in my office looking through files when I heard a knock at the door. I looked up from my desk to see Max in my doorway. Max is a Caucasian male, shorter than my husband, but a sharp dresser. Image is everything to Max, as he would remind us often. His hair was cut sharp as well. Ok, so he was a handsome man for a white guy, but his attitude was too much to bear.

I smiled at him, saying, as I looked back down at my paperwork, "What can I do for you, Max?"

I heard him laugh. "Well, my love, you can do a lot of things for me, but as I heard before from your husband ...Ellis is it?"

Confessions in Whispers

I looked up at Max.

He continued, "Well, Ellis would not approve. By the way, how is the funeral payments coming along, Neka?"

I cut my eyes at him, and then lowered my head down again to my work. I could hear him taking a seat in front of my desk, and all I could think of was, "Go away Max, there is no way in hell I am going anywhere with you."

I could hear Max clearing his throat. "Look Neka, come on, let me take you on a vacation somewhere, you know how much I adore you; I know this has been hard on you. Dealing with this situation…"

I cut him off, looking him in the eyes. "Look Max, thank you for your concern. I am grateful to know you do care about me and that you are not trying to get into my panties…"

He chimed in, "You mean your thongs right, I can't see you wearing panties with a figure like yours."

As my eyes narrowed at him, my tone deepened. "Max, do you have any idea what my husband would do to you if he heard you say that to me?"

Max smiled as he stood up. My gaze stayed on his face until he brushed off his suit.

"Nothing, he is not around right now to say anything, or do anything right now, isn't that right, Nekalia."

I started to yell at him, but he turned around, and walked out of my office closing the door behind him. I leaned back in my chair and huffed. How dare he speak about Ellis that way?!

I could call Ellis, have him come up here and kick that arrogant bastard's ass, but I know he is asleep. He has to go to work tonight. I decided to ignore Max and get back to work. I had too much shit on my mind to deal with Max today. I had to get through this day first, and then deal with an appointment in a few days. One I was not looking forward to at all and I just didn't need any more pressure on me.

I worked through my day like normal but left the job feeling down, depressed, and just plain shitty. When I got home, I got undressed, hopped into a hot bath and drifted off to sleep. I was woken

Confessions in Whispers

suddenly by a voice, "Don't drown in there, baby."

I jumped up looking where the voice came from and saw Ellis standing in the doorway in his uniform.

He laughed at me as I splashed water at him. "Stop doing that! Stop standing in the doorway like that, you scared the hell out of me, Ellis!"

He laughed again as he walked over to the tub and kneeled down to kiss me. I looked up at him.

I said, "Why are you home so early anyway."

He helped me out of the tub, and then wrapped a towel around. "The Lieutenant said some of us could go home early if we wanted to, so I was the first to put my hand up. It's been a slow night anyway."

I let him lead me to our bed. Ellis made love to me, and then asked me about my day as he held me. When I told him about Max, he sat up and leaned against the headboard.

"You know what Neka, you tell Max I will come up there and beat the shit out of him if he doesn't leave you alone."

I smiled, patting him on the chest. "I already did, baby." I knew I hadn't really told Max that but if made Ellis feel better, then that was good for me.

Ellis hugged me tighter. "Neka, don't ever let me go baby, no matter what, let me stay with you."

Tears slowly fell down my face. "Ellis, baby, you are my husband, I love you more than anything in this whole world. I will never let you go."

He smiled and closed his eyes to go to sleep. I watched Ellis's sleep; he is so handsome, brave and above all, he is all mine. I couldn't be prouder to have a better husband than Ellis. I cozied up to him, and he wrapped an arm around, pulling me in closer and I fell asleep.

*

I woke up the next morning smiling, and I could smell my breakfast next to me. I opened my eyes to see my mom sitting next to me. I rolled my eyes as I sat up. "Momma what are you doing here, and where is Ellis?"

My mom smiled. "I came to check on you, and Ellis has gone."

Confessions in Whispers

I shook my head, scratching it. "He must have gotten a call. So, you made me breakfast?"

My mom placed the tray in my lap, motioning me to eat. "Neka, are you going to the therapist on Friday?"

I stopped eating. "Momma, I am eating, let me finish my food before you start in on that. You already know how hard this is for me anyway."

My mom placed a hand on my knees, rubbing it. "Baby, I know it is, but you have to pay those funeral fees and move on from all this. I want all of this behind you before I leave you alone again."

My mom was dying; she never said what from because she knew I took my daddy's death just as hard. I didn't want to listen to this nonsense of funeral fees and going to a therapist for grieving counseling. Looked at my mom, she smiled at me with her sweet brown sugar cheeks.

"Momma, I will deal with the therapist on Friday, ok momma."

She smiled big; she was pleased. I finished my breakfast, then hopped in the shower, and then got dressed for work. I left the house feeling weird. I couldn't understand why my mom wanted all her funeral stuff paid for so fast. Then I thought about Friday, I had to go see this grieving counselor Michella Hodges. My mom recommended her to help me get through this whole process. I was not ready to face the truth and that was just it. I didn't want to look at the pain my momma was going through. I wanted to pretend it was not happening. That's what was keeping me sane. Pretending my life was fine with Ellis, he was the perfect thing in my life, without him I would never get through this.

While at work, Max tried to talk me into going away to the Bahamas again. He claimed I needed a real vacation from all that was happening in my life. I rolled my eyes at him and continued with my day. I had dealt with enough drama with my momma to have deal with this bullshit from Max. I did need to relax. Then I got a phone call. I answered, "Hello."

The voice on the other end was a woman. "Hello, is this Niklia Jamerson?"

Confessions in Whispers

I corrected her quickly. "My name is Nekalia Jermson, and who am I speaking with?"

"My apologies Nekalia, I am Doctor Michella Hodges, we have an appointment on Friday together. I just wanted to talk to you and see how you are doing?"

I sighed. I knew who had called her, my momma! I quickly answered her "Look. Doctor Hodges, we do have an appointment on Friday, but I do not want to discuss anything until then, okay."

"I completely understand, Ms. Jermson."

I began to inhale and exhale quickly. "I am Mrs. Jermson! I will see you on Friday!"

Slamming the phone down, I tried to get a hold of myself. I was losing it fast. as I laid my head down on my desk trying not to think of Friday. I just didn't need this right now. I heard a knock at the door, and I jerked my head up. It was Patrice.

I sat up, wiping my face, and motioned her to come in. She quickly walked in. "Neka, what's wrong?"

"Pat, my mom had the doctor call me today, to remind me of my appointment with her on Friday."

Patrice then sighed. "Neka, your mom is worried about you, we all are, even Ellis is worried about you. I know that if anyone was more worried about you, it's Ellis I smiled. She knew all too well to bring his name into a conversation would brighten my day.

I laughed. "Yes, Ellis is worried about me, he doesn't want me to leave him, he told me so last night. He was worried I would just forget about him, and then he would be all alone."

"Girl, you couldn't forget about Ellis if you tried. He is only the love of your life, I know. Deal with these funeral payments have been hell to you, but you will get through this. Just tell the doctor that you are fine and that this is natural for you to grieve this way. If she can't understand it then tell her I said go to hell."

I laughed at Patrice. She walked around my desk to hug me. She knew how hard this was for me. She was always making it easier on me than harder.

I went home feeling much better. I walked into my room, and just fell on the bed. I fell asleep almost instantly after an exhausting day.

Confessions in Whispers

I was woken up by a touch, the sensation of someone massaging my back. I then felt kisses on my left ear and the side of my neck. I smiled as I opened my eyes to see Ellis.

He cupped my chin in his hand, kissing me. "Neka, baby I am home."

I rolled onto my back. I smiled up at him, caressing his beautiful face. He smiled back down at me.

"You had a rough day, huh?"

I nodded as he gathered me in his arms holding me close. "Does this have to do with Friday by any chance?"

I hugged him tighter. "My mom is on a real trip. She had that doctor call me today, to remind me of the appointment I have with her on Friday. I just do not want to deal with this right now. My mom is dying, and her biggest concern are these damn funeral payments!

"Ellis she is driving me crazy, she wants me to go to this grieving therapist to help cope with all this shit. She has no idea that all of this stress and pressure is making it harder to say goodbye."

Ellis repositioned me to as he lied down next to me. "You do know that you are not alone in this, don't you? I am here as long as you need me to be. You know that right, baby?"

I snuggled up to him, whispering, "I love you Ellis, never leave me ok, always stay with me, I have no idea what I would do if you left me."

Ellis laughed. "You know, ever since the first day I met you, I was in love with you. Your smile calms me, your touch comforts me and your love is something I need, and never want to forget. I am here for you always, Neka, as long as you want me here, baby."

We fell asleep and when I woke up the next morning, I could see that it was going to be another long day. Ellis was there holding me. I attempted to move but felt him grab me closer. "Where do you think you are going?"

I laughed while pushing him off of me. "I have to go to work unlike you, Mr. Jermson."

As I stood up, I was suddenly forced back down to the bed. I looked up to see Ellis with that devilish expression on his face again.

Confessions in Whispers

I shook my head. "No! No Ellis, I am going to be late for work, later baby, okay?"

Ellis nodded at me, as I jumped off the bed and ran me a shower. I came back out to see him lying on the bed in the "Come and Get Me" position. I ignored him and walked over to the closet to pick out my suit to wear to the office. I picked two, then turned around to look at Ellis.

"Which one, baby? The black stripe one or the beige and cream one?"

Ellis pretended to concentrate. "I love the beige and cream one, remember I bought that one for your first interview at the hotel. You look stunning in it."

I smiled, blushing a little. Ellis had bought this one for me, I was so nervous about the interview at the hotel then.

I laughed. "Ok, I will wear it today, how about that?"

Ellis nodded in approval, and then motioned to the shower. I wasn't in the shower a few minutes when I felt his hands caressing me. I laughed as I turned to face him. Ellis picked me up, placing me against the wall. "Sorry, I couldn't resist, I need you right now."

We made love in the bathroom, as we finished, I heard someone call my name.

Ellis shook his head. "Neka, I love your mother and all, but did you have to give her a key to the house. You remember what happened the last time she just showed up. She caught us naked in bed and you didn't want to have morning sex with me for a month!"

I remembered and laughed, but by the look on Ellis's face he didn't find that funny at all.

"Ok, I will distract her and make her go downstairs, ok."

Ellis pushed me towards the door. "Hurry, I am getting cold."

I grabbed his towel, throwing it at him. "Cover up and keep those buns warm for me, ok."

He shook his head at me as he wrapped his towel around his body. I wrapped my towel around me, and I stepped out of the bathroom.

"MOM! What are you doing here?"

Confessions in Whispers

My mom stood in the doorway with both hands on her hips yelling, "I have been calling you for ten minutes. Why didn't you answer me?"

I pointed at the bathroom door. "I was in the shower."

She sighed with relief; she had become so jumpy lately. She sat on the bed. "I spoke with Doctor Hodges the other day; she told me you got terribly upset and hung up on her. Why are you so mad? You haven't been trying to kill yourself again, have you? Remember your promise, I go first before you. I will not bury my daughter before me, do you understand?"

I sighed as I sat down on the bed. "Why did you bring that up? Why do you insist on bringing up bad memories, and events? Do you have any compassion for this situation at all! You know I took it ridiculously hard when Ellis and I lost Nicolette. Ellis had a nervous breakdown to see his first-born die. I thought it was all my fault and I just wanted him to feel better, so I thought if I was with her, he wouldn't be sad anymore."

I started to cry. I heard the door open, and Ellis came out. He came and sat next to me. I cried into his arms.

"Ellis didn't want it that way, now or ever. Just go to the grieving session it will make you feel better, ok baby," Momma said.

"Ok, I will go, but I do not want to hear any more about this situation or Nicolette till then, ok momma?"

Ellis looked at my mom, nodding he agreed with me that all this was not good for us.

My mom nodded. "Okay."

I then realized that mom hadn't said hi to Ellis.

"Good, now say hi to Ellis. He has been waiting on you to speak to him."

My mom nodded her head, waving to the right of her.

"Hello Ellis, help my daughter get through this, ok."

Ellis and me both looked at each other, we were sitting on the left side of her, why did she wave to the right side? I realized that my momma's sight was going.

Confessions in Whispers

She left without another word. Once alone, Ellis hugged me. "You are a strong woman, Neka, baby. I never once blamed you for Nicolette, I told you then that it was God I was mad at, not you, but I am not even mad at him now, because remember if she had lived, even though I wanted her so very much, I would have lost you. Nekalia, you are the most important person in my life, I would die over and over again just to be with you."

I knew Ellis was trying to make me feel better. I got up and started to get dressed for work. Ellis got dressed too, he was meeting his boy, Clayton, to play some ball on his day off.

We walked out together, and I kissed him goodbye. Then, I got into the car. As I shut the door, I looked out of the driver side window at Ellis. He leaned down and kissed me deeply.

"I will see you later baby, you have a good day at work. Don't worry about your mom, she will be fine."

I smiled, and then drove off to work without a care in the world. The workday went by without any headaches, I was late, but I didn't care. I realized that I wasn't going to go insane to make others happy. As long as Ellis and I were together and happy, that's all that mattered. So, I let my day fly by me. I couldn't wait to get home to work on dinner for Ellis and me.

I left work, and then headed to the store to get some food to cook for tonight. While I was in the store, I ran into Ellis's sister, Sherry.

"Hey Neka, how are you doing?"

I smiled. "I am fine; I am just getting some food to cook tonight."

She nodded, then said, "How are the payments coming?"

I shook my head. "Sherry, I do not want to discuss this. Ellis told me I didn't have to deal with it until Friday, so I am not going to." "My brother did always have a way of dealing with things, so if that's what he said, then ok. It was good to see you, Neka."

Sherry left without another word. I just could not understand why everyone wanted to talk about this now! My mom's condition was not getting any

Confessions in Whispers

better, and I just didn't want to handle all the drama with the funeral fees right now.

When I got home, I went into the kitchen to start dinner, I didn't even want to change. I was hungry and I just knew Ellis would be too. I turned to see a shadow in the doorway. I jumped back screaming as Ellis walked through the doorway. "You are still the scariest woman I know!"

I marched over to him, punching him in the arm, screaming "YOU SCARED ME, ELLIS! Damn, why do you have to stand in the doorway like that anyway?"

"Ok, I am sorry, I didn't mean to scare you, baby, I meant to surprise you."

I picked up an onion I had dropped on the floor, walked over to the sink, and washed it. I began to tell Ellis that I had seen his sister, Sherry, at the store today.

Ellis jumped up on the counter, picking up an apple from our fruit basket.

"Oh really, I miss Sherry, how is she doing?"

I shrugged my shoulders. "She is fine, I guess, she mentioned the funeral fees too, I think she wants to help me out with them. What do you think, Ellis?"

"If you want her to help you with the payments, then let her baby. I do not see why you have to pay for the whole thing anyway."

I smiled, walking over to him and standing between his legs. "This position looks backwards, doesn't it?"

Ellis stared down at me, and winked as he hopped down, then grabbed me, placing me on the counter, and then stood between my legs.

"You're right this is much better." Ellis then kissed me. We were getting heavy into it when the phone rang.

Ellis looked at the phone. "Don't get it now, let's play before dinner."

I pushed him back. "Ellis, let me at least see who it is."

I looked over at the caller id, it was my momma. Ellis looked at me shaking his head, He picked me up, throwing me over his shoulder.

"Oh no, she messed up a good morning, I will be damned if she fucks up our night, Night momma!"

Confessions in Whispers

Ellis carried me into the living room, as I struggled to get free. He laid me on the couch, and then jumped on top of me. I hit him on his chest, and I screamed, "Ellis Nicholas Jermson, you are heavy!"

Ellis looked down at me. "Oh, so we are using government names now are we, Nekalia Dymond Murphy."

I laughed; he knew I hated him to call me by my full name. I looked up at him, then pouted.

"Oh no, not the 'I have to get my way' face. What is it?"

I pouted some more "You forgot to add something to my name."

Ellis smiled, then slyly said, "Uh huh, and what may I ask did I forget in your name?"

I pushed him, and he picked me up. I then pulled him close to me, wrapping my arms around his neck. I whispered in his ear, "You forgot Jermson."

I could feel the heat of his body rise as he looked back down at me.

"Oh, I would never forget such an important detail Mrs. Jermson. I will always be honored for the day I made you my wife, Neka. Don't you ever forget that?"

I began to cry; I was so lucky to have a man as wonderful as Ellis. He wiped my tears away. "I didn't say that to make you cry baby, I said it to let you know I am only yours in life and in death."

I kissed Ellis; we made love on the couch. I could die the happiest woman in the world because of Ellis.

I woke up the next morning alone, I sighed.

"Ellis must be on his day shift now; he isn't home."

My stomach began to growl; I remembered that I hadn't had dinner last night. I had Ellis instead and even though, a meal like that was great, I needed real food in my belly.

I got up and walked into the kitchen. As I was getting down the cereal, I looked over at the answering machine. I had nine missed calls and nine messages. I shook my head saying to myself, "Momma, really you called that many times."

Confessions in Whispers

I didn't bother listening to the messages, because a few minutes later, I heard the front door thrown open.

In came running was my mom, yelling, "Neka! Nekalia! Honey, are you ok?"

Shaking my head, and rolling my eyes, I said to myself as I came out of the kitchen, "Ellis, baby you were right, I should have NEVER given her a key to the house."

My mom sighed in relief as she held her chest. "I called you nine times last night, why didn't you answer me?"

I sat at the dining room table, looking up at my mom as I placed my bowl on the table. "Mom, I am fine. Ellis and I fell asleep on the couch. I didn't even hear the phone ring."

My mom nodded saying sarcastically, "Oh, and where is Ellis now, upstairs?"

I rolled my eyes. "No, he is working his day shift now momma, you can be so arrogant about Ellis sometimes."

My mom sat at the table. "I am sorry, Neka, I know I have given Ellis a headache with busting in on you two in bed, and always coming by without letting you know, but I am still your momma, and I can worry about you too."

I smiled; she did mean well, but sometimes my momma was a real trip. I finished my breakfast.

"I know that tomorrow is the appointment, I am so scared, I don't want to do this now."

My momma sighed and hugged me. "Nekalia, baby I know this has been hard for you, but after tomorrow you will feel much better, you will see."

My momma left. It was my day off and I had to deal with the reality of tomorrow. I had to deal with this. I wanted Ellis; he would make me feel better. I was about to go upstairs to lie down when I looked up to see Ellis walking down the stairs.

"Has she gone?"

I blinked. "What are you doing here goofy, aren't you supposed to be at work?"

Ellis shook his head. "I asked for the day off because I know tomorrow is the appointment. I knew you would need me through this, so I decided to stay home and just be with you."

Confessions in Whispers

He walked over to me, picking me up. "I will always be here when you need me, Nekalia."

I hugged him; I knew that I could always depend on Ellis to be there for me. I would really need him to help me get through tomorrow. I just knew I would break.

Ellis and I decided to go out and have a couple's day. We went to the park where Ellis took me on our first date. We watched a bunch of kids play for a while. Ellis saw an adorable little girl, then said, "She would have been so beautiful, Neka, she would have looked just like you with my eyes."

I looked down, then back at the little girl, then up at Ellis. "She would have been a daddy's girl for sure, I am sorry that my body couldn't keep her."

Ellis wrapped his arms around me, I leaned back into him. "Neka, you do not have to apologize to me anymore baby. Nicolette wouldn't want her mommy to cry all the time, I am just sorry I couldn't give you another baby."

I looked up at Ellis; he would have been an amazing father just like he is an amazing husband. We left the park and headed home. I made dinner for us, and we used the good China, and dressed up for the occasion. Ellis loved having candle lit dinners with me. He wore his wedding tuxedo, and insisted I wear my wedding gown. I walked down the stairs once I was dressed, Ellis stood at the end of the stairs looking more handsome than when I married him.

He extended his arm to me as he led me into the living room. He had moved the couch, tables, and loveseat out of the way to leave a big open space. Ellis smiled at me as he led me into the center of the living room, and then put on some music. We danced, in all my life, I had wanted a man who could dance, and Ellis was the man who could sweep me off my feet. He spun me round and round.

We ate dinner together, chatting about old times and laughing. I felt a pinch in my heart; I rubbed it as I looked up at Ellis, who looked at me concerned.

"We might have used too much pepper in the steaks, huh? You have a little heart burn, baby?"

I sighed. "Yeah, a little heart burn."

Confessions in Whispers

I looked down at my food; suddenly I didn't have an appetite. I felt them coming down my face, I tried to wipe them before he could see them, but I was married to a police officer who paid attention to everything.

Ellis got up from the table. I tried to tell him I was fine, but I could tell in his eyes it was too late. Ellis kneeled down to me. "I am not leaving you, Neka. Don't you worry for a minute that tomorrow will change anything?"

I looked at Ellis, falling into his arms, crying my eyes out in frustration. "I don't want to say goodbye to her, I don't want to say goodbye to anyone! I don't want to feel this way at all Ellis, baby, take the pain away forever."

Ellis knew what I meant. "I will not allow you to take your life. You have to live for Nicolette, for your mother, your friends, and for me."

I looked into Ellis eyes; he would never let me just leave him.

Ellis then said, "Tomorrow, I will be here at the house waiting for you."

I shook my head. "I want you outside in front of the car waiting for me, okay?"

Ellis held me close, I felt him get choked up as he tried not to cry. "I will be there, Neka, if that's what you want me to do, then I will be there."

We tried to enjoy the rest of the night, but it didn't work. We took off our clothes, leaving them in a heap on the floor, climbed into bed and just held each other till we finally fell asleep.

*

When I woke up, I looked to see Ellis standing in the doorway.

"Why do you stand there?"

He smiled at me; he was in a white suit. I sat up.

"Where are you going in that?"

"I have an appointment today too; I need to go for a review." It will be over by the time your appointment is over, I will be at the car okay."

I nodded. I watched him walk out of the bedroom, and then heard him go down the stairs. I looked at the clock. It was time for me to get ready for this stupid appointment.

Confessions in Whispers

I got into the shower, got dressed and looked in the mirror saying to myself "Neka, you can do this today, Ellis would want you to be brave and strong. You can do this."

I grabbed my keys, locked up the house, jumped into the car, and headed to Doctor Michella Hodges office. I arrived a little early as I sat in the waiting area. I looked at an adorable little African American girl sitting by herself talking to herself.

She looked at me. "You're Neka, aren't you?"

I was surprised. "Why, yes I am. How did you know my name?"

The little girl smiled, she looked so familiar to me. "My daddy told me about you, he said you are beautiful, and he wanted me to meet you."

I looked puzzled. "What is your name?"

She smiled, stood up, walked over to me, then hugged me.

"I am Nicolette, mommy."

I gasped.

"You will always have me, mommy. Don't cry anymore, you make me sad."

I started crying, as I hugged her.

"I won't anymore, Nicolette. My baby girl, oh God, you are so beautiful."

Her beautiful ebony face started to fade. I suddenly felt myself being shook. I sat straight up in the chair, looking around the room, calling out "Nicolette! Nicolette!"

I felt someone patting me on the shoulder. "Nekalia! Nekalia, are you ok, honey?"

I looked up to see my momma looking down at me. I tried to regain my composure as I stood up; I realized that I had been dreaming.

I looked at my mom. "Momma. What are you doing here?"

My mom looked at me., "Come in Neka."

She led me into the doctor's office. Once inside, I saw Patrice, Sherry, and even Max there. I looked at the woman sitting directly in front of me as she introduced herself.

"Hello Nekalia, I am Doctor Michella Hodges, please have a seat."

She motioned to a chair next to my momma. I sat down. "What are you all doing here?"

Confessions in Whispers

Doctor Hodges then smiled. "Nekalia, do you mind if I call you Neka?"

I shrugged. "I don't care if you call me Neka, just answer my question."

"I asked for some moral support for you, because frankly you don't know me, so I always ask for family and friends to come to support the grieving person because they are familiar. Do you understand?"

I nodded; I did feel a little better that they were all there, even Max.

Doctor Hodges then began. "Neka, we are here to help you grieve, about your loss. Are you ready to grieve?"

I sighed looking at my mom.

"It has been really hard to deal with this for a long time, I love my mommy so very much, I just can't get over the fact she is dying."

My mom cleared her throat.

"What? Neka that's not what we are her for, I am not dying."

I looked at my mom. "But you have had cancer for the past year, mom, see how strong she is, such a fighter."

Doctor Hodges looked at me, puzzled.

"Oh ok, so why do you think your mother is dying?"

I blinked; I couldn't believe she hadn't told them.

"My mom has been going through this for a year, she has been going to chemotherapy and everything. Momma, I can't believe you haven't told everyone."

My mom looked at me, shaking her head. "Nekalia, I have been cleared from cancer for almost three years now, you know that."

Doctor Hodges interrupted. "She might not, in cases like this, people tend to only remember up until the incident. They have a block of anything during the incident or after."

"Why are you talking like I am not here? I know what is going on here; you want me to talk about Nicolette, right? Look I have dealt with the death of my daughter, thank you very much.

Confessions in Whispers

"Ellis and I have done all we can to put it past us, we almost had a divorce due to it, but we fought through it, and we are doing fine now."

Max's face became red as he stood up. "Neka! You have not dealt with this, and that's why we are here. We are not talking about your mother or the death of your daughter!"

I looked up at Max; he was concerned about me, I felt like crying as I looked down at my hands.

I then heard Doctor Hodges say, "Neka, you are not ready to grieve about it, are you?"

I looked up at her. "I have no idea what you are talking about, there is nothing else I need to grieve for."

Patrice started to cry.

"Oh, Pat what's wrong?"

Patrice looked at me. "I love you Neka, but you have to get this out love, you are scaring me."

I looked at her. She got up and began to walk out of the room when I ran over to her and hugged her. "Patrice don't go. Stay with me, I need you right now, okay."

Pat looked at me. "Are you going to face this or not, because Neka, if you are not going to face this, then I am leaving. I can't watch you do this to yourself anymore."

"Okay," I said.

I was going to face it for my friends, for my momma, and for myself. Patrice hugged me, then sat back down. I turned to everyone, then sat back down too.

Doctor Hodges said, "Ok now that you are ready to grieve. What is it that you want to grieve about, Neka?"

I dropped my head, I closed my eyes, and I could hear Ellis's voice saying, "You can do it now, baby."

I looked up at everyone and cried, "I don't want to; you have no idea how hard this is for me. I don't want to let him go."

Sherry started to cry.

"Dr. Hodges, it's been three years since my brother's death. I understand it all too well how Neka feels. My brother was my hero! He was everyone's best friend; he was my only real friend in my life. When he died a piece of me died with

Confessions in Whispers

him, I could not eat, or even sleep. I didn't want to get out of bed or anything."

I looked at Sherry, she then said, "When I saw you at the store, and you said Ellis told you didn't have to deal with this yet, I was jealous. He was my brother and he stayed with you, he kept you company. I just wanted to know why he just left me one day. I used to see him too; he would stand in my doorway. Tell me I was okay and that he would always watch over me."

Doctor Hodges then looked at me. "What do you want to say about Ellis, Neka?"

I looked at everyone; they were in pain, and this hurt them too. Then I remembered what Ellis told me, "I will be with you as long as you want me here."

I smiled and said, "Ellis is alive to me; he lives at home with me. He keeps me company, we make love, and we live through this together."

Max looked at me. "Nekalia, Ellis has been gone for three years; he died on duty when he took over the day shift. He was shot and killed. You were at his funeral, we all were, and you lost it. You won't pay the funeral fees because you do not want to deal with the fact that your husband has gone! We all have offered to help you pay the cost of the funeral, but you must go down to the funeral home yourself and sign the papers."

"For Christ's sake, Neka, you keep talking about him as if he were still alive, even referring that he would come kick my ass for flirting with you! Now, he will always be with you in the heart, but come on Neka, you say you make love to him, you cannot make love to someone who is not there, that simply crazy."

I stood up yelling, "Crazy! Is that what you all think of me? I would rather have him here with me than to bury him away and forget him! Ellis is everything to me, after I lost Nicolette, I thought I was going to lose him too, but Ellis told me himself that he would rather lose the baby than to ever lose me."

"How crazy is that he would die without me, so he stays with me. I am lost without him; I will not just forget about him as if he never existed!"

Confessions in Whispers

Doctor Hodges sniffed. "I lost my daughter in a car accident a few years ago, I couldn't cope, she was my world, so I started living like she was still here with me. I got up every day, getting her ready for school, driving her there, picking her up. People looked at me like I was crazy too. My family, friends, and eventually my own husband left me because he could not handle 'my fantasy world" anymore.

"One day, my daughter herself told me that it was time for her to go. I begged her to stay with me, but she said I could finally live without her and move on. I know all too well about how you feel."

"You do know how I feel; Ellis said he would stay with me as long as I needed him, he was so afraid I would just forget about him. I have ensured him that I would NEVER forget about him. I cannot do it. If you want to call me crazy then do so, if you do not want to deal with me then do not, but I will not leave my Ellis's side."

"He comforts me, I can live with this. You call me crazy but how am I crazy if I know I can go to work and deal with everyday simply fine, and know when I get home, he will be there to keep me company. How can you call that crazy? When he died, I lost my mind, I would not eat, work, or sleep."

"I couldn't even get out of bed. When Ellis came back to me, he told me to get up and keep moving. He told me I could be better. Ellis is my world and until he says it's time for him to go, I will embrace every moment that I get with him."

"Neka, you are right," Dr. Hodges said.

Gasps went through the room as Dr. Hodges explained. "Neka is very right as long as Ellis is around, she can do anything that is normal. Now, this may seem crazy, but this is actually a large part of the grieving process. If he won't let her go, and she doesn't want to let go herself, she can never live a normal life. Neka, you are so brave to deal with this as long as you have, and not lose it completely."

My mom jumped in screaming, "This is insane Dr. Hodges. I can't leave my daughter like this, I fear the day she will crack and take her own life, like when she tried after Nicolette died."

Confessions in Whispers

I looked at my momma saying, "I wanted to end it before I came here, I begged Ellis to help me do it, but you know what, he wouldn't do it. He told me I had to be here and move forward with all of you for Nicolette, for my friends, for you momma and for him.

"I am getting better; I can see it now why he always stood in the doorway. He comes from heaven that way and he watches over me. Ellis is my sanity; without him I will go insane. I will never be the Nekalia you all know and love. So please stop trying to stop me from being with him."

"You don't have to encourage me if you don't want to. I have learned in the last three years that I don't need your blessings for Ellis to be around. He stays with me because he knows I need him, and maybe one day he will leave me, but by that time I will be able to handle it better than right now."

Patrice stood up. "I am here for you, Neka, I will not hinder you anymore about Ellis. He is helping you through this more than I thought, see you at work girl."

I smiled as she walked out the door.

Next was Max, he shook his head then leaned down and kissed my cheek. "You tell Ellis, that I said I would take care of you, you mean more to us in the living than he will ever understand."

I was stunned by his words, but I smiled as he walked out of the door too.

Sherry stood up next hugging me. "Tell Ellis I was so happy yesterday to see my niece. She is beautiful, tell my brother his little sister misses him dearly and to stop by sometime, okay."

I was completely shocked Sherry had seen Nicolette too; I smiled, nodded, and laughed as she walked out the door.

Last was my momma, she stood up, shaking her head.

"Here Neka, it's the key to your house, I will not burst in on you anymore, I can't watch you like this, you aren't the daughter I raised."

My heart almost stopped, was my mom walking out on me? I got upset and slapped her across the face. She gasped.

Confessions in Whispers

"Out of everyone, I knew you would be the one to stand by me, even if no one else did. You are the only one to turn your back on me, your only child!"

My momma cried. "Nekalia, you tell Ellis I said I want my daughter back one day, you hear me." She hugged me. I dropped to my knees as I watched my mom walk out on me.

I sat there for a few minutes in a trance with tears pouring down my cheeks. Then, I saw a shadow standing over me. It was Dr. Hodges. She helped me to my feet, then said, "She will come around Neka, don't worry. My husband did finally, after my daughter left for good. You deal with this the best way you can. Grieving is about doing what we have to do, no matter how insane it may be to anyone else. We have to learn to cope with what is happening in our reality."

I smiled at Dr. Hodges; she was right. I put the key in my purse.

"She acted this way when my dad died; she always needed space to get her own thoughts in order."

I thanked Dr. Hodges for the intervention and left. I walked out feeling free of my own worries and doubts. I was free to live as I pleased without worrying about what other people thought or felt about our situation. I walked out to the car and there leaning on the hood was Ellis.

He smiled at me asking, "So how bad was it up there? Did they label you insane for wanting me around?"

I smiled at him punching him in the side. "Yes, but what is insane is the fact that I am happier with you here with me like you are now, not the fact of what people think how it should be." Ellis laughed. "Fuck them, baby, I am here as long as you need me, let's go home and have dinner."

I laughed as I got into the car, leaning over to kiss Ellis. "This is my sanity, being with you, always Ellis, I love you."

Ellis smiled as he kissed me, whispering, "I will always be here baby, I love you too, Neka."

I drove home with Ellis and understood now that my world was different from the norm, so what if I am happier this way.

Confessions in Whispers

I was sad that my momma didn't understand me and my choice, and she may never get it. After Ellis died, I went crazy for real. I tried countless times to kill myself; poison, cutting my arms, but nothing worked. So finally, I strangled myself. It was at that time when Ellis walked in "Neka, baby what are you doing? You can't do this! I won't allow you to run away from life anymore."

I got down from the dining room chair; I was wearing my wedding dress. I was shocked to see Ellis standing there in his wedding tuxedo; I ran over to him and hugged him. He was real; he smiled at me stroking my hair.

"Did you think I really would just leave you, not even death could keep me from you."

Ellis then looked behind me shaking his head. I turned around to see what he is looking at, and I stood amazed to see my lifeless body lying there. Ellis walked me over to my body. "Baby, you can't come back to me like this, you have to go back."

I shook my head. I was finally with Ellis. Why would he make me go back?

"I will be right with you when you wake up, I am not going to leave you, now go."

That's where my sanity began; Ellis brought my dead lifeless body back to life. When I woke up, Ellis was there. I then realized that I could live on as long as Ellis was around.

People will call you crazy for talking to yourself, acting strange, but within my own mind I now know that my insanity was my bliss, and without it would be insane.

I still live with Ellis, and I am completely functional. I am still friends with Patrice, Sherry, and even Max. My mom is still away, she will not condone my behavior, but I am not worried because Ellis says she will come around soon, and if she doesn't, to hell with her.

Nothing will change my mind on my decision. If only people knew I was dead before and Ellis was the only one who made me come back and bring my sanity back, they wouldn't be calling me crazy anymore.

Confession 4

Secrets of an Adopted Son

I stood in front of the modern day five-bedroom house. I watched the shadows tentatively as they moved quietly. The light suddenly revealed her face. I sighed as I looked up at my wife, Angel Seasons Mathis's face.

The tears fell as I couldn't even call out her name to ease this endless pain I felt in my chest. I looked around the immaculate house; the lawn was cut, and the trash was out. I sighed again, then I heard laughter coming from the side of the house.

I walked around the house to investigate my baby girl's bedroom. Joylyn Mathis, she is no longer a baby anymore, as I saw a fully grown teenager standing in front of the mirror talking on her cell phone. I looked around her room, she still had all the stuffed animals. I smiled suddenly. I saw a picture of me and her on her nightstand.

I couldn't take it anymore and I began to walk away I heard the window open. I paused as I heard her calling my name. I walked to her window looking into her eyes, she smiled and hugged me.

I couldn't have her touch me, and I pushed her back from me. I look into her eyes, and then I covered up tighter in my dirty trench coat and hid myself behind a tree. "I am sorry Joy honey; daddy can't let you touch him. I have to go princess."

I run away stopping by the mailbox, grabbing the contents, shoving in the items from my pocket, and running away into the night.

*

I ran and ran but I couldn't escape her voice calling me, "Daddy." I was no longer her father; I was no longer a man at all but a mere monster. I looked down as the night took over me once again.

I looked up to the sky. It was a clear night; the stars seemed to shine brighter but not for me. I couldn't enjoy its shine; this monster I was doesn't deserve to be happy or be blessed by its beauty.

I ran again until I reached my alley. I walked into the pitch-black darkness and hid among the

Confessions in Whispers

shadows. In the dark, no one could see my shame. I was safe in its confinement. I settled myself in for the night; I cuddled in my blanket I stole last year. I turned on the flashlight and removed the contents from my pocket.

    I smiled to myself as I looked at the pictures of Angel and Joy. This is how we communicate now; I go by the house every June tenth. Over the years that date was not as torturous as it used to be. I looked at the letters from Angel and Joy. I cried as they pleaded for me to once again come home. I cried because I couldn't, I was no longer human. I could never go back to them, I was no longer Marquise Mathis, and I wasn't even a man anymore. I was a bum.

    I wasn't like the regular bums of society; no, I even praise their strength and respect their fight to survive. I have begged all these years for death; I have tried countless times to take my life but not even God wants me in his presence. I looked around the metal box I have made my home, for my canister. I find it, open the lid and placed the pictures and letters inside. I have collected them for eight years now. Joy is now sixteen years old, a high schooler. I tried not to think back on the past, I have missed out on so much of my little girl's life, but it's my own fault.

I have thought about this countless times, nothing has changed yet. I thought back to the beginning. I was born to Shylynn Harris Mathis, on October thirty-first. My mom died giving me birth. My dad, (I never got to know his name) he was gunned down on the way to the hospital. With no family to claim me, I was put in an orphanage. I should have known I was cursed from the start. I was a ward of the state until I was three, when Damon and Shante Seasons adopted me.

They looked like a perfect educated African American family who couldn't have children of their own but looks can be so very deceiving. Things seem to go fine through my toddler years but after I turned eight, things changed suddenly. My adopted mom Shante was sneaky, she had a devilish smile that charmed any man she met. Damon ended up having a huge drinking problem. They were always fighting, with Damon usually

Confessions in Whispers

leaving. He wouldn't return till morning, sometimes two days later. Shante was a freak; she liked kids a little too much. She always wanted a hug from me; she would have me lie between her legs, wrapping them around and humping me. I was eight. I had no idea this was abuse. I didn't even know the meaning of it. After a month or so of that, I had to take off my clothes and do it naked. I didn't understand back then that she was wrong, but I did as I was told.

That went on till I was nine, I was an over developed boy at that age, had a little chest hair and even my dick was good size. Shante took me to her friend's house "showing" me off. I would have to stand in the center of a living room naked as these women all wanted 'Hugs and Kisses'. I learned oral sex from all these women. Before I knew it, I was having sex with women for money for Shante.

I would go to a woman's house claiming to be a yard boy or something. I would have sex with her in whatever way she wanted, get paid, and then leave. Simply, I was a child prostitute. Shante loved the live shows best. This is when a fellow "Mommy" would have her kid perform with me. The first girl I had to perform with was Staci. Staci Hunter had been a child prostitute since she was five, she was professionally trained. She did everything - anal, bdsm, you name it, and she did it. She walked into the room in her costume, bowed to the women, walked over to me and unzipped me. I just stood there frozen as she sucked me off. I couldn't get over the feeling.

   I think I like fucking and getting head best. We performed, and then serviced the women there. Yeah, they wanted Staci to 'kiss' too. This was my life. At home Shante wanted her own private time with me. She never asked, she always told me. I didn't have a choice I don't think. She would come into my room once Damon was asleep or gone, and I would fuck her for hours or until I couldn't go anymore. She would get mad when I couldn't perform and got beaten for it. I worked on it; I never stopped till she said, "I can't take anymore."

   I had problems countless times. I was always hard. I couldn't help it; I was always working. So,

Confessions in Whispers

when I was at school, I would have a hard on all day. I tried to jack it off in the bathroom a few times, but it wasn't helping. I was attracted to older women and young girls. I couldn't control myself. By the time I was eleven, I was like a machine and like a horn dog at the same time. I would try to trick the other little girls in my class to sleep with me. I had a crush on one cute light skinned girl name Tonya Clear. She was my type and she reminded me of Staci. I begged her to come into the woods with me. When she finally did, I asked her for a kiss. She smiled and kissed me. I then asked to touch her under her skirt. She was scared at first, but I wrapped my arm around her telling it was ok, that I wouldn't hurt her. She smiled at me, then let me do it; I was losing my mind. I had her lie down and I got on top of her.

She got scared and begged me to stop. I got mad; I wasn't used to hearing no. I held her down and kissed her forcefully. She struggled to get away from me; I don't remember what happen next but when I finally came back to myself, I saw Tonya crying uncontrollably by a tree. I looked down and almost threw up at the blood on my dick. I looked at her and asked her, "What happened?"

She turned to me and yelled, "You raped me!"

I was stunned by her words; I felt them before I could stop them. I was crying, I looked at her and said, "I'm sorry."

Tonya seemed to see I was sincere; she crawled over to me and hugged me as I cried in her arms.

Tonya then said, "I won't tell anyone okay Marquise, I know you didn't mean to."

I looked at her and said, "How do you know that?"

Tonya then said, "My stepdad does it, he has been doing it for years. He has never felt sorry about it."

I sat in complete shock. "I'm so sorry Tonya, I have no idea what came over me." Tonya kissed my cheek, and we went back to class. The rest of the day I could feel the shame. Every time someone looked at me, I would blurt out, "I'm sorry." I was laughed at so much that I finally ran out of the classroom and headed home.

Confessions in Whispers

When I got home, I found Shante in the kitchen. She smiled at me, and I walked over, kissing her before sitting down at the table. I then looked up at her and said, "I raped a girl today."

Shante turned to me with a shocked look on her face, then she smiled and said, "How did it feel?"

I shook my head saying, "I don't remember all of it. I just remember is her saying no and then I blacked out."

Shante shrugged her shoulders as she brought me a sandwich and a plate of chips. She sat on my lap.

"Now baby, some girls don't understand it's your job to serve them yet, so you have to teach them, even if you have to take it to make them understand."

I nodded that's the kind of teachings I got about sex; take it no matter what.

So, by the time I was fourteen, I didn't take no for an answer. My next "playmate" was a brown skinned girl named Yasmin Christie. She liked me; she told all her friends we were dating. I didn't mind, I wanted her anyway. So, one day I asked her if I could walk her home from school. She was excited. We walked to her house and her parents weren't home. She let me in, and I led her to her bedroom. I sat on her bed motioning her to sit next to me. We kissed a while, and then I placed her hand on my dick.

  She jumped. "I'm a virgin, I can't do that Marquise." I told her it was fine and said, "Let me eat you then."

  She looked scared but agreed to that, so I used all my techniques I had learned. Once she had cum at least three times I said, "Let me stick the head in at least." She smiled and nodded. I put the head in, but I didn't stop there. I started pushing. She tried to push me back, but I held her down telling her to relax.

  She started to scream; I got mad covering her head with a pillow as I pounded her. Once I came, I let her go. She just lay there crying, I wasn't in the mood for her tears. I got up and got dressed. As I was getting dressed, she hit me with a lamp. I grabbed her by the head and slammed her against the wall, then pulled her hair.

Confessions in Whispers

"If you dare tell anyone what happened I will kill you, you hear me!"

She nodded her head and I let her go. Then I sat down next to her, caressing her face. "Come on now, tell me the truth, it was good right, after you relaxed."

She smiled at me. "Yeah, it was baby."

I smiled; she was getting with the program. I kissed her, and then we did it again this time without all the drama. I left her house feeling weird. I couldn't explain it. I felt bad about Yasmin, I couldn't shake off this bad feeling, but there it was again - my shame, my guilt. I ran back to Yasmin's house banging on the door. Yasmin's mom answered. I fell to my knees saying over and over, "I 'm sorry."

She looked at me weirdly until I saw Yasmin. I ran over to Yasmin, fell to my knees, and said, "I am so very sorry, Yasmin, please forgive me."

Yasmin helped me to my feet and walked me out the door to the corner. "I forgave you already Marquise; I know this isn't you. I could tell in your eyes you were confused, Look, you need to talk to your mom and ask her why you feel this way."

I knew it made sense; I did need to talk to Shante about these feelings. So, I kissed Yasmin on the cheek and ran home. When I got home, I walked into an argument. Damon was drunk again. I shook my head and headed to my room when I heard my name being called. I walked into the living room.

Shante ran over to me screaming, "Don't you dare put him in the middle of this, Damon!"

I was confused. "What's wrong Daddy?"

Damon pushed Shante out of the way, then grabbed me and hemmed me up against the wall.

"Daddy my ass, nigga you have been fucking my wife!"

I shook my head. "Nah, daddy I would never…"

He cut me off by punching me in the stomach. "Fuck that! I am not your damn Daddy! People are talking about the two of you; they are telling me what they heard from this house when I am not here!"

Confessions in Whispers

He went to punch me again; I closed my eyes bracing myself for the next blow when I heard a crash. I opened my eyes to see that Shante had hit him over the head with a vase.

Damon fell, she had me help her put him on the couch and cover him up. Once he was taken care of, Shante walked over to me and rubbed on my dick. I moved her hand. "Hey, I am not doing that shit with him right there." Shante's eyes narrowed at me, then she pushed me against the wall whispering in a low tone, "You're mine and I can have you whenever and however I want you, do you understand." She unzipped my pants and sucked me off. I bent her over the couch and fucked her, watching for Damon to move at any moment but he was out. I was enjoying myself to much I slapped her on the ass; I pulled her hair, and she came and came. Once she had her fill, I took a shower and went to bed.

The next day was a Saturday, and that feeling crept back up on me. I couldn't shake it; I got up and got dressed. I went downstairs. Shante had breakfast ready for me. Damon was gone; she smiled as I kissed her. I sat at the table and asked her "Shante, what's with this feeling I have once I take a girl?" Shante smiled and sat on my lap again; I was getting tired of this shit. As I pushed her off "Is this all just a game to you, some freaky sexual training? Answer my damn question!"

Shante stood there with her hands on her hips.

"I don't care what feelings you are having; you are property to me. I don't care what you do; you must come back here to me. Your feelings are little concern to me. If you ever push me off you again, I will throw you out on the street! Do you understand me?"

I was once again defeated; I played it off by walking over to her, wrapping her in my arms, kissing her neck, massaging her breast telling her bend over the kitchen table.

I fucked her till she was satisfied. That's the only time I am ever in control - when I am fucking someone. I left the house and took a walk to the park.

My life is a blur now, I had no idea what the fuck to do. Why did I feel like shit, and want to apologize every time I slept with a girl? I was trying my best back then to come up with an answer, but it wouldn't come to me. I was sitting there when I heard my name being called. I looked around to see Staci.

She sat next to me. "What's the matter with you, Marquise?"

"This feeling I have when I take a chick I like."

Staci laughed. "You actually feel guilty! Boy you better get with the program. I don't anymore. There is nothing you can do about the way we were raised. I have sex with men and women now."

I looked at her kinda shocked, but why had she had been in this life longer than me? Then it made sense to me; if there was nothing, I could do to change it then why fight it. I grabbed her and kissed her on the neck. She pushed me away, then grabbed my hand taking me into a men's restroom. We fucked in one of the stalls not caring who heard us.

Staci called out to the men listening to us. "You perverts can watch us for a hundred."

We fucked all afternoon in that restroom. I made me a cool seven hundred by the end of it. I went home and looked for Shante. I found her in the bathroom just getting out of the shower.

I grabbed her; she laughed telling me to stop, but I knew she wanted it. I took her in the bathroom. As I was banging her, I heard the front door open, Damon was home.

I turned her to the bathroom door, bending her in front of it telling her, "Don't moan, just answer him when he talks."

She nodded, and then locked the door. I heard him coming up the stairs as I stirred inside of Shante. She tried not to moan as he walked to the door.

"Baby, you in there?"

She cleared her voice. "Yes, I am in the shower, I will be out in a minute."

I pushed harder into her; she gasped which made Damon say, "Baby you ok in there?"

She quickly replied, "Yes, I changed to cold water when I wanted hotter water, baby. I will be out soon."

Confessions in Whispers

I listened to Damon walk away, and then pulled out, pushing her down onto her knees and made her suck me off. She did, and I loved it, when I am in control. I made up my mind that I would be in control always. I didn't care if someone's feelings were hurt.

I raped from eight to thirteen. I had sex with various older women for money. I went with the program. I had no feelings, I was exactly what Shante said, "I was property, I was meant to serve women no matter if they wanted it or not."

So that's what I did until I was seventeen years old. By this time Shante had finally had her a baby, it was a little girl they named her Angel. I played with Angel, she was a sweet little girl, but my appetite grew as well.

I was dating Staci then and we had a ball fucking adults together. She was the only one who understood my cravings and helped me every time to satisfy them. One night I was babysitting Angel, when Staci said she wanted to fuck, right in front of Angel. We did, and I didn't care if she watched. When I was done Angel asked if she could play. I smiled I played with her for a while. She had to learn. I knew Shante would have her sooner or later. When the door was thrown open.

Damon and Shante stood there in shock as I quickly got dressed. Shante ran over to Angel asking her what happened, Angel smiled telling her we were just playing.

Shante stood up and backhanded me screaming, "What have you done to my child, Marquise?!"

I turned and looked at her screaming, "I only did what you trained me to do! She wanted to play so we played!"

Damon jumped on me, punching me over and over. I fought back pushing him off me.

"What, it was ok for me to fuck her all this time, but I can't get what I want when it comes to Angel!"

I pointed at Shante. "You made me this way, now you know how I hate it!"

Shante grabbed Angel who was trying to run to me screaming, "You Monster, you should be put in jail!"

Confessions in Whispers

That's exactly what happened. I was sentenced to prison for ten years for molesting Angel. The judge didn't even have pity on me when I told him about the abuse at the hands of Shante. He didn't listen to me at all, I was a pedophile. While I was locked up with the other criminals, I got my ass whooped for being a pedophile.

Once I finally explained what happened, most of the dudes in there cut me some slack. Others kept warning me to watch my back. I spent those ten years trying to think about my life. Where in the hell had it gone wrong? The counselors in prison didn't really talk to me. My years flew by me like lighting and before I knew it, I was getting ready to be released.

The conditions of my parole were simple, stay the hell out of trouble. I couldn't be around kids unless they were my own. I wasn't allowed near schools, parks, or anywhere kids were playing. I could not be there.

I wasn't interested in fucking a kid after being locked up that long, I needed a woman! I had to report to my parole officer twice a month. I didn't have a place to stay now that I had fucked it up with the Seasons. I was now twenty-seven years old with no job, with a felony record and no money. What the fuck was I going to do?

As I walked out of the prison, I saw an attractive red bone girl standing in front of a car. I began to walk in the opposite direction of her when I heard her say "Marquise?"

I turned around. "Yeah, how do you know my name?"

She smiled at me and ran towards me. She wrapped her arms around me, but I pushed her away. "Whoa! I don't know you. What do you want?"

She looked hurt as she said "Marquise, you don't remember me at all?"

I shook my head, then she blurted out, "I'm Angel, Angel Seasons."

I blinked at Angel, and then said, "What are you doing here? How did you know I was here?"

She smiled again, then explained everything as I got in the car with her.

Confessions in Whispers

"Well after they arrested you, Momma wasn't the same. All she talked about was this brother I had. I wanted to see you so badly, but Momma said she had messed that up for me. So as time went on, all she would do was talk about you. She would spend all day talking about you."

I shook my head., Shante was crazy. Angel continued "Well, after a couple of years, she told me that you weren't my real brother. It was then that I started looking at you as my Prince Charming. I fantasized about you constantly. It was a few years ago that I ran into that Staci girl. She told me where you were and I now here I am."

We were at a red light.

I sighed. "What do you want with me?"

Angel kissed my cheek. I turned and just stared at her as she drove. I hadn't been kissed in ten years, and now that she had done it, I didn't know what to do with myself.

I leaned over to her and kissed her back on the cheek. She grabbed my hand and I held hers; she had given me new hope. She got me a hotel room and told me she would take care of me until I could get back on my feet.

I didn't have any doubt in Angel; she always did exactly what she said she was going to do. She bought me some food and we talked.

I couldn't keep it in as I said, "I am sorry about what I did to you back then, Angel."

Angel looked at me, then sighed. "Momma told me how she used to treat you. I understand how you felt."

I was surprised she could understand when I didn't even understand it then.

She continued, "I never held any grudge against you Marquise, Momma wouldn't let me. She felt terrible once they locked you up; she tried to kill herself many times. She wrote you so many letters saying she was sorry. She never sent them because she thought you wouldn't accept them after what she had done to you. Daddy left Momma after he found out the truth about what Momma did to you. He was to hurt to come and apologize to you too.

"Before he left, he told me to tell you, his son, he was sorry for never protecting you, and blaming

Confessions in Whispers

you for Shante's behavior. Daddy had been one of Momma's victims, he was jealous that she had found a replacement in you."

All the shit Angel told me started to make sense; I didn't know that Damon had been one of her victims. Shante had used her power to control the emotions and actions of men to get whatever she wanted, as well as train them to hurt and deceive the rest of the world.

I am lost in her devilish game even now; I know that just the sound of her voice would grab a hold of me and suffocate me. Angel took me to the store to buy some personal items, and bought me food, then she left.

Alone in the hotel room, I am lost once again. It was the nights that haunted me most. Even though I felt it was my comfort it was also my doom. At night I would have endless nightmares of girls screaming, ringing in my ears. The endless pleads for me to stop, and I could see my rage clearly. I lay in the fetal position praying for peace, but their voices echoed with questions I can't answer… "Why did you do that to me? Why are you hurting me?" I shook uncontrollably.

I woke up the next morning in a cold sweat. I ran to the bathroom to throw up. This was a daily process even when I was in prison. I would awake, disgusted at myself of the things I have done in my past. I stared at myself in the mirror as I knew how the day was going to go.

I would go out and rape the first pretty thing I saw. I could see the monster creeping up on me; I turned away from the mirror and ran back to the bed. I would not leave the room today. I know it's best I stay inside, away from regular people.

I jumped suddenly at a knock on the door I shook my head as I walked up to it, opening it. I looked down to see Angel smiling up at me. She hugged me suddenly and for some strange reason, I was at ease. She bounced in with food; I smiled as I took a seat at the table. She talked, rambling about her day at school, classes, homework, and teachers.

I listened attentively. She was so cute in her boot cut jeans and tie-dye t-shirt. Angel's auburn hair was pulled back in a ponytail. She was beautiful to me, she was kind and different, and I believe that's what makes me feel at ease.

She isn't my prey; she is my friend, something I have never known. When I was younger, I kept to myself. No one would have ever come near me if they knew my true nature. I smiled at Angel as she continued talking about her day. Then she grew quiet, looking at me with concern. I begin to panic, I wondered, "Am I wearing my monstrous form on my face in front of her?"

She sighs, "Marquise? How do you feel about me?"

I am shocked at first as I laugh at her question. I look back up at Angel, her eyes are narrowed at me. I have pissed her off. I quickly say, "Angel, you do understand that we could never have a normal life."

She looked disappointed at first then says, "Marquise, I love you! I know that with me, you could have a real life."

I grabbed her, hugging her tightly; she knew the words to say to make my heart melt. Angel held me tightly, and for the first time in my life I didn't have a feeling to knock her down and take her. I just wanted to lie there in her arms forever. I pulled back from Angel looking into her brown eyes. "Ok, we can be together."

   I watched her face light up like Christmas as she tightly bear hugged me. I held her firmly, letting my lips graze her forehead. I knew then she would be the only one to make my heart melt now.

   After Angel left, I went to the mirror and looked at my reflection. For the first time in a long time, I saw me. I had new confidence with her love. I went out into the world with a new beginning. I put in for jobs, I explained my past carefully to people and although most didn't hire me, I didn't give up. I knew someone would.

   A man with a construction company by the name of Tyler Hampton hired me. He was a good man; he believed I needed this job. He always had a theory about the type of job you do, having something to do with your personality. He also told me, "Marquise, there are no little girls around here, you earn my respect by doing your best, nothing less."

My boss was a black man with a father like personality. He was older than everyone else who worked for him; he was our mentor, our dad, and our friend. I worked hard for Mr. Hampton. He always encouraged us to do our absolute best, to not be afraid to make a mistake because we would never learn to do it right if we didn't mess up. In no time, I was able to afford an apartment and I moved in with Angel. She was so excited, and she didn't want to live at home anymore with Shante.

Shante had found a new piece of "property" to play with. I didn't want Angel around her Momma's madness anymore. I had lost the best parts of my life following all her bullshit orders.

Angel and I lived together for a long time. She was the best thing in my life. As long as I had her I would be fine. Angel kept the monster inside me at bay. She eventually talked me into going to college. I asked Mr. Hampton one day about it, and he said, "Look Marquise, I believe and always have that a good education makes a strong young man."

I laughed. "Did you go to school, Mr. Hampton?"

He smiled at me walking me into his office to show off not only his bachelor's in architecture, but his master's in business administration as well.

Mr. Hampton then said, "It took a long time for me to build everything I have son, I had to take many bullshit jobs in this field, but I worked hard. I never gave up on my dream. I took all I learned, and I taught you boys how to earn a living worth having, son. School is a particularly important part of that, so yes, I say go Marquise."

I took the advice Mr. Hampton gave me and enrolled into the community college, Harrison Technical. I really liked the construction field, but I had always wanted to land me a degree in social work.

I understood the underlining pain from being unwanted, used and abused. I wanted to be different, and somewhere in my mind, I felt I could do it. So, for the next two years I worked hard to pass all my classes. With Mr. Hampton and Angel's help, I finally graduated.

Confessions in Whispers

I then started looking for jobs in my field. This would be one of the hardest times of my life. Because of my felony conviction, it almost became impossible to get a job in my field.

I was a registered sex offender, and since this job would have me near children, I practically wasn't deemed fit for roles in social work. There was no way anyone would hire me. Just when all hope seemed lost, I landed a job in a women's halfway house. I would be one of three social workers there. Since there were no children there, it was safe. I worked there for the next seven years.

My life was good and finally in place. I believed I had beaten my past finally. I was going to therapy, and I married Angel in a secret wedding. I even invited my dad, Damon. Angel and I didn't bother inviting Shante; she didn't care that Angel was even gone, but I just knew if she knew I married her daughter she would start problems.

A year after Angel and I were married, we had a beautiful daughter, Joylyn Mathis.

Seven years would go by before my past came back to haunt me. I was working at the women's halfway house talking with my clients when she walked in. She looked like shit, but I recognized her without a second glance. She walked in with her normal "fuck you" attitude and sat down. She didn't even look at me at first till I said "Staci?"

I watched her for a moment; she tried to shy away from me. I reached out to touch her, but she turned away from me. I backed up and said again, "Staci? Is that you?"

Staci turned her head to look me in the eyes. She blinked looking me over, and then jumped out of the chair hugging me screaming, "Quise! Oh my God, Marquise is it you?"

I hugged her back, embracing my old friend. I pulled back from her then asked, "What the hell happened to you?"

Staci tried to fix herself, brushing her hair with her hands and straightening her jeans and tube top. She sat back down.

"I got caught up on some bullshit, you know, but I didn't do it."

I nodded as she talked; I looked over her file. It said Staci had been put in prison for prostitution.

Confessions in Whispers

I looked at her. "Staci, are you still doing this?" Staci looked offended and I tried to explain but she snapped at me.

"Doing what? Don't you look at me like that Marquise, like you didn't do it too!"

I stood up and closed the door to my office, then turned around saying, "That was the old Marquise, I am a different person altogether now, Staci."

Staci rolled her eyes. "Yeah right! When is the last time you fucked a little girl?"

The words stabbed me like a knife. I sat back in my chair unable to speak for a minute, my body was shaking like a fiend.

I shook my head yelling, "I am not that man anymore! I have a wife and a child now, Staci. I have a little girl of my own and I would kill a man dead if anyone ever touched her!"

Staci smiled at me; I could see the demon in her eyes. I turned my head and covered my ears, but I heard the words anyway. Staci's voice almost changed into a demon's voice as she whispered, "You miss the feeling of power, don't you Marquise."

I looked her dead in the eyes. "No, that so-called power our so-called parents gave us almost destroyed me! Staci, look what your mother has done to you, you are a mess." Staci raised an eyebrow. "At least I am honest about who I am Marquise. Unlike you, you hide behind this desk, acting like we didn't rape little girls together for fun. You haven't changed. You are still a monster just like me. You just haven't had the chance to really let it out is all, but you mark my words, Marquise Mathis. It's coming, oh yes, your test is coming. You will want the taste so badly that it will consume you."

I stood up turning my back to the wall. Staci walked up behind me and caressed my back with her nails. I felt the feeling, she was testing me. I screamed in my head "FIGHT MARQUISE! YOU ARE MARRIED NOW! THINK OF JOY AND ANGEL!"

I snapped out of my trance, turning around to face Staci. I looked her in eyes.

"I am not like you anymore Staci, I am not a monster anymore."

Confessions in Whispers

Staci smiled, backing away from me and grabbing her things. She headed for the door. As she reached for the handle she said, "Once a monster, always a monster, Marquise. You are no different than me, you are just brain washing yourself into believing so."

She then took something out of her purse and placed it face down on the desk, blowing me a kiss as she walked out. Once she was gone, I walked over to the desk and picked up a photo. When I turned it around, I gasped!

It was a picture of Angel and me when she was five. I closed the door to my office and locked it. I sat at my desk admiring the picture a while. I smiled at how cute she was as a little girl. Suddenly I felt it, I tried to think of something else, but it was too late, I was hard. I cursed myself but then I looked down at the picture again and I felt my dick throb.

I screamed at myself. "Marquise, she is your wife now! Stop it! You wouldn't look at Joy like that!"

My mind then wandered to my beautiful little girl. She was turning eight soon. I still had to get her birthday present and set up her party. She was getting big too; she was developing nicely as well. She has way more body than her momma did at that age.

I caught myself. "What in the hell was wrong with me? Marquise no, you are not that person anymore."

I cleared my head, shoved the picture in my pocket and got my stuff ready to go home. I closed my office and headed home.

Angel had cooked a great dinner and my princess had painted a new picture for her daddy's office. We ate, I read to Joy, and then I took a shower. I was lying in bed, Angel said, "Are you ok, Marquise baby?"

I turned to her. "Yeah baby, I am fine." I turned back around. Angel held me from behind, kissing my ear. "Marquise, I know you baby, talk to me."

I faced her looking into her eyes; I always felt better when I was near her.

I cleared my throat. "Baby, I feel weak. I had a relapse for a minute today."

Confessions in Whispers

Angel caressed my face softly. "It's ok Marquise, remember what the therapist said, 'It will get harder before it gets easier, baby. Do you want to take it out on me?"

I was shocked by her words, and I stared at her. I could feel the monster in me boiling inside of me. He wanted to take her, he wanted to tie her up and beat her. I shook the image away, jumping out of the bed and running out of the room. As I reached the stairs, I jumped back to investigate in a mirror.

He was standing there staring at me, the monster. I couldn't move, he held me captive for a few minutes. Angel ran out to get me, I snatched away from her.

"Don't look at me! Don't touch me!" I ran down the stairs towards the door.

Angel caught up to me screaming, "Marquise, you can't run from this! You have to face this head on, baby!"

She grabbed me this time. I turned around facing her, then broke down in her arms. I held on to Angel for dear life. She stroked my head.

"Baby, I am here. I won't let him take you from me!"

She grabbed my face with both hands forcing me to look at her.

"DO YOU HEAR ME, MARQUISE MATHIS! That monster has no power as long as you continue to fight him off. I will not let him take you from me!"

I hugged her tight; Angel always knew what to say to snap me out of one of my episodes.

I then heard a small voice. "Daddy, are you ok?"

I turned to see my little princess standing at the bottom of the stairs with tears in her eyes. I motioned for her to come to me, and she ran into my arms. I hugged her tightly.

I had woken up Joy again with one of my fits. I felt so, ashamed of myself as I picked her up, carrying her back to bed. Once I knew she was asleep, I went to bed holding Angel tightly. I needed to see my therapist tomorrow before it was too late.

The next day I called my therapist Dr. Peter Winedale. I spoke with his secretary Deloris. She told me that Dr. Winedale was out of town and won't be back till Monday. I told her to make me an appointment for Monday. She made my appointment and told me she could prescribe me some medication to get me through the weekend.

I begged her to do so, telling her I had an episode last night. She put in my prescription and told me I should be able to pick it up in an hour. The date was June tenth. That was the day that changed my life forever. I was waiting around the house, trying to occupy my time till I could get my prescription. I was sitting in the house alone watching T.V. Angel was at work and Joy was at school. I had called off work because I wasn't feeling well. Whenever I have an episode, I do not go to work the next day because I am weak and can't control myself well.

I was watching T.V when I heard him, I tried to ignore him at first, but he started screaming. I fell to my knees covering my ears, but I could hear still hear him calling to me. "Marquise. You miss the power, don't you?"

I screamed out, "No! I DON'T! I DON'T WANT THIS ANYMORE! WHY CAN'T YOU LEAVE ME ALONE?!"

I could hear him laughing at me. He was taunting me. I tried to block him out, but he was getting stronger. I crumbled to the floor shaking; I reached for the clock on the end table knocking it down to me. I looked at the time, I only have thirteen more minutes before my prescription would be ready.

I was struggling; he was taking over me again. I kept my eyes on the clock; I needed something else to concentrate on. I was still on the floor screaming for this monster to leave me alone when the door opened.

I looked up to see Joy standing in the doorway. She was smiling, running over towards me.

I screamed out, "Joy! Honey, go to your room!"

She tried to say something, but I yelled again.

"Joy! Please go to your room! Lock the door and under no circumstances do you let me in or come out!"

She ran up the stairs crying. I tried to regain my strength enough to get to the phone. I reached for

Confessions in Whispers

the phone, dialing Angel's work number. I got her on the phone. I was screaming. "Angel! Get home now! Come get Joy out of house now!" Angel screamed into the phone. "What is she doing home this early! I am on the way! Stay on the phone with me, Marquise!" I began to black out, I shook it off. I felt the pain as I shouted, "ANGEL! HURRY!"

Angel yelled back into the phone. "Baby, try to fight it! Don't let it take over you! I am coming Marquise, hold on baby."

I tried to hold on, I tried to listen to Angel's voice only. I felt dizzy as I saw a vision of Angel, she always keeps me sane. Her image was blurry in my mind as I continued to fight this urge that was growing stronger. I beat the floor yelling to Angel, "Hurry Baby! I can't hold on anymore."

She tried to tell me something, but it was no use. I couldn't hear her as I blacked out.

When I come back to myself, I looked around to find myself in Joy's room! I looked around the room again; I had broken through the door. I started to cry as I turned to look at my daughter.

Joy was lying still on the bed; I ran over to her. She was unconscious. I grabbed a hold of her, shaking her, begging her to speak to me. She stirred, then opened her eyes looking up at me. She immediately fought to get out of my arms. I was relieved to see she was ok as I held on to her tightly.

Joy continued to fight with me as I tried to apologize to her. She then bites me, and I let her go. She ran towards the door, then looked back at me. I couldn't look at her face, all I could see were the bruises on her body and the blood running down her leg.

I fell off the bed to the floor, crying. I suddenly heard the door fly open. I heard Angel's voice downstairs, and then I heard her scream. I can only imagine the expression on her face as Joy ran into her arms, to see what I had done.

I looked for something to end my life with, but I couldn't see a thing to take me out.

"I can't do this anymore," I said to myself. "You finally have to come to grips with this Marquise; you are as Staci said, you're a monster. Look what you have done to your own daughter! You can't change, you were stupid to think you ever could!"

I cursed myself for another ten minutes. I made my choice to leave them. I wasn't normal, I never was.

It killed me; I couldn't take it anymore. I got up and ran down the stairs. I looked at Angel's face, she yelled out to me, "Marquise!"

I wiped the tears from my face. "I am no longer your husband Angel, and Joy, I am no longer your daddy, I am a monster, and I can't be with you anymore. I am sorry."

I ran out of the house. I could still hear Angel calling my name. I ran away, and as I ran; I saw images of Joy's bed covered in blood. The images burned into my mind and would not fade. Suddenly, I could hear the screams of little girls, and then I could hear my Joy's voice. I fell to my knees in the middle of the street. A car stopped right in front of me. I leaned on the car, annoyed it didn't hit me and take me out of misery.

The man tried to help, but I yanked away and continued to run. I wandered the streets all day. People looked at me and I mumbled, "I'm sorry."

They are all looking at me, they can see it! I shouted at them saying, "I 'm sorry! I know you can see it! I am monster and I am sorry!" I wandered to a house familiar to me, it was Shante's.

*

I walked up to the door. I was about to knock. I saw her standing there, staring at me. She grabbed me and hugged me,

"Marquise! Oh, my baby, you're home!"

I hugged her back, and then looked into her eyes.

"I hate you! You did this to me!"

Shante's face changed. She pushed me back. "No one saved me when it was me, so why should I give a damn about you!"

I stepped up to her face.

"So instead of stopping it, you continued it! You preyed on me and Damon, and whoever you have now! All because no one saved you from it! You trained me all these years to the point that I can't even function without you! I raped my daughter today because of YOU!"

Shante started to shrug her shoulders until she heard me say, "Oh no, don't act like you don't care, she is YOUR granddaughter after all."

Shante's head snapped up., She held on to her chest. She started to cry.

"You! YOU ARE FUCKING MONSTER! You took my baby and now you have taken my grandchild!"

I was in no mood for her bullshit. I grabbed her by the arm. She struggled to get free from me, but I had a firm grip on her. I threw her on the couch; she looked scared. I rolled my eyes.

"Don't you dare play innocent now! This is your entire fucking fault, you told me to serve them even if they didn't want it!"

She turned her head away from me trying to cover her ears, but I moved them, screaming in her face, "YOU WILL LISTEN TO ME! You did this! You made me into this monster! I didn't want to be this way; I wanted a better life with Angel and Joy! I tried my best to fight the demon you poisoned me with, but he got the best of me today. Don't you understand I raped and beat my daughter unconscious today all because of you?!"

Shante looked up at me.

"I'm sorry, Marquise. I am sorry for all I have ever done to you. The man who raped me when I was younger was your dad. The woman you were born to, was my best friend Shylynn."

I felt my knees grow weak and I dropped to the ground.

Shante sat up. "Marquise, I am so sorry. I did it because I couldn't forgive your dad for what he did to me. He made me a monster too and even now I can't stop it".

I couldn't believe it, all this time I was the prey for revenge for my dad's actions! My blood boiled, my rage was unmeasured as I stood up and slapped the hell out of Shante. She fell off the couch and onto the floor.

"I know I was wrong, but I am sorry, Marquise!"

I didn't want to hear that shit now! I jumped on top of her as she screamed. I grabbed a hold of her neck and started to choke her! She gagged in my arms, as I squeezed. She beat at my hands as I watched the tears stream down her face.

I suddenly couldn't do it. I let go of her.

Shante grabbed me, begging, "Please Marquise, kill me, take me away from all of this."

I turned to her. "I won't give you mercy when you never showed me any. Fuck you, Shante. You tortured me my whole fucking life over some grudge you had with a man I never knew."

"I am now this monster because you couldn't let it go, but you want to know what I think? I think you like being a monster. You are addicted to the power, and it consumed you!" Shante sat on the floor crying. She wiped her tears. "You're right, I do love the power, but I didn't want that life for Angel. So, when she left and never came back, I thought it for the best before I did her like I did you."

I walked over to Shante, kissing her on her forehead.

"Goodbye Mommy."

I read the hurt in her eyes and all over her face. I had hit the one nerve she couldn't power her way out of her heart. She grabbed me from behind before I left.

"You can beat this Marquise, I can't. I have done this too long, but you can. I know you can. Forget all I have done; all I have said. Get help son, I love you Marquise."

I left Shante's house feeling lost, I finally understood the truth behind her games and her power trips, but I understood it too late. There was no help for me now. I went to the drug store and got my prescription. The damage had been done, but at least I could keep the next episode away for a while.

I quit my job and just wandered the streets. I took all the money out of my personal account. I was no longer a normal part of society. I was a monster even though I knew no one could tell by my appearance.

I felt they could read it all over my face. I bought a trench coat and a hat. I didn't want people to stare into my guilty eyes. I eventually would find a safe haven in an alley I would name my home. Even though I expected to find the police waiting on me when I walked by my house, there was never any there. It became a ritual I would do every June tenth.

I would steal cards, candy, toys, jewelry and anything I could get my hands on to shove into the mailbox during the night, along with a letter to let them know I was alright.

Angel and Joy would leave me pictures, letters, and even money. Though I was no longer around them, I felt close to them this way. This way, they were safe from my episodes and my guilt. I hide myself away from them like a ghost; I might as well be dead in their eyes.

It was best for me to forget them until June tenth, but I lied to myself. They never left my mind. I longed for Angel's touch and Joy's smile. I hide in my alley to keep myself from harming anyone, and it's been this way for seven years now.

Even as I hide myself in this place now; I claimed myself the worst, the bottom feeder of society. I stayed away from everyone. I only go by the house on that day; it's my birth and death all at once.

I walked the streets knowing people can see my guilt even now. I cover up in my blanket when I hear a voice. The voice was familiar. I turned my flashlight on to see who was calling my name.

I looked to see Joy standing in the alley way. I turned away from her.

"Joy, it's too late for you be out here, it's dangerous, go home please. I am no longer your daddy. I am no longer human."

I can hear the tears in her voice.

"I am not going back home without you daddy! Now you listen to me. I know that when I was a child, I didn't understand what you were going through, but I am not a little girl anymore. I have looked into all of this, and you can fight this! Momma is dying and you aren't even there to take care of her!"

I walked out of the alley and stood in the light as I hear the news of Angel dying. I straightened my clothes. "Please tell me that not true, Joy?"

Joy looks at me. "She is dying in spirit daddy, she needs you. You come by every tenth of June, you never speak to her, she writes to you all the time to come home, we both do, are you going to do this forever?"

I looked at my daughter, I have caused more pain and heartache than good.

"I stayed away because of my condition; I thought I was doing what was best for you and your mother. I couldn't forgive myself for what I did to you, Joy. You are the most precious thing in my world beside your Momma. I couldn't believe I hurt you the way I did.

"I couldn't stand you hating me like all the rest of the other little girls I have hurt over the years. Can you really tell me you could forgive me for what I have done? Could God give me another chance to be the man I was before that fucked up day?"

Joy wiped the tears from my eyes.

"Yes. I can forgive you for what you did to me that day, I have already. I cannot forgive you for running away like a coward in the night missing out on most of my life, but daddy, it's not us who needs to forgive you, it not even God who needs to forgive you. It's you! Daddy you have to forgive yourself for what happen to you in your life, the whole thing."

"You can't keep fighting it if you can't even forgive yourself for it. What are I and momma supposed to do? Wait until the day there are no gifts or letters in the mailbox to know you are dead! Then, not know where you are to bury you! You would send us through that, daddy? How selfish are you going to be about this?"

I looked into Joy's eyes, she meant it. She was right; I had to forgive myself first before I could get better. I couldn't bear to put them through any more pain. I couldn't die in this alley where no one would know where I was. It would kill Angel for sure, and then even in death I would not be able to forgive myself.

I remembered what Shante said. "I could fight this, I had done it before, and I could do it again."

I went back into the alley, grabbed my canister and walked back out. Joy's face lit up when she saw me standing there with her.

I looked up at the sky. "Marquise, I forgive you for everything you have ever done to anyone. Give

Confessions in Whispers

yourself the life you were meant to have. God keep me this time, don't let this monster take me ever again.... Amen." I turned to my daughter. "Ok Joy, please take your daddy home."

Joy hugged me and I let her. She cried in my arms as I hugged her back. It had been years since I hugged my princess. I got into her car, and we drive off to the house.

*

I hesitated to get out, but I did. Joy opened the door to the house, and I heard her voice. My heart filled with joy as I watched her walk down the stairs. She stopped, staring at me.

She screamed. "MARQUISE! BABY YOU'RE HOME!"

I grabbed Angel, hugging her tightly. I kissed her all over her beautiful face. She cried in my arms as I grabbed my daughter and hugged them both.

I made a promise there and then that I would never leave them again. I have had one hell of a life; it was dramatic, tragic, and full of pain, tears, redemption, and love. The secrets of my life are my family's, no one else apart from a select few know the details of my life. Now I am a happier person; I killed the monster inside me all together. I am a father and a husband again and I will never turn my back on my family again.

My daughter saved my life; she found me and brought me back home with her. I would have never found the strength to face my demons and win without her forgiveness. Thank you Joylyn and Angel, you are the true Angels who saved my life.

Confessions in Whispers

Confession 5

The Color of Red

Dear Diary,

Fuck this shit! There is no need to keep up appearances any longer! This bastard thought his ass was slick, and yes, I played the fool for him. To all his bullshit mind games! Yes, I can admit it now, I was the dumb ass who loved him so much to the point that he controlled my every move, but after what I have read from this little slut, fuck it!

I am going to kill both of their asses. Since they want to be together so fucking badly, I will bury both of their trifling asses together. I can't believe this shit, all this shit I have ever done for this man was for her!

How could she do this to me, we're family. I am her fucking aunt, but you know what? Fuck it now, they both have to go!

Thinking about these letters I am holding in my hands got me mad as hell. Look at this bullshit. Over the last three years of our marriage this was going on! I always wondered why he switched up on me so suddenly. I thought it was some kind of a break down, he needed this to feel whole again and me being stupid, I would do anything for him.

Damn you, Maxine! You should have left his ass then, but you didn't. You stayed enduring it all.

I paused a minute. I was trembling all over thinking of it all! I looked down at the paper and then looked at the handful of letters I was holding. Placing my pen down a moment I picked up the first letter. I tried to pace myself as I opened it slowly starting to read it aloud.

*

"Trimaine,

I see you like me, huh? You are married to my aunt. Max, you know dat, don't you? I don't care if you are married or not, you are fine and all. I can't fuck with you though. Besides you're a weak man, and I don't want no weak ass man. I need a man who can take control; he gotta know how to keep me in check.

My Aunt Max runs your ass, I ain't seen no reason for me to fuck with you. You are no real man, just cause you got some bread, don't mean shit! I can fuck a drug dealer and have that bread! You gonna have to show me some real man status before I even think about giving you a peek of my goodies. Kisses (got your dick hard, don't I) LOL, Nell."

*

I dropped the letter watching it float to the floor. That's when it all started - from this one letter. My nightmare began....

A couple of weeks later, Trimaine and me were at my sister Zena's house for a dinner party. Zena is my baby sister, she is also Shanell's momma. I remembered that night clearly. Shanell was walking around in a high black mini skirt, lace blouse showing off her breasts and stripper high heels. Her bronze and black streaked hair was up in a bun on the back. She was a nice-looking girl; she and Zena had the same medium skinned tone and hazel eyes. For a sixteen -year -old she dressed too grown for me.

I remembered talking to Zena about a party she and her boyfriend Daryl were throwing the week after next.

Zena said, "Maxine, you and Maine have to come with us to Tripp's next week to celebrate Daryl's promotion."

I smiled at my baby sister, nodding. "Girl, we will be there, I will just have to remind Trimaine."

I turned around looking for Trimaine, but I didn't see him anywhere. I started to search the house for him.

When I finally located him, he was outside on the patio smiling and talking to Shanell.

I smiled thinking, "He is such a good role model for her."

As I walked over to them, Shanell smiled at me. I tapped Trimaine on the shoulder. He turned around. The frown on his face made me feel uncomfortable.

Confessions in Whispers

I quickly asked, "What's wrong, baby?"

Trimaine rolled his eyes at me. I was amazed; he had just been all smiley and cheery with Shanell, and now that I had appeared he had an attitude!

Oh, hell no, this shit was not going to fly at all. I said, "Would you like to have this conversation in private?"

Trimaine looked at me. "No, I wouldn't, now leave. You're bothering me."

He turned his back on me and continued his conversation with Shanell with a fucking smile on his face!

I stood there a minute thinking to myself, "Oh no, this mother fucker didn't!"

I tapped him again. The next thing I remember was blacking out! When I blinked my eyes, I realized I was sitting on the floor looking up at Trimaine and Shanell.

I felt intense pain along my jaw line on the left side of my face. My eyes almost popped out of my head as I realized Trimaine had hit me!

I blinked again and started to get up, but Trimaine bent down whispering to me, "Don't you fucking move, you sit there until I want you to get up."

I froze. I couldn't move. Trimaine had never hit me before, and now that he had all my big talk was out the window as I just sat there.

Trimaine stood up smiling down at me.

"You're fucking pathetic! All that shit you used to talk about what you would do to man who hit you. Shit I just hit you and look at you just sitting there. You make me sick."

I couldn't do anything. I just sat there with this horrible throbbing sensation coming from the left side of my face. Shanell stood there looking down at me, she shook her head and walked away with Trimaine. They had left me alone still sitting on the concrete.

"Max, what in the hell are you doing? Why in the hell are you just sitting there?"

I was in shock! I couldn't believe Trimaine; my husband had hit me in front of my niece! She didn't do anything to help me either, she just looked, but I thought back then she was too scared to do anything, thinking he might hit her.

Confessions in Whispers

I sat there for almost twenty minutes before Zena found me. She was so upset to see my face and screamed, "Sissy! What happen to your face?!"

I lied; I didn't want her to know what had just happened with Trimaine. So, I tried to smile, but it hurt like hell.

"Girl, I tripped on the doormat and hit my face on the side of the door."

Zena helped me to my feet. We went into the bathroom. When I looked in the mirror, I started to cry. The whole left side of my face was swollen. I turned away from the image, disgusted at what I was seeing. I sat on the toilet.

Shaking my head, I just could not comprehend what had just happened. We had been married for almost nine years, he had never, I meant never even looked like he wanted to hit me, let alone talk to me like that in front of anyone.

Zena gave me an ice packet for my face. I pretty much stayed in the bathroom for the rest of the night. I didn't want to alarm anyone with the condition of my face. We left a few hours later; Trimaine helped me to the car.

As we were headed home, he apologized to me.

"Baby, I have no idea what made me do that to you. Let's go the store and get you some medicine for your face, okay."

He smiled at me, taking my hand, and then kissed it. He caressed my swollen face lightly. I had to forgive him, he didn't mean it, but we had to talk about this in the morning.

I exhaled deeply; I was a fool. I really believed that shit back then, that he didn't mean to knock me on my ass. I looked back down at my diary; yes, it had to happen now. I had to end their torturous game before they killed me.

I closed my diary for the night; tomorrow I would go get everything ready for June seventeenth. I didn't need to remember anymore dates; they had all happened in a blur anyway. All that mattered now was June seventeenth. I hid my diary and the letters as I heard the keys of the front door. I went downstairs to greet my husband. I would stay the faithful wife he has always known for now, no need to let him know what awaits in six more days.

Confessions in Whispers

I will be the last one laughing in the end. I will have them both, and I will have no regrets. They didn't care about the pain, and the emotional burden they were causing me, then why should I care about the pain, and oh yes, the endless pain I would cause them.

I placed myself in the position that he had trained me to be in when he arrived home. On my knees, head down wearing a red silk night gown that he had bought me. As the door opened, I heard his breathing. He smelled of a scent that was quite familiar to me, it was hers. He had gone to see her again, that's why his ass was late. No matter, I was no longer concerned with the affair my husband was having with my niece.

No! I smiled to myself as he grabbed by my hair, yanking my head upwards. I look into his eyes with a fake concerned look on my face. Pathetic, aren't I? He had no fucking clue that I was numb to the whole act now, nothing hurt me anymore. He shouted in my face because I hadn't answered him. I make myself cry, as I pleaded for him to forgive me. Trimaine slapped me across the face, and I crumbled to the floor. I didn't even look up.

He grabbed my hair again, yanking me to my feet. "How many fucking times must I tell you to look up at me when I come through the door!"

He slung me towards the wall; I braced myself as the pain speared through my body. I had gotten smarter, and I now wear a body suit, so the impact wasn't as bad, as the first time was.

He broke two of my ribs the first time. I bounced off the wall, falling to the floor. Damn that hurt! I enter my inner self and the pain disappeared. I could see all the blows but couldn't feel a thing. To me, it was all a routine, all a blur.

I woke up the next morning without any real memory of the night before. As I opened my eyes, I saw blood on my sheets; yes, Trimaine had beaten me good. I would have to wash these sheets before he got home. I laughed to myself; I know it was sick, but all of this was so amusing now, there was nothing else I could do but laugh.

Confessions in Whispers

I rolled over on my back looking at my vaulted ceilings, yes, I lived in style. Trimaine was a highly paid business consultant, and I was his beneficiary if anything were to happen to him. I got up and looked in my hiding place for my diary. I pulled it out and sat at the little table in the corner where I usually look out the window to watch the birds. I opened my diary to the next page to write.

Dear Diary,

I laugh to myself thinking there are only six more days. Last night like many other nights is a complete blur, I couldn't tell you what I did, or what he did. I found myself sleeping in bloody red stained sheets again.

Trimaine must have had him a really good time. Oh well, he better enjoy it while he can. Today, I have to buy a few things like the bullets, the rope, the poison, the gun, the plastic bags, and lastly, the dress.

Oh, there are a few other things I need to get but I will think of those later. This whole situation has me going crazy. Last night yet again, he came home smelling like that heifer! She has no morals; just a little hot ass slut is all. No matter, yes, I said it, no matter. She better enjoy him while she can.

I pull out another letter looking at it. It read: "Trimaine!

Damn, I didn't think you had it in you to smack her like that! Oh baby, you turned me on with that shit! Ok, I guess you do have a little real man status in you. You are still not ready for these panties though. I need a man who can handle his woman; I mean I will have to want to do anything for you. Now I know you had her sitting there looking stupid and that was funny as hell. Make her degrade herself. You know what I mean do, something unthinkable like hmmmm, like piss on her! I will give you a kiss if you do it. You gotta let me see it, so video tape it! I know you can do it my big man, Nell.

*

Yeah, I remember that night. He came home from work, talking shit, and he sounded wasted. He stumbled inside the house, shouting my name. I came running down the stairs thinking there was something wrong.

I asked franticly, "Baby! What's wrong?! What happen?!"

Trimaine looked at me saying, "Nothing baby, I just want to hold you is all."

I rolled my eyes, helping him up the stairs. We stopped halfway to the bathroom, and he said, "let me go pee, baby?"

I helped him into the bathroom, and I let him go, but he grabbed my arm.

I looked up at him. "What in the hell is wrong with you, let me go!"

Trimaine got mad, he pulled me over towards him, blowing hot drunk air into my face.

"Let's have some fun, baby?"

"Maine, you are drunk, hurry up, pee and come to bed."

I tried to walk away from him, but he pushed me into the bathtub. I hit my head on the tile, I felt dizzy as hell. I tried to remain conscious, but I blacked out.

A few minutes later I was woken to water being poured on me. Some got in my mouth, I coughed and gagged. It wasn't water, it was pee!

Trimaine was standing over me, peeing on me! I tried to get up, but he punched me in the mouth knocking me back down. I cried in the tub as I couldn't move. Why???? All I could think was why was he doing this to me? What in the hell was he thinking?!

Confessions in Whispers

I lied there feeling totally degraded as my husband pissed on me, videotaping it on his phone. Once he was done, he wiped his dick on my face and left.

My mind wandered in circles, I just sat there for while covered in urine! I cried silently to myself as I ran the shower over me. I made it as hot as I could stand it, I didn't just want to wash away the urine. I wanted to wash away the shame. Yes, the endless shame I felt.

I had to let this go on; I hadn't once tried to stop it. So, was I the one to blame for all of this going on? Was there something as a wife I wasn't doing to fulfill my husband's needs?! Once I cleaned up, I went to bed. Trimaine was fast asleep.

I would ask him in the morning about this whole thing. The next morning, Trimaine woke up with a hangover, I quickly got out of bed and made him some tea thinking that would help, then gave him some aspirin. He smiled at me, stroking my hair. "Thank you, baby, you take such good care of me."

I paused a moment, there in that one sentence was the man I fell in love with. Tears flooded my eyes as I hugged him.

He embraced me and kissed my forehead. Suddenly a flash back hit me about last night. I looked up at him. He gasped looking at my face.

"Baby? What happened to your face?"

I blinked, he had no clue he had hit me last night, he didn't remember any of it! I realized that he must have been so intoxicated that he blacked out.

"You hit me last night."

Trimaine grabbed me, holding me close. "Oh Max, I am sorry baby, I have been looking online at these sites, with women being submissive. I just want to add some spice to our relationship, and you seemed to not be interested."

I pushed back from him. I yelled, "Maine, there is a better way to ask me for something kinky, than to hit me!"

Trimaine looked at me then I saw his face change. He shoved me off the bed, and I hit the floor. I gasped.

He said, "You don't love me!"

Confessions in Whispers

He got out of the bed; he looked like a giant from where I was sitting. He continued, "You hate me, don't you?"

I was at a loss for words, what in the hell was he talking about?

I screamed back at him, "I do love you Trimaine, but I have no fucking clue what you want from me!"

He started pacing the room; his sweet medium chocolate features seem to melt away into this monster.

He leaned down grabbing my chin, I tried to wiggle out of his grasp, but it was no use; he was too strong. He pulled me forward, then yelled, "I want you to do what the fuck I say, stop questioning me and just do what I say!"

I saw his hand rise backward, I didn't want to be hit again, and I stretched my arms out screaming, "I will do it! Baby I will do anything you want me to do, please don't hit me again."

He smiled as he lowered his hand, placing both hands on his hips. Then a terrifying smile came across his face. The ice- cold chill that ran up my spine froze my soul. He was no longer my loving husband; he was a monster, and I was now his slave.

    I shuttered to the thought of that smile he gave me. Yes, from that day on it just got worse. He had a new thing he wanted to "try" every day. And yes, all of this shit I would do for him, just to make him "happy", to prove I "loved" him. Days turned into weeks, and then months. By the time I knew it, it had been three years. Now I know the truth, my anger was now hatred. He fucked me over for that little bitch, and I will show him.

    I remembered the countless things he made me do, but one night sprang to my mind more than any other.

    I looked down at the letters, twelve in total. But only a few meant anything to me. Just a few of them stood out to me, the ones that caused me so much pain.

    Dear Diary,

Confessions in Whispers

    I know I have neglected you but planning out my anniversary has drained me. I am still here looking over the letters. I am still shocked at a particular one, that I can't stop looking at; it gives me shivers thinking of it now.

    Countless days went by without a reason why he was treating me so bad, and soon my reason for living was to serve them both. Nothing mattered and all I wanted in this world now was his approval. I had lost all self-respect in the years I endured his twisted fantasies.

    Death was no longer my biggest fear, being lost to him was. I had no way to escape, even though my physical body could leave, my mind was trapped within his words and hands.

*

    I pause a moment picking up another letter. This one would give me some reasoning to his newfound madness as it read,

*

    "Wow, Maine, Baby, you really do know how to handle her ass now, but baby I want you do something more devilish to her now. I know you asked me the other day, why did I do all of this shit to her to begin with.

Well, you see my daddy and my aunt had an affair together when I was little, which caused my momma to go crazy for a while. She apologized and everything but fucked that! She fucked up my home! My daddy left mad one night and died in a car accident that night.

So, since she loves dick so much, I have an idea. I know some horny boys at my school who would love a crack at her. You set it up baby, and we can fuck upstairs while they tear her apart, you game? Nell.

*

Tears form in my eyes as I remember De 'Shaun Mathieson. Yep, I had slept with my little sister's husband years ago. Shanell would have been no more than like eight years old at the time.

De 'Shaun was my boyfriend first. We had dated in high school; we were engaged to be married first! She stole him from me; she slept with him on my prom night! Zena was always fast; she was

Confessions in Whispers

almost as bad as Shanell. She got him drunk and slept with him on my prom night.

I never forgave him or her because she became pregnant! My momma told him to marry Zena or go to jail. He married her, but he begged me to forgive him for years. I could have if he hadn't married her, but since he had, I wanted my revenge. You're damn right I slept with him, but I was getting back at Zena not Shanell. Oh well, no matter now, that was her problem if that's the grudge she wants to hold against me. I cried more than anyone at De 'Shaun's funeral. He was the love of my life then until I met Trimaine, I was completely lost.

*

I closed the diary. I didn't want to remember De 'Shaun. It hurt too much to think about him and his beautiful face. Tears dropped, but I wiped them away. I cleaned the house and got back into my submissive position, waiting for my husband to come home. When Trimaine got home, he beat me, and slapped me around. For me, it was all over in a matter of minutes, I hardly remembered a thing.

The next morning, it was all the same. I woke up in bloody sheets again. I smiled; it wouldn't be long now. As I went to my hiding place to retrieve my diary, I sighed as I opened it. Not many entries in it, I agree, but the ones I was writing helped me fuel my anger to rage. I clearly remembered a memory of one of my "Lessons" as I write,

Dear Diary,

The night she asked him to set me up was the final straw for me. I was tied to a twin bed that he had set up in the living room. I was blind folded for a good minute, until I heard the voices. Male voices, a lot of them. I became terrified. I heard heels tapping on the hardwood floor of the foyer. I knew there was at least one woman with them. I called out to Trimaine, but he would not answer me. I remembered thinking to myself, "What in the hell are you going to do to me now?"

My question was answered as I heard him clap his hands together.

"Have fun, Max."

Confessions in Whispers

I called out to him again, but suddenly I felt hands all over me. My clothes were ripped from my body. I remembered I was screaming, struggling to get free but I couldn't move. I was raped over and over again for hours. Laughter, chuckles, and high five slaps went around the whole time. When it was all over, I woke up to see Shanell with her arms wrapped around Trimaine.

She smiled at me. "You got exactly what you deserved, finally his all mine now."

My eyes bulged out of my head as Trimaine leaned down to kiss her passionately. I yelled at Trimaine, but he never took his eyes off of Shanell.

I yelled at her. "How in the hell could you do this to me, I am your aunt!"

She looked back at me, rolling her eyes.

"So what? You took someone from me, so this is fair play." I didn't realize then who she was talking about. Trimaine walked her out to the car. Once she was gone and he had come back in the house, he looked at me.

"Well now you know. I don't love you anymore."

He walked over to me and untied me. I slapped him across the face, and then tried to run. He grabbed me by the hair and slammed me to the floor. I lost all my breath. I crawled on the floor to get away, but he jumped on me beating me unconscious.

From that day on I was numb. I couldn't feel anything. I wasn't allowed to leave the house anymore or talk to my family. Shanell came to the house and I was now the servant. She spat at me, slapped me, and even kicked me a few times. I was given a red silk night gown to wear symbolizing I was a whore. I was to never speak any longer unless I was spoken to first. This was how it was even now. I closed my diary for the night. I shivered at the lessons I had learned. I got back to my numb existence and serve my master.

*

A few days ago, while I was cleaning Tremaine's office, I knocked over one of his book holders and I saw the letters fall out. I picked them up, looking over them. I sat on the floor as I felt the tears flood my eyes. I was amazed as I saw the truth vomiting out.

He had done it all for her. Everything was her fault; she was fast just like her momma. She had written him all these letters, sent sexual pictures of her to him. She fueled his perverted fantasies with her words and pictures. I read them all, they explained all my pain, humiliation, and the void. The last letter was written a couple of days ago.

"Maine,

Look my love, I am ready to be all yours, but we both know that bitch won't give you a divorce. So, let's kill her, so then we can be together forever. I love you Trimaine, you have proven to me that you are the man for me. I am so very proud of you. Let's have babies together and live happy from now on. What do you think baby? We can do it after your anniversary and tell everyone she left you. We can poison her, and then dump the body outside of town. Come on baby, let's finally end this and be happy. I love you so much. Nell.

That's when I started planning. Days have passed, now it was now June seventeenth. I had everything ready. Trimaine wanted to celebrate our anniversary together. He went to work early that day when I woke up. I wrote a last entry in my diary that day.

"Dear Diary,

This is the last letter I will be writing to myself. It's all come to this. They will both now go to hell where they belong. I will feel no remorse for them, as for the last three years there was no forgiveness for me. I have everything I need, even down to my beautiful evening gown. Tonight, I will end my suffering and I will be reborn anew. Goodbye Trimaine, Shanell and Max."

I closed the diary, bittersweet I would think it was. I had ended my old life to get ready for a new one. I went to prepare for tonight. I was happy; our first and last time together would be bittersweet. I cooked dinner; we would have steak, mashed potatoes, and green beans.

Confessions in Whispers

 I asked him to invite Shanell over, since she loved my cooking so much. He thought it was a great idea. Shanell arrived a little later. I let her and Trimaine sit as the heads of the table. She wore a little black dress and smiled sweetly at Trimaine. I wore - to their surprise- a red evening gown. I wore my long light brown hair in an up do. I wore long red gloves and deep red lipstick. Trimaine couldn't keep his eyes off me. Shanell was a little jealous, she tried to smile as she said, "You look like a high price prostitute!"

 Trimaine and she laughed at me together, I laughed too. I then served them their meal. I sat in the middle of the both of them. We all enjoyed a beautiful dinner. Once dinner was over, I stood up to toast them both on a beautiful life together. Shanell looked shocked.

 I said, "I love you both, you have given me a beautiful new life and I want to thank you."

 Trimaine seemed choked up. He tried to say something but suddenly felt dizzy, then passed out on the table. I turned and looked at Shanell who ran over to him trying to shake him awake. I stood up, walking behind her and whispering in her ear as I grabbed her hair, "He's dead."

Shanell screamed as I dragged her into the living room. Where the twin bed was set up once again, I threw her on it and sat on her as I strapped her up. I laughed as she struggled to get free from me. I then stood up, walking to the foot of the bed looking down at her smiling saying, "Shanell, you really could have come to me and just asked me why I slept with your daddy. I would have told you everything, how your mom stole my husband from me. She had you, and how I couldn't forgive her then, so I slept with him later."

"It's not my fault you found out about it. You didn't have to take it to this level though; we could have talked it out. Your mom and me did, we are closer than ever. You, however, couldn't let it go; you blamed me for him dying."

I wiped the tears from my eyes.

"You corrupted my husband, but I have to blame him too, he didn't realize you didn't really love him, you just wanted to get back at me."

Confessions in Whispers

Shanell cried, "Daddy talked about you all the time. He told me one night when I was thirteen, that you were supposed to be my mommy. I hated him for saying that. He was supposed to love mommy, not you! I hated you both for it. So I had this sixteen year old guy I knew who worked on cars. He messed up his brakes, he promised me that daddy would be able to live through it, but the way the truck hit him, he never made it."

I dropped to my knees, I covered my ears, and I couldn't believe what I have just heard. She killed him; she was the reason De'Shaun was no longer here!

I cried from my soul; her jealousy had to be stopped. I wiped my eyes, then stood up when I heard the knock at the door. I opened it to see the young men who had raped me two months ago. I had run into them bragging about it at a store one day. I offered to pay them to play with my niece for me.

I smiled as they walked into the living room with me.

Shanell screamed at them, "I know all of you, I will tell on you."

I smiled, crossing my arms across my chest.

"This is fair play isn't Nell, you had them rape me, so I had to have them rape you."

I sat on the love seat and watched them tear her apart; I was blessed to not know exactly who they were. She would have to face each one face to face. I smiled then looked to my left as I watched Trimaine wake up. He stumbled into the room. He stood there in shock watching the boys raping Shanell.

He turned to me, then begged on his knees for me to stop them. I stood up watching him graveling at my feet. I smile as I slapped him across his face.

"You're pathetic! All these years you played this little game to win her over and look at her now enjoying every minute of those boys raping her, you ought to be ashamed of yourself." I then pulled out the gun from the side of the loveseat.

Trimaine begged me not to kill him. I laughed.

Confessions in Whispers

"I am not going to kill you; I am going to give you a choice. You can do it yourself or kill the both of you, don't matter to me."

"What if I don't want to do either?"

"Boys, please bring me the video camera."

I showed Trimaine the footage I had collected over the last couple of days, then the letters from Shanell.

Trimaine then said, "Baby, I'm sorry."

I laughed. "Baby? I haven't been baby for the last three years Trimaine. Now you can do that or have the police put you both in prison for an awfully long time."

Shanell screamed out weakly, they had worn her out, "We're family! You can't do this to us."

The boys began to leave, and I handed one of them the evidence, then said as I walked over to the closet to collect my bags, "There is no trace of evidence that I was ever here tonight, I wore gloves the whole night. The boys wore condoms so as you can see, they cleaned the living room before they left. So that leaves you two alone in the house.

"Trimaine, you always did like the color red. Now at last, so do I, I sat the gun on the post of the stairs, then walked out.

I wasn't out the door a few minutes when I heard the scream from Nell then two-gun shots, I smiled thinking of blood pouring from her lifeless body, and then I heard the second shot and heard Trimaine calling my name.

I paused a moment, then I walked back inside to see the bloody mess. Ahh, it was the most beautiful sight I had ever seen. The color seemed to calm me. There was not a bit of fear in my heart or in my eyes. The bloodstained scene brought me peace, and I smiled as I looked around to see Trimaine crawling toward me.

He looked up at me saying, "I love you Maxine, I am sorry for all the pain I caused you." I laughed out loud at the delicious irony of it all. I wanted to watch him bleed to death, but I had a flight to catch.

Before I walked out of the house, I turned to Trimaine and said to him as he took his last breath,

Confessions in Whispers

"I always thought that blood was thicker than water, you and Shanell proved me wrong, enjoy hell Trimaine."

I don't even shed a tear as I think back at what happened that night. I was on a cruise when the police questioned me. I gained Trimaine's insurance money. I burned the diary. I didn't really need it; it was my reason to force myself to do it, the constant reminders of my pain for the last three years. The letters from Nell gave me the right push to harm the one I loved most. Her greed and obsession gave me all the fuel I needed to end my torment.

I moved back into the house once the scene was clear. I shake my head and smile at the living room every time I walk into it. As I slip my gloves on and walk down the basement steps, I smile at the pathetic figure strapped up against the wall. As I reach for the whip, I smile, slapping it against my red boots.

The old Max is gone; I was no longer weak. I raise the whip up high and listen for the cracking noise when I hear him scream.

I almost climax as I hear him shout, "Oh. Thank you, my sweet Lady."

I am happy to hear my new name said loud and clear. Max was gone; she died on June seventeenth; she will never return again either.

Trimaine and Shanell had given me a new life, a new name. I am now obsessed with the lifestyle I had to endure for three years. I hit my slave over and over again, happily remembering every beating under the hands of Trimaine, my body tremble with excitement. I became obsessed with the color red, now as well. Trimaine's favorite color, the color he gave his whore! Oh yes, the color of passion, hate, and finally at the end, my revenge and my name, Lady Rouge.

Confessions in Whispers

Confession 6

Switching Shadows

I was ashamed of myself now! Why in the hell did it take this long for me to be ashamed? I walked into the bar, looking for a place to sit and decided to sit at the end. I asked the bartender for some Hennessey with ice. I needed a drink. I know I promised my wife I would quit, but tonight I needed it.

How in the hell did I come to this?! Three years later and now I was upset about my decision. I sipped on my hinny. I was a wreck now, and I couldn't even look in her face the same anymore. Tonight, I would let this shame out. I was just waiting.

Suddenly, I saw him. I know it was a risk, but it was a risk I had to take. He looked at me as he took his seat. I couldn't even look him in the face.

I just mumbled, "You want a drink?"

He shrugged his shoulders and nodded ed as I order him the drink of his choice.

He sighed as he took a hit of his drink.

"You asked me out here, now what in the hell do you want?" I looked around the bar for an empty table. I found one by the pool tables, then motioned for him to follow me. We sat at the table.

I sighed then began,

"When I was younger, I fell in love with a beautiful young girl called Evelyn Cider. She was one of the most beautiful girls in my high school. She was supposed to marry this asshole at our school, his name was Nickolas Sanderson. He was the quarterback. I was on the yearbook committee; I was a nerd, a nobody. Well, during our senior year, that asshole went and got himself killed in a drag race with some college kid.

Evelyn couldn't get over it; no one understood her, she would go to his grave every year without fail. I began to follow her there; I became her companion. I would help her grieve through it and eventually she fell in love with my compassion. I

Confessions in Whispers

married her after I finished college. We tried for three years after that to have children, nothing.

We almost gave up hope....

*

He just rolled his eyes. "What the fuck does any of this have to do with what you have done?!"

I sighed, pacing myself, then said, "Everything, just let me finish."

He sat back in his chair and pulled out a cigarette. As he lit it, he motioned with his lighter for me to continue. I sighed, closing my eyes momentarily.

"Evelyn became very depressed. She cried most of the day. We almost considered adoption because we wanted a child so badly. We even went to a few adoption agencies to find a newborn baby. In the end Evelyn couldn't go through with it. She wanted her own child.

"There was nothing in this world I wouldn't do for Evelyn. So, we went to the doctors, countless doctors, trying to figure out the problem. We found out that I was the problem. I was not producing strong enough sperm. So, they put me on a strict diet, changed my underwear and even gave me pills to help me strengthen my sperm count.

"A year later Evelyn was pregnant! We were so happy! I made Evelyn take off work the whole time. She was pregnant! I went out and got two more jobs to support us.

"I was so excited that by the time I knew what we were having, I was damn near set! I went out and bought so many types of diapers, bids, wipes, bottles, you name it I bought it. Then we found out we were having a boy!"

I paused a moment, I tried to refrain from crying. I laughed it off.

"I will admit I cried when I heard I was having a son. I couldn't help it I was overjoyed! Nothing made me happier in this world. When MY son was born, I cried, I named him Marcus after me. Holding him that night in the hospital, I made a promise to him, that I would always protect him."

I looked up at him. He sighed rolling his eyes.

"But you hurt him right, you disappointed him, didn't you?"

I lowered my head.

Confessions in Whispers

"I have spent so much time lately wondering how in the hell did all this happen?"

I remember the first time I saw Shana Gibson; I froze. I can't even explain it. Maybe it was her sun kissed skin, dark amber eyes or thick lips….

He shook his head, disgusted at me.

I raised my hands. "I am sorry, but I had to tell you exactly what I thought of her. I am sorry if you can't handle it."

He wasn't listening to me, that's fine. I started to get up and leave.

He jumped up. "Where the hell are you going?!"

"You told me you would listen to my story, now you are sitting there ignoring me, so I am going to leave.".

He sat down motioning for me to sit back down too,

"Alright I'm listening."

I sat back down, and paused a moment, then said, "Are you going to listen to me now or just sit there and ignore me?"

He crossed his arms in front of him.

"Yeah, I'm listening."

I wondered if this was a good idea after all but continued anyway.

"She was so much younger than me. Hell let's face it, she was old enough to be my daughter, but that didn't stop our mutual infatuation. I met her when she was only twelve years old. She was dating my son then. He was so proud to have her on his arm. I was proud of him too; he had found his Evelyn. For years they were inseparable, he loved her as much as I loved my Evelyn.

"It wasn't until Shana was fifteen that her true feelings were even brought to my attention. I was taking her home one night after one her dates with my son, when she started telling me that she liked me. She told me the story about how she grew up without a dad, and how she was scared of all of her mother's boyfriends because they had all raped her as a child.

I felt sorry for the girl."

*

He sat up in the chair.

"What?! She told YOU about that?!"

Confessions in Whispers

I nodded. "I guess she didn't think my son could handle it."

I continued. "Well, I started to watch over her, like the dad she never had. One night she called the house real late begging me to come and get her. She was crying that she had locked herself in her room, trying to keep one her mom's boyfriend's out! I could hear the man yelling at her through the door. She was pleading for me to come get her. I jumped out of the bed, got dressed, and headed over there.

"When I got there, sure enough he was still there trying to get in her room. The front door was open, so I ran up the stairs. I beat the guy's ass and kicked him out! I threw him out the door. He yelled, "Hey man, I live here!"

"I told him I don't give a fuck and to come back when Shana's mom was home. He got in his car and drove off. I went back into the house to check on Shana. I knocked on the door softly letting her know it was me."

"She opened the door slowly looking out to see me standing there. She ran out to me and sobbed in my arms. We sat on the couch till her mom stormed in screaming, "What in the hell is going on here?!"

"I stood up and introduced myself again as Marcus's dad, then explained how some guy that claimed to live there tried to rape her daughter. She just rolled her eyes and tapped her foot. She didn't care, she was more pissed off that she had been called off from her damn job!"

"Yeah, he stays here. You know what, I don't have time for this shit, so you watch her then. I have to go back to work."

"I was surprised, I watched as this woman walked back out of the house and back to work!
"I sat with Shana for a while. She lay on my chest, cuddling me. She kept telling me about how brave I was, and she wished she had someone like that to protect her. I reminded her that she was dating my son, and he was just as brave.

She shook her head that she didn't agree with me. We watched a movie, then as I was about to drift off to sleep, I felt a rubbing sensation. I looked down and saw her rubbing on my leg! I jumped up

Confessions in Whispers

protesting that this wasn't right. She was dating my son for Christ's sake! She smiled at me telling me about how she had always liked me, and that Marcus was a little boy, he could never protect her like I did.

"She then looked at me with those amber eyes. '"Besides, aren't you bored with that lame sex with your wife.'"

I paused. Sure, I was bored but I never thought I would ever admit it out loud. I loved Evelyn, but she wasn't trying anymore to turn me on, let alone have sex with me.

Then I thought about my son. He was young but so was she. Shana was fast, much faster than my son could possibly handle. I shook my head; I couldn't go through it. She then crawled towards me grabbing my shirt. I looked down at her as she smiled up at me.

"At least let me do something to thank you for saving me."

I said, "A simple thank you will do."

She wasn't hearing it. She whipped me out and started sucking me off! The rest is history; we slept together. I was so lost in the moment I couldn't think straight, and before I knew it, I had come.

"Before I left, she said something to me that left me feeling weird. She said, '"You and Marcus should switch places more often."'

On my drive home I thought about that, I had switched places with my son! I couldn't shake the feeling as I walked back into the house at seven-thirty in the morning! My wife was in the kitchen with my son.

"'BABY?! What was so important that you ran out in the middle of the night?!'"

I looked at my son, and then said, "'Shana called me.'"

Surprise came across their faces.

"'She was attacked by one of her mom's boyfriends.'"

Gasps echoed the kitchen as my son jumped up, running to the phone. Once he was out of the room Evelyn said, "'Oh my God Marcus! What did you do?'"

I sat down explaining everything except what Shana did afterwards. Do you know what? A while ago, everything seemed pretty cut and dry, but it was Shana's appetite for me that was insatiable; she wouldn't stop. "She sucked me off and wanted more. She wanted it any place! Once she sucked me off in the bathroom of my own house! It didn't matter where, it could be the house to the backseat of my car. We eventually called it "Switching Shadows." She was switching little Marcus for big Marcus. The affair would go on for a year. I was mad at myself for not stopping it sooner, but by the time I knew it I was obsessed.

"I was falling for her, that devilish smile, her fire hot touch and those dark amber cat-like eyes. She was sucking me in fast! The more Evelyn denied me sex, the more Shana begged me to fuck her. When she called me telling me she might be pregnant one day, the whole situation changed.

"I got scared, but I agreed to take her and my son to the clinic, because we both had been fucking her and we didn't know who the father was! The whole time I drove us to the clinic I prayed it was Marcus's, not because I didn't want a baby with Shana, but because he loved her so much!"

"I looked at them through the rear-view mirror and smiled as he talked to her, trying to hold her hand, but she wouldn't let him. I saw the expression on his face, and I wanted to pull over and give him a hug. She had hurt his feelings. She looked up at me and smiled.

"'Marcus, are you okay, son?'"

He looked up. "I am a little nervous, dad, were you this nervous with me?'"

I laughed. "'Yeah, I was.'"

"When we arrived at the clinic, I told my son I had to get some blood work done. We had two different doctors see us. The results would be back within a week. A week later, I was scared to death as we walked back into the clinic again for the results. The doctor to see us was my doctor.

"My son said he was going to the restroom. I sat there alone with Shana.

Shana said, "'I hope it's yours.'"

There was nothing I could say, I didn't want to think about the baby right now, I was worried about the outcome if it was mine. The doctor came out congratulating me. I sat there in a frozen state for a minute, as my son walked in.

He smiled, shaking his head at the doctor as he patted him on the back saying, "No, it's mine, this is my dad. I know we have the same genes and all, but that baby is mine."

The doctor looked at my son, confused. Then he raised his brows at me. I turned my head as I listened to him tell my son.

"'I am sorry young man, but this baby can't possibly be yours.'"

I remember turning to look at Marcus's expression as he laughed.

"'Why in the hell not?!'"

The doctor tried to calm Marcus, but he wasn't hearing it as he shouted, "WHY IN THE HELL NOT?!"

The doctor then took a long sigh. "Because there was an extra X-chromosome found in the baby's DNA, and your dad is the only person with that extra chromosome.'"

I would never forget his face. Pure shock, pain, and anger as he turned towards me.

"'WHAT THE FUCK IS HE TALKING ABOUT, DAD?! HOW IN THE HELL CAN YOU BE THE DAD?!'"

"I couldn't look in his eyes anymore. I lowered my head. The secret had come out and now I couldn't even look my own son in the eye! I saw his feet only as he stood in front of me. I felt his breath and saw his tears hit the ground. All I could say as I rose my head to meet his painful expression was, "'I'm sorry, son.'"

"I felt a blow to my jaw, and I fell to the ground. Yup, I deserved that. I looked up to see Shana lying across me. I wasn't quick enough to stop him as he slapped her across the face! I jumped up, throwing him into the wall. "'MARCUS! What in the hell is wrong with you, you never, ever put your hands on a woman! I taught you better than that!'"

He pushed me away, a hardened expression on his face as his tears ran down his face.

"'I thought you also taught me that a real man doesn't cheat! Oh, I guess we missed that lesson together huh, dad!'"

Confessions in Whispers

"I stepped back from him and just stood there; I couldn't say anything. I watched as my son shoved passed me, walking out of the door, and then running towards the exit. Before he left, he cried, "'WHY DAD? Why did you do this to me? Hell, why in the hell did you do this to mom?!'"

All I could do was lower my head as I heard the clinic door slam. I looked over at Shana who was still on the floor holding her face. I helped her up and we walked out of the clinic."

"As I walked out, the doctor ran after us giving us information and a checkup appointment. I took Shana home and told her to call me tomorrow. Then I went home. I didn't have a clue what I would find when I got there. I knew by this time that Evelyn knew, and she was probably burning my shit in the front yard. I almost didn't even go home to face it; I knew I had fucked up and there was no amount of apologizing that would fix this. I also knew not coming home would only make this shit much worst. So, I went home to face the piper. When I drove up the driveway, I saw Evelyn standing outside waiting. I parked in front of her.

She stood there; hands folded in front of her chest. She was pissed off. I knew because she didn't even look up. I paused a minute thinking if I should just leave. No, I had to face her, she would never forgive me if I just left like a coward".

"As I got out of the car, I heard her say, '"Three Hours!"'

I blinked. '"Huh…What?"'

She finally looked at me, her eyes were bloodshot from crying.

'"Three hours, I have been standing here waiting for you. THREE FUCKING HOURS!"'

She marched up to me pushing my chin upwards,' screaming "Oh, don't you dare play like you are ashamed now MARCUS! You weren't ashamed when you were out hurting our family or better yet, fucking your own SON'S GIRLFRIEND!"'

She slapped me across the face. '"WHY?! What made you hurt him! I don't even care about me; I am a woman I can get over it! But I can't get over you hurting Marcus! YOUR ONLY FUCKING SON! We spent years trying to have a child; you got two

Confessions in Whispers

jobs to support us so I wouldn't lose him, and this is the shit you do! WHY WOULD YOU DO THIS SELFISH SHIT TO HIM?! Marcus' whole life was that damn girl, and you knew it! I know I stopped fucking you, but damn Marcus, we could have talked about it and handled it!'"

"She slapped me again, and again screaming, "YOUR OWN SON! WE BEGGED GOD FOR A SON AND YOU WOULD DO THIS SHIT TO HIM!'"

Her words stabbed like daggers. I cried. I had begged God for him; I had envied so many men for their sons before I had Marcus and now, I had done this to him. I grabbed Evelyn trying to apologize but she fought me.

"'FUCK YOUR SORRY MARCUS! You didn't even go after him!'"

"He thought somewhere in his mind he could forgive you, if you were really sorry you would have gone after him, beg for his forgiveness, but you stayed with her and it broke him.'"

I shook my head. "'Evelyn, I didn't want to make him madder at me; I knew I had hurt him. I was trying to give him time to cool off.'"

Evelyn walked over to me, caressed my face, and then kissed me. That kiss ended in us making love, but this time we did every dirty thing I ever wanted to with her. Once we were done, we went to sleep. The next morning Evelyn woke me up saying, "'Okay, Marcus, it's time to get up and get out!'"

"I blinked as she pulled the covers off me! I jumped out of bed.

"'Evelyn, baby what are you doing?!'"

She looked at me wrapped in a robe.

"'I can forgive you Marcus, but not till Marcus forgives you! There is no way you will be able to make this right by him, so you have to go.'"

She was right. I couldn't make it right by him, so I left. As I walked down the stairs, I saw all my stuff sitting at the front door. I began to walk towards the door when I saw Marcus. He looked at me. I walked over to him and gave him a hug.

"'I'm sorry son, Marcus.... '"

Confessions in Whispers

He pushed me off. "'Your son Marcus Jr. is dead, my name is Trayvell, and his dad is dead.'" That was the name his mom wanted when he was born.

I stood in shock that he didn't even want to be called by my name anymore! I picked up my bags.

"Trayvell? You tell my son I will make it up to him some day." He nodded and I left.

"I didn't go to work…"

He interrupted me.

"How were you going to make it up to him?"

I shrugged my shoulders. "I don't know."

"Okay, continue."

"Shortly after I was kicked out of my house, I got a phone call from Shana. She was a wreck! She was crying about telling her mom about her being pregnant! She said her mom had a fit. "'I am not taking care of no babies, get the fuck out!'" Her mom kicked her out! I drove over there to see Shana standing outside of her mom's house banging on the door. She was begging her mom to let her stay. I drove up the driveway as Shana ran over to the car.

"'She locked me out Marcus!'"

As I got out of the car, Shana's mom came out throwing Shana's clothes at her. She shouted art me. "You tell Marcus she is HIS problem now!"' Shana started crying, I helped her get her things. Her mom was throwing this entire girl's stuff, breaking some of it, and calling her a slut and a whore.

"I helped her get the rest of her things, then we got a hotel. We only lived there a week. I got us an apartment and Shana's mom signed Shana over to me. We lived together. She continued to go to school and had to deal with everyone. They called her a whore too. Marcus didn't tell anyone about the baby not being his but said she had cheated and had got pregnant by some random guy. She came home many times, crying in my arms about how hard it was to deal with him mad her like that. I tried to tell her that he would forgive us one day, but that just didn't seem possible. Eventually I transferred Shana to make it easier on her. I didn't want her to lose the baby due to stress.

"When the baby was born, it was a boy. We named him Mark Trayvell Bradwell. He looked just like my son! I cried holding him in my arms. I missed my son! I had fucked up with him badly and now he hated me. I married Shana on her eighteenth birthday. It was a small wedding with a few of her friends and some of my family who hadn't disowned me due to the divorce with Evelyn."

He shook his head at me.

"You are damn right I married her, yes I loved her, she did mean something to me. I had to marry her; she had my child after all."

He looked at me. "I mean it made sense to fuck your son over more by doing that, right. You didn't think that might seem like you were rubbing it in his face?"

I paused. I had never thought about it like that, would he really think I did it to rub it in as if I wanted this to happen all along?

"I didn't do it to rub it in, I did it because it was the right thing to do, by her."

"Did it never occur to you that maybe your son would hate you more for marrying her, for choosing her over him?"

I threw my hands in the air, then rubbed the back of my head.

"I didn't choose her over him. I did what I taught him to always do, stand by his girl, even though it was a fucked-up situation. I had to stand by Shana regardless."

He smirked. "So, if your loyalty was so high, why didn't you think of your wife during your little sexual crusade?"

I paused; he was right. I didn't think of Evelyn while I was fucking Shana, or her true feelings when I married her. "Evelyn and I have come to terms with that dreadful year, we are still friends and have moved on with our lives. I tell her all the time I wish her nothing but the best, and I am sorry I couldn't be the best she deserved."

"Well, my new marriage is an interesting one. With her being younger than me, she likes stuff that doesn't make sense to me. We still have great sex and all, and she cooks ok, but she is spoiled. Shana is an excellent mom though; Mark doesn't want for anything."

Confessions in Whispers

I paused a minute as a tear collected in my eye. "Ok, now for the reason I asked you here. About six months ago, I went to the doctor because of some chest pains, and they found a large tumor in my heart. I knew it was because I had hurt Evelyn and Marcus. I had always promised my heart to Evelyn, forever. I had broken that promise and now I was dying for it."

I looked at him, a concerned expression crossed his face. I didn't deserve it. I reached across the table to touch his hand.

"Marcus, I spent all these years hoping you would forgive me. I can finally make it up to you."

He grabbed my hand, tears building in his eyes. "YOU CAN'T JUST GO LIKE THAT! You owe me your life! You hear me, damn it! You stole mine, you left me for so long and you bring me here to tell me you're dying on me!"

I let the tears flow down my face.

"Come outside with me, Marcus."

We walked outside.

"Marcus, take a ride with me."

We got into my car, but I let him drive. He asked me many times if I was alright whenever I coughed. That long story took a lot out of me.

We reached a lake and I had him park.

I asked, "Do you remember this place son?"

He nodded. "It's where you taught me to swim."

"This is the place I made you a man, son. You were your own man."

I sat up straight. "Get out of the car, Marcus."

He didn't hesitate as he got out of the car, he was about to walk over to my side to help me out when I said,

"Just stand there and wait for me."

He went and stood by the water. I watched him for moment. In an instant he was a little boy again in my eyes, tears fell as I watched young Marcus turned calling my name, "'Daddy, come on! Let's get in the water.'"

I had remembered in seconds all the great times we had at this lake and the day I finally taught him how to swim. I also remembered Evelyn, her chocolate skin, her warm smile, and her gentle

Confessions in Whispers

touch. I had the perfect family and I had messed it up.

As the vision faded, it brought me back to my present. Marcus standing as an adult waiting for me, I sighed as I opened the glove compartment taking the gun and the letters out. He had his back towards me as I got out of the car. He spun around as he heard the car door slam, his eyes were wide as he stared at the gun in my hand.

"OH MY GOD MAN, YOU DIDN'T BRING ME OUT HERE TO KILL ME, DID YOU?!"

I looked down at the gun, shaking my head. I handed it to him with the letters. He took it, confused. Then he looked to see me fall on my knees facing the lake.

He gasped. "You would do it this way! You would just leave her, no...Them like this!"

I turned my head to look at him over my shoulder. "This is not about them, Marcus. This is about you son!"

I looked at him, shaking with the gun in his hand. "I know that three years ago you wanted to kill me. I killed your dad, then Marcus, and I killed my baby, Evelyn's husband. I don't have much time left, don't let me die without making it up to you son!"

I was crying now. I heard him ask me, "How does killing you make this up to me?"

I cleared my throat.

"I have signed our marriage license, apartment, car, and even our son's birth certificate under Marcus Trayvell Bradwell

He gasped. "What?"

"I stole your life back then, I stole your son and wife, when I had my own. She still loves you Marcus, I never let her love me completely. I always left that love for you there. I need you to do this son!"

I turned back around and waited. I heard him coming closer, my heart kept racing so fast as Marcus placed the gun to the back of my head, and I smiled. I then raised my head. "Marcus, son she needs you, besides me. You, her and your mom, know about the baby, no one knows he is even mine. He looks just like you son, he needs a father,

Confessions in Whispers

and she needs a husband. Marcus, I switched shadows with you forgetting one thing."

I could now feel the pressure of the gun on the back of my head. "What?"

I smiled again as I said, "Your shadow will always cast higher than mine because when I die, you will leave a shadow standing for both of us."

I could hear him crying. I closed my eyes.

"Marcus, my boy, my miracle, my son, it's time to pull the trigger, give the letters to the girls... It's time to switch back son. I know you are just as much of a man as you were learning to swim on your own.... I love you Son."

I heard the clicking of the gun and smile at how proud I was of him. The last thing I heard was him saying.

"I love you too dad, and I forgive you" As everything fades to black.

Confession 7

The Devoted Daughter

Please do not judge me. I couldn't help it; no, I can't explain why I did it. Or maybe I can, I loved him so much. He was handsome, brave, caring, and he loved me back. I had known him all my life. I lost my dad when I was young, around eight or nine years old. My mom, Claire by then flipped from one man to another, she never kept one around more than six months at a time.

She always told me she wasn't getting married ever again. Lying bitch is what she was, hateful ass too. I didn't like any of her boyfriends she had any way, they were all assholes. Either they thought they were players or had no jobs, trying to use my mom for her money. I could never understand why she didn't just find a decent man and chill out. Never would I have guessed that she would try to find that perfect man when I was seventeen years old.

She found it in Malcolm Ingram. Malcolm was my mom's best friend and he practically raised me through all of my mom's years of going through men like they were the yellow pages. Malcolm is a fine milk chocolate man. He wasn't only my mom's best friend but mine as well. Whenever I had a problem, I would go to him.

He was a professor at the college I wanted to attend, Graymont University. For years I had a huge crush on him. My mom never thought twice about him in all these years. It didn't happen until I came home crying. Malcolm was over our house helping my mom through another disaster relationship she was in. When I walked into the kitchen in tears, Malcolm looked up at me.

"Rica, what's wrong?"

I started to say something when my mom said, "Malcolm! You're helping me right now! Rica go to your room and have your nervous breakdown there, we're busy!"

I just stood there for a minute in shock, then ran to my room slamming the door. I sat on the bed still crying. I hated when she did that shit! She was always hogging Malcolm. Whenever I needed someone to talk to, she always "needed" him. I tried to calm myself and chill.

After a while, I finally was calm. I heard a knock on the door. I looked up to see Malcolm standing in the doorway. He smiled.

"Rica, you, okay?"

I dropped my head. I heard him sit on the bed.

"Come on baby girl, talk to me."

I couldn't resist his voice; it was so smooth and low. Malcolm's voice always sent shivers up my spine. I looked up at his chestnut eyes which were always warm and sincere. I could always feel loved and safe within them. I sat up clearing my throat, then said, "Terrance is an asshole!" Surprised at my statement, Malcolm laughed. He then lied down motioning for me to lie on his chest. I loved cuddling with him, lying on his chest as he stroked my sandy brown hair.

"Do you want to even know what happened?"

Confessions in Whispers

He laughed again. "I thought you were going to go in on him, so I just got comfortable."

"Ok, so I am at school and my friend Beatrice asked me, '"Am I going to the prom?"' I said, '"Of course I am, Terrance and I are going together."'

She then told me that wasn't true. I said, '"How come you said that?"'

She then told me that Terrance is going to the prom with someone else! I asked her who and she told me Devon Clarke!"

I started crying again and Malcolm hugged me. He asked, "So what did Terrance have to say?"

I wiped my face. "That bastard came up to me during lunch saying things like, '"Oh, I don't think it's gonna work out with us!"'

'"Oh, so it's not going to work out with us, but it's going to work out with you and Devon, huh?"

"He just shrugged his shoulders at me. So, I got mad and slapped him in the face! He then mushed me down on the ground calling me a stupid bitch."'

I was crying so hard by now that Malcolm sat up and just held me.

I pushed him back from me, crying "He broke up with me right before prom and now I don't have a date! Mom already bought my dress and everything!"

I looked up at Malcolm; he smiled.

"Well, do you still want to go?"

I nodded yes. Malcolm caressed my face which made me feel like I was going to melt, then in his low sexy voice said, "Rica, will you go to the prom with me?"

I was stunned, I was speechless.

He smiled at me, then kissed my forehead. "I will take that as a yes."

I jumped in his arms hugging him, Malcolm was the best! I ran downstairs and told my mom. She looked sour at the news. "Malcolm, you don't have to do that. Rica can go with one of her friends or something."

I couldn't believe it; she was fucking hating! I started to say something when Malcolm tapped me on my shoulder shaking his head.

"Claire, I already told her I would go with her, I'm not taking it back."

Confessions in Whispers

My mom put her hands on her slender hips, rolling her hazel eyes. "I said no, isn't she supposed to be going with that Terrance boy anyway?"

Malcolm shook his head; he already knew that my mom was a spoiled ass brat! He sat down on the couch. "Claire, he broke up with her. I am going to take her, so she is not embarrassed."

My mom huffed and started to protest again, but Malcolm covered his ears.

"La, La, La...I'm not listening; I have made up my mind." My mom laughed trying to get him to move his hands away from his ears. Malcolm moved them.

"Are you done arguing with me?"

She smiled. "Yes, okay she can go with you." Malcolm stood up and smiled slyly. "I wasn't waiting on you to approve, we were going regardless, just didn't want to have my phone blown up about it is all."

My mom rolled her eyes again and that was it. Malcolm was taking me to prom.

The prom night finally arrived! By Saturday, prom night! I was super excited as I got dressed in my sheer coco brown and tan silk gown. I looked in the mirror at my suntan almond skin, I was truly glowing. I was going to prom with Malcolm Ingram. My mom came into my room.

"You look beautiful, Rica."

I turned to my mom.

"Thank you, Momma." "You should thank Malcolm for having pity on you to decide to take you to the prom; he must be pretty desperate for a date."

I frowned at her. She was always saying stupid shit like that about Malcolm.
She always said she was only friends with Malcolm because he gave her money and would listen to her talk about her real boyfriends. Pathetic if you ask me, Malcolm was always there for her ungrateful ass and for me.

There was nothing my mom couldn't ask of him that he wouldn't give to her or me. I finished getting dressed when the doorbell rang. My mom went to get the door. I walked down the stairs, and when I reached the bottom, I stood next to my mom in complete shock.

Confessions in Whispers

Malcolm was dressed in a dark chocolate suit with a cream color button down shirt. The whole package was complete with his chocolate brown hat and baby boy smile. He stared at the both of us laughing.

"So, I take it I look good, huh?"

My mom and I nodded at the same time. He then looked at me, his eyes roving from the top to the bottom.

"Rica, you look exquisite."

I smiled delightedly as I walked up to him. I stood next to him, and then told my mom to get the camera. She frowned and came back five seconds later claiming she couldn't find it. I couldn't do anything else but shake my head, blowing under my breath, "Yeah, I bet."

Malcolm then wrapped his arm around my shoulders. "That's cool, I always bring my own anyway, here take a picture, Claire."

I smiled as he handed her the camera. She snapped a quick picture of us. Malcolm looked at the picture shaking his head. "Claire! You only got me in this picture! Now stop playing and take the picture!"

I rolled my eyes; she was so evil I couldn't stand her! This time she looked in the camera and took a few good shots, and then we were off to prom.

*

He was the most handsome man there. The girls drooled around him, and the boys couldn't do nothing else but respect his swagger. I was standing by the door waiting for Malcolm to bring me some punch when Terrance and Devon walked up. Terrance laughed. "So, you brought pops with you, huh?" I tried to ignore him, but he carried on talking.

"Rica! You hear me talking to you?"

I faced him. "Correct me if I am wrong but aren't you here with Devon, back up!"

I turned around again as I heard Terrance say, "FUCK YOU, RICA! That's why you had to get your pops to babysit your ass for prom!"

I was going to say something back, but Devon said, "He doesn't look like her dad."

Confessions in Whispers

Terrance snatched her hand and shouted, "BITCH! Did I tell you to say something...No I didn't, so shut the fuck up!"

Letting Devon go, Terrance then turned back in my direction. Before he could say anything, I said, "You have got a nerve to speak to me after what you just did to Devon!"

"BITCH, I oughta!"

Malcolm walked in between us.

"Nah, young man you are walking up on the wrong one here, homeboy."

Terrance stepped up in Malcolm's face. "NIGGA. Step off, I'm talking to Rica, not you!"

Malcolm stepped back. "I'm not playing with you little boy, get out of my face."

Terrance laughed, then went to punch Malcolm, but Malcolm grabbed his arm, pulling it back and slamming Terrance to the floor, then he twisted his arm around, folding his hand down. Terrance struggled, crying for Malcolm to let him go. Malcolm eventually did.

"Now, you enjoy your prom with your date, and leave Rica to me."

After Terrance and Devon walked away, Malcolm asked me to dance. I could have died a happy girl in his muscular arms. The scent he was wearing was intoxicating as we danced slow to the jam. I was lost in his arms and felt he was just as lost in mine as well. Afterwards, we took some professional photos, danced some more, and then went out to eat. And then later, we ended up in front of my house.

Still in the car, Malcolm said, "Rica, I had an amazing time, thank you for being my date."

I laughed, "Shouldn't I be saying that to you?" Malcolm sighed deeply. "I am going to admit something to you that I have never told anyone."

"Sure, what?"

Malcolm cleared his throat. "I never got to go to prom."

I was speechless that he never got to go. I asked, "Why?"

"Well, when my prom came around, my mom was in the hospital. I had a choice to make. Go to prom or be with my mom before she died."

Confessions in Whispers

I suddenly felt emotional, but Malcolm caressed my face. "You don't have to cry Rica; it was the best choice I ever made."

I hugged him tightly; he needed this, and I was so happy I was able to share this moment with him. As I parted from him, I got lost in his eyes again. Malcolm wouldn't look away from me and my eyes couldn't leave his. He leaned in and kissed me! It was slow, lingering, and passionate. I wrapped my arms around him, and our kiss deepened. It seemed to last forever.

As Malcolm pulled away from me, he gasped, and his eyes grew wide. I turned around to see my mom standing behind us!

She had both her hands on her hips, staring at us with her eyebrows raised! Malcolm jumped out the car. "OH GOD, CLAIRE! I'm sorry I didn't know what came..." She cut him off. "I allowed you to take my daughter to prom and you do this!"

Malcolm tried to explain but my mom wasn't hearing it! She screamed, "Rica, get out of the car now!"

I got out as Malcolm was still trying to explain. I walked towards the house. Malcolm reached to touch my mom's shoulder, but she yanked his hand away.

"GET THE HELL OUT OF HERE, MALCOLM! I'm calling the police!"

I grabbed my mom's arm, screaming, "NO MOM, he didn't do anything, it was my fault!"

My mom turned around slapping me across the face. "YOU SLUT! You put him up to this, didn't you?" Malcolm grabbed her while I stood there in tears. He yelled at her.

"Claire! You didn't have to hit her, hit me, I did it!"

She snatched away from him trying to attack me again, but Malcolm grabbed her as I ducked.

"Rica! Run, go to your room!"

I ran into the house, to my room locking the door. A few minutes later I heard my mom fighting Malcolm up the stairs. She reached my door.

"YOU WHORE! I'M GONNA GET YOU! YOU HEAR ME, RICA!"

Confessions in Whispers

I screamed back, "I HATE YOU! YOU ALWAYS RUIN EVERYTHING!"

It would be another two hours before my mom would stop screaming at my door, by then I was every "Bitch", "Slut" and "Whore" in the book. After she had stopped, I was finally able to go to sleep. I cried most of the time as I slept because my mom said she was going to call the police on Malcolm!

*

When I woke up the next morning, my mom was downstairs in the kitchen. I sat at the table for breakfast. She smiled and even said, "Good Morning."

I was confused, hell, I was more than confused, what in the hell was she so happy about. I wanted to ask but I liked the mellow mood, so I kept my mouth shut. I kissed her goodbye and went to school.

At school everything was cool, everyone was still talking about how Malcolm slammed Terrance at prom. Terrance didn't have anything to say. He just rolled his eyes talking, "Oh yeah, I bet none of y'all would come at me like that."

Everyone laughed at his ass; he was so stupid. School went by like a blur; all I could think about was that kiss with Malcolm. I started to wonder if he had the same feelings for me as I had always had for him.

I was still upset that mom told Malcolm he couldn't see us or talk to us. I was going to call him when I got home. When I got home, I saw Malcolm's car in the driveway. I went inside to find Malcolm and my mom in the living room. I sighed with relief that she had forgiven him. I walked into the living room and sat on the couch. Malcolm didn't look happy, but when I looked at my mom, she was all smiles.

I was confused. "Okay, what's going on here?" Malcolm lowered his head again as my mom beamed with joy. "I got married today!"

Now I understood why Malcolm was upset. I turned to her.

Confessions in Whispers

"Momma, come now, which one of those deadbeat bastards have pumped your head full of nonsense?"

She stood up beaming with pride as she said, "Rica, you are so silly honey, no sweetheart. Malcolm and I got married today."

I stood up suddenly; that was why he couldn't look at me!

I turned to my mom who was still smiling as she said, "This is our arrangement, so I don't call the police and have his ass sent to prison!"

I marched towards her slapping her across the face, yelling "BITCH!"

Malcolm grabbed me holding me back from beating her ass! My mom walked up to me as Malcolm held me. She whispered in my ear, "He is all mine now, little girl."

I stopped struggling and just sank to the floor. Malcolm held me as I cried in his arms. I looked up at him.

"How could you?"

He wiped the tears from my eyes. "She threatened me Rica, she promised she would call the cops on me. Do you have any idea what that would do to my career? Baby girl, I couldn't let her do that shit! I begged her to stop with the jealousy act and let this go! She wouldn't, she kept going on and on. Finally, she came up with this shit to wipe the slate clean."

I hugged him tightly saying. "She forced you to marry her, that bitch!"

Malcolm held me tightly. "Rica, you have to believe me that I don't see this as a real marriage! She did it all this because I told her how I felt about you!"

I was surprised that he had the same feelings as me! I was about to say something else when my mom walked into the room. She placed both hands on her thick hips. "Aww, doesn't that look cute – a father and daughter moment. Okay break it up, Rica go do your homework. Malcolm, baby come give me a massage."

I started to say something when I felt Malcolm holding my arm, shaking his head. I jumped up grabbing my book bag and glared at my mom as I passed her, running up the stairs. Once I was in my room, I slammed the door. That Bitch! She did this shit on purpose! My life became instant hell.

She started having loud sex with him. Kissing and touching him and being all over him whenever I was in the room. For a while Malcolm protested, and she would remind him about the report she wrote for the police. He began to 'act' right.

A year of that and he was like a robot. Malcolm was devoted and loyal to my mom. One night while Malcolm was working, I caught my mom fucking one of the boys from my school that lived in my neighborhood. I then took it upon myself to relieve Malcolm's pain. Fuck her, she had a great man, and she was cheating on him! So, when Malcolm got home, he went to take a shower. I called out like I was leaving and even walked out the front door waving at my mom.

I then climbed the tree next to my window and got back into the house. She knew he would be in the shower for an hour. I slipped inside the bathroom, locking the door. I heard Malcolm say, "We had a deal Claire, not when I am in the shower!"

I undressed and got into the shower with him. He was about to yell, then gasped.

"Rica! What are you...?"

I stood there in silence at first, I was embarrassed. I looked down at my feet.

"She can't have you; I'm the one who loves you. I won't let her take you from me."

Malcolm stood there. I could hear him breathing heavily. I looked up at him, and he just stared at me. I walked up to him and caressed his face. He turned his head to kiss my hand. Malcolm suddenly pulled me close to him. I wrapped my arms around him as he kissed me. Our embrace lit a fire in me as Malcolm kissed me all over my body.

I whispered, "Take me, Malcolm."

Malcolm shook his head. "No, Rica not like this, let's wait a while then we can, okay."

I nodded as I washed Malcolm's back. From then on, we would sneak around to fool around.

Our favorite times were on my way to school. In the car, Malcolm would snuggle up with me and caress me. One night, my mom came home announcing that she was pregnant!

Confessions in Whispers

Malcolm shook his head because he knew it was not his. I looked at him.

"You okay, Malcolm?"

He applauded my mom. "Congratulations Claire, you slut!"

My mom marched over to Malcolm and slapped him across the face. "It's yours!"

Malcolm laughed. "How in the hell do you think that? We fucked with condoms!"

My mom smiled. "Well, I poked holes in them before you come to bed!"

Malcolm became enraged as he went to attack my mom. I jumped in front of him.

"Malcolm, calm down please!"

He looked down at me, and then calmed down turning his back to us. I spoke to my mom, "You are an evil bitch, you know that! Look what you have done to us!"

She rolled her eyes. "I don't care! I'm having his baby and that's that!"

She left the room leaving Malcolm and me alone. He said, "I will be damned if I have a child by her!" He sank on the couch looking at the ceiling.

Suddenly it came to me. I sat next to Malcolm.

"Rica, what are you thinking about?"

I blinked out of my trance. "Then, let's kill her." Malcolm laughed at my suggestion till he looked back at my face again. He cleared his throat.

"Rica, you aren't serious, are you?" I shrugged my shoulders.

"NO, we can't do this ..."

I threw my hands in the air. "What Malcolm? She did this shit on purpose! She married you to keep me from doing it and now she is pregnant by you! This shit is not fair!"

Malcolm held me as I cried in his arms. "It's okay Rica, I will think of something."

I pushed him away. "You haven't come up with anything yet! You just let her run over you!"

I started to get up and run, but he grabbed my arm. "Rica, she wasn't playing that she would put me in jail for kissing you, baby you have to believe me I would fight her if I could. I love you!"

I turned around and hugged Malcolm; he loved me. He wanted out of my mom's marriage, but he

Confessions in Whispers

didn't know how to get away from her. I made up my mind that I would make a way.

I stood up whispering to Malcolm, "Come to my room tonight." I didn't wait for an answer as I stomped up the stairs to my room.

I lied on my bed thinking but nothing would come to me. Later that night I made love to Malcolm. He came in my room once he was sure my mom was asleep. I let him take my virginity. It took all my strength not to be loud. He felt amazing. When Malcolm was ready, I begged him to come inside me.

Malcolm kissed me as he came deep inside of me. He then went back into my mom's room. That's when it all started. Days turned to weeks and weeks into months as my mom got bigger. I slowly started mimicking her, I gained weight like her. She ate so much and so did I. She never once asked me about my sudden weight gain. I spent hours at the library looking up information about being pregnant, time length, and delivery.

I paid close attention to my mom's mood swings, cravings and everything. I mimicked it all, even all my friends kept asking me if I was pregnant and I told them yes. After a while Malcolm started paying attention once I threw up in the bathroom. He asked me about it one day.

"Rica baby, are you pregnant?"

I smiled at him sweetly. "Yes, I am."

Malcolm placed his hands on his head. "Rica, what are we going to do about this? You know your mom is going to find out it's mine!"

I caressed the side of his face. "No, she won't, she doesn't even have a clue. She will never know it's yours baby, I promise."

Malcolm seemed to calm down as he grabbed me and kissed me. I hugged him; he didn't have to worry; I would handle all of it. I waited patiently for my mom to have her baby. She looked so beautiful that she was glowing. I helped her as much as I could. I made sure she was eating the right foods and taking care of herself.

Confessions in Whispers

She asked me one day when I was washing her back in the tub, "Rica, why are you being so nice to me?"

I shrugged my shoulders. "Well, I suppose I am a little excited about having a little brother or sister." My mom smiled leaning against me. "I didn't ever think you would just get with the program. Malcolm has been nice; we will be one big happy family finally, huh?"

As I helped her out of the tub, as her water broke.

I looked at my watch smiling, it was time. She begged me to take her to the hospital. As I drove, I smiled telling her to breathe in and out. We were ten minutes from the hospital when I drove right pass it. My mom yelled, "Rica! You missed the hospital, honey!"

I looked at her. "I know. I know a mid-wife who wants to deliver your baby, mom."

She was in too much pain to argue with me, she screamed, "Well, then hurry the hell up and get us there then!"

We drove for another twenty minutes, and then stopped in front of the abandoned house.

"Where in the hell have you brought me, Rica!"

I hopped out of the car, then helped my mom out. "She stays here; she is inside, come on mommy."

My mom allowed me to lead her inside. It was much nicer there, and she sighed in relief asking to see the mid wife.

I nodded as I sat her down in a comfy chair. I walked down to the hall and walked into a room, smiling as I put on the white lab coat. I then returned to my mom. She looked up at me impatiently yelling, "Well, where the hell is she?!"

I smiled about to say something when my mom screamed, "Get that stupid smile off your face!"

I frowned, and then laughed. I walked over to my mom who looked confused.

"Sorry mommy, I am just so excited. Come on, let me take you into the delivery room."

I helped my mom up telling her that the mid wife asked me to prepare her, and she would be down shortly. As we walked to the room I said, "Now, just lie down and relax. The midwife will be with you shortly, ok."

Confessions in Whispers

She lied there breathing in and out as she tried to calm down, suddenly she screamed as her contractions began. She screamed for the midwife. I smiled as I started to strap her down. She was kicking and screaming and so I tightened the straps.

Once I was, finished she looked at me saying, "Rica! What in the hell is going on here?!"

I sighed. "You just had to have him, didn't you? You couldn't just be a real mom and be happy for me! You had to steal my man!"

She laughed, then screamed because of the contractions. "Your man! You pathetic little girl, you have no idea what the hell you are talking about! Malcolm is your dad!"

I stood back, stunned for a moment, then shook my head screaming at her, "NO! You're lying, you always lie!"

She laughed at me. "Girl, I got pregnant by him when he was just about to graduate college, I didn't want to ruin his life with me having his baby so lied and said it was someone else's."

My mom's words punctured a hole in me. If Malcolm was my daddy, then I had just made love to my dad! I was knocked out of my trance with my mom's screaming.

I got the supplies out and started to deliver the baby. It took seven hours before it was born. As I cleaned the baby boy, I collected the blood and the aftermath of the delivery and placed it in an icepack.

My mom sighed, "Rica, that's why I was so upset when he kissed you like that in the car after prom. I needed to protect you, do you understand now, sweetheart?"

For a moment, just a moment I did, but looking at the baby I realized I didn't care. I let my mom hold the baby as I walked over to a closet and pulled out a newborn car seat.

My mom asked, "Rica, why did you bring me here in the first place?"

I smiled at her as I dragged out the gasoline. Her facial expression was classic and priceless.

She screamed, "HELP! POLICE! HELP ME!"

Confessions in Whispers

I shook my head as I pried the baby from her hands. "No one can hear you, so shut the fuck up!"

The baby began to cry, and I rocked him back to sleep. "Now look what you did, you made him cry."

As I placed the baby in the car seat I said, "Do you really think I care about all that bullshit you just told me now? I love him and he loves me. We are going to be together and raise this baby as our own."

I picked up the car seat and the items for the house and walked outside to the car, strapping my new baby boy into the car.

I then walked back inside the house and started throwing gasoline around the house. I reached my mom's room. She was trying to escape. Oh no, she wasn't!

I walked over to her and punched her out cold. Then picking her up, I strapped her back in the chair. I remembered the breast milk.

I pumped as much milk as I could from my mom, then kissed her forehead whispering in her ear, "They are both mine now mommy, rest in peace Bitch!"

I threw gasoline around the room and on her.

I walked outside and locked the door behind me. I got into the car, still covered in blood, and then drove the car to the end of the driveway. I got out and then pulled out a bottle of gin. I dropped the key in and placed the rag inside.

I lit it and threw it in the window. I got back into the car and drove back home and found Malcolm wasn't home yet.

I set up the house. I poured the mixture of blood and water on the living room floor and lowered my body. I then covered the baby. I threw away all the evidence and sat in the living room waiting for Malcolm to come home. He walked into the house an hour later. As I screamed for him, he dropped his bags rushing to my side.

"Oh my God, Rica baby, oh my God, are you okay?"

I smiled at him saying, "Isn't he beautiful?"

Malcolm nodded as he kissed my forehead. "Where is your mom?"

Confessions in Whispers

I pointed at a note lying on the table that said my mom left him after finding out I was pregnant as well.

Malcolm helped me to the bathroom to clean up. We cleaned the baby, then took him to the hospital. The doctor was amazed that I was fine, and that the baby didn't even rip me. The baby was healthy as well. We took him home and Malcolm started on his new nursery.

Malcolm and I were married the following year after no one could find my mom. We even put out a missing person's report, but nothing ever came up, so the judge nulled the marriage of my mom and Malcolm. That made Malcolm extremely happy. The house fire was on T.V and the police still had no clue what happened.

I smiled at the footage, as I cradled my son in my arms. Malcolm said, "DAMN KIDS, they probably did it."

I laughed. "Baby you're probably right, but I am sure it must have been for a good reason, don't you think?"

He laughed too. "What reason would anyone have for burning down an old abortion clinic?"

I shrugged. "I am just saying it would be a shame if that was all for nothing."

I am happy now; I have a wonderful husband and now two beautiful boys. I know my mom would have been so proud of me; in the end I ended up just like her. I lied, cheated, and murdered my way to get what I wanted. Now she can rest in peace knowing I am well taken care of by my daddy, Malcolm, and my baby brother Clarence & son, Malcolm jr.

Confessions in Whispers

Confession 8

Tangible Justice

Sighing, I opened my eyes and asked myself, "What is Justice? Some fairy tale bullshit that people in the Justice System call upon when they know damn well, they can't fix shit!"

What am I supposed to do now?! Just leave it alone, let it go? Pretend this shit never happened? Fuck that, I 'm going to get my justice the best way I know how.

I paused, folding my hand in a prayer. "Lord, please forgive me for the actions I am about to take, but I can't wait for a system that doesn't do as it claims, any longer. No matter the outcome, I need this pain in my chest to heal!"

I rubbed my chest as I finished my prayer. I looked out the window. I was saying this prayer in my car as I sat outside of this motherfucker's house! It took all my courage to finally do this, I had planned it out carefully. I was here, no time to back down now, Elliott.

I tried to control my breathing; I was so upset that I couldn't even breathe right! All I kept saying to myself was, "I waited, I did... For months after the fucking trial, I waited with no answer! So, fuck them now!"

Again, I prayed to the Lord for help begging Him, "Lord, you must believe me, I gave them a chance!"

I was shaking now; tears streaming down my face as the images came back to me so vividly...

I look up at the sky as I wiped my face.

"Lord, all I want is peace. I pray, I go to church, and I believe even after my close call in my own past. I am a good person Lord!" I sighed, then wiped my eyes again as anger set in.

I screamed, beating the steering wheel. "These tears will not be for nothing! I will have my justice!"

I look up to see the front door open. I almost lost my cool as I watched HIM smile, hug, and kiss his children.

Confessions in Whispers

I was disgusted, "Fuck that fatherly bullshit, 'White boy' playing nigga!" I prayed again "Lord, again if there is another way, please tell me."

I listened but only heard dead silence. I understood. "Thank you, Lord."

This confirmed my decision. I put the car in drive and followed closely behind them. I followed them for miles. I parked my car down the street walking the rest of the way. As I walked up on them, I could see them chit chatting about something. I walked up to the driver side window and knocked on it with my gun.

He looked at me with eyes full of shock. I nodded to motion him to roll down the window. All I could think to myself was, Fuck that, I'm scared shit now!

I pointed the gun at him and screamed, "GET OUT!"

He hesitated as he opened the door. I yanked it wide, shouting in his face, "Don't fuck with me, Drason! Get out of the fucking car!"

He got out and raised his arms in the air.

The woman in the car jumped out screaming, "What are you doing, Elliott?!"

I pointed the gun at her and pointing my finger at him not to move.

"Do you want this to be about you? Your husband and I have unfinished business to attend to, don't we Drason?"

As I waited for his answer, she said, "He's my husband, this is already about me!"

I ignored her and told him to come with me. She started to move again, and I pointed the gun at her.

He shouted, "Drayia! He's right, this is not about you, and we do have unfinished business to attend to, just take the car and get the hell out of here!"

I looked at him with a frown thinking, "He could save his wife, but not her!"

My blood boiled as I shouted, "Let's fucking go!" He nodded we walked away to get into my car. I opened the door on the passenger side, and then pulled the handcuffs from my back pocket, tossing them to him to put them on.

He snapped them on, and I checked to make sure they were secure. I helped him into the car.

Confessions in Whispers

As I drove, neither of us spoke. There was nothing to talk about. I looked in my rearview mirror at him. He had his head down and eyes closed.

"You want to pray now! Nope, I'm sorry homeboy, God can't save you now!"

I pulled into the driveway of my house. As I parked, he looked up terrified; he should be. Where else would be a more appropriate place than where it all began? I slammed the door and marched around to his door opening it, saying in a low tone, "Get out."

He looked up at me and then tried to escape, I shook my head, no. Fuck that now man, your ass is going to die today! As I pushed him to walk towards the door, he looked over his shoulder at me. "Come on man, not here! Please!"

I dug the gun into his back. As I was about to say something, I heard my name being called. I grinded the gun further into and turned my head to see my neighbor Jackson Hilt. He waved from his car. "What's up, Elliott man! You are still coming over for the game, Sunday?"

I nod at him. "Yeah, after church, it starts at five-thirty pm right?"

He nodded as he got into his car. I watched him drive off, and then I turn back to this scary ass nigga. I frowned at him as I pushed him forward with the gun. I pushed open the door; I didn't even bother locking it this morning.

I pushed him hard inside, he tripped on my carpet and fell. He was pissing me off! I grabbed him by his work shirt and yanked him to his feet.

I then point with my gun towards the basement door. He walks towards it and opens it with both hands. He looked down the stairs. I pushed him down the stairs and he rolled to the bottom, out of breath.

I casually strolled down the steps and closed the door behind me.

"Now we can begin."

I stepped over him, and then helped him up. There was a muffled sound coming from around the corner. I shook my head, and then pushed him around the corner. He gasped at the sight on the other side. I had made a homemade torture

Confessions in Whispers

chamber, but what he was shocked about was seeing her chained up against the wall.

"NO! Come on man, no!"

"Oh, what's wrong man, you didn't want to see her?"

I pushed him towards the wall, then chained him up next to her. I walked over to her. I had left her there all night in nothing but her bra and panties. Her skin looked ghostly pale. I kissed her cheek as I ripped the tape off her mouth.

"Good afternoon, baby?"

She screamed in agony, and then started crying. I laughed.

"Oh, what's wrong, baby?"

She twisted and turned in the chains.

"I need to pee, Elliott."

I heard her but I pretended not to. I placed a hand to my ear, "I can't hear you baby, what did you say?"

She gets red in the face, screaming, "You heard me, Elliott! I have to pee!"

"Oh, I'm sorry, you need to pee, huh."

I walked over to the sink in the basement pulling out a bucket and sliding it under her.

"Ok, now you can go."

I even walked over to him, turning him and myself around so she wouldn't be embarrassed.

She screamed, "What the fuck, Elliott! You expect me to use this!"

I sighed, still turned around.

"Hurry the fuck up or I will make you hold it again!"

I could hear her crying. She shouted, "I HATE YOU ELLIOTT!"

I shrugged my shoulder as I said coolly, "The feeling is mutual baby."

I heard her cry as I listened to the sound of her peeing into the bucket. I laughed as I turned to look at her face. Her face was bright red.

"Don't look! Stop staring at me!"

Clapping my hands, I laughed. "What? I have already seen how dirty you can be, what else is there?"

I then walked over to him, unlocking his cuffs and pointing the gun at him to strip. He took off

Confessions in Whispers

his clothes, leaving on his boxers. I chained him to his place again. "Okay, maybe now we can begin again."

He looks at me. "What the fuck man! Why in the hell do you have us chained up like slaves!"

"Oh no, not like slaves, no. Slaves were innocent people who were kidnapped for monetary gain. You two are chained up for being demons of Satan!"

She laughed at me. "YOU"RE CRAZY, ELLIOTT! You have always been crazy!"

I walked over to her. "Yes, I have. Just like I was crazy about you, I married you didn't I, Kristal?"

She looked down, but I raised her chin up with my finger looking into her eyes and shook my head. "NO! NO! Don't look down baby, answer me."

Her green eyes were now red as she nodded her head. Letting her go, I then turned to him. He looked away, and I jump in his face.

"Oh no homeboy, you are not innocent in this, you knew better than anyone motherfucker!"

He looked at me. "Look, it doesn't have to be like this, Elliot."

I punched him in the stomach; he leaned forward. "You did this shit over a bitch! You lost your fucking mind, friend, and then hired some bullshit lawyer to get you off."

He was still coughing. "I didn't have choice; I couldn't do that to my kids or to my wife, man!"

That was it; I lost it. I punched him in the face, stomach, and chest. He started to cough up blood. I stopped; I was losing my cool. I calmed down, then walked over to the fold out table I had placed in front of them.

I tried to control my breathing as I picked up the blue folder opening it. Tears ran down my face as I stared at the picture. I then flipped to the medical report. I read it over it, trying not to get upset. I turned around and wiped the tears from my face.

I pulled out a large metal rod and swung it over my shoulder. I stared at them. The looks on their faces were priceless.

I sighed, closed my eyes, and prayed to God.

"Lord, please forgive me for what I am about to do, if I shouldn't do this, please give me a sign."

I waited. Nothing but silence.

Confessions in Whispers

"I have prayed over and over for months now to ease this pain in my chest, for him to give me a different avenue to take, but it has come to this." I paused for a moment, "Kristal, you knew I loved her, she knew there wasn't anything in this world that God wouldn't let me give her."

So why did you do it?"

She shook. "I was lonely Elliott, you were always at work, and you were never around anymore."

"Okay, I had been busy, but I was trying to pay the damn bills and put food on the fucking table!"

I turned to him waiting for answer. He looked at me. "Man, I didn't know, Drayia wasn't giving it up, man."

Now that I heard their excuses, I could do this with a clear conscious.

"Almost six months ago on March thirteenth, I came home from work to find my Deacon in bed with my wife. When I caught them together there was a fight. I started to kill this nigga. He ran out of the house, jumped into his car and backed out super-fast..." I paused a minute as the image became clear. I started to cry. "He didn't look in his rear-view and smashed his car into my little girl's bike with her standing in front of it! He doesn't stop as he impaled my daughter into her bike!

"He just drove off, leaving me screaming. I ran over to check my little girl, she was barely breathing at this point; she whispered, "Daddy, Daddy."

I was crying now. I looked up to see they were crying too.

"What the fuck are you two crying for?! I don't remember either of you doing a fucking thing to save her! I had to watch my daughter die in my fucking arms!"

I slammed the rod on the floor which made them both jump. I screamed, "Nothing! She died in my arms! She was twelve fucking years old! And you!" I pointed at him. "You got off for her murder! You hired that fancy ass lawyer and got off!"

I picked up the rod and whacked him in the knee; I heard the break. His scream echoed around the room. I watched as his leg swelled. "Kristal, you claimed that you passed out, but what you did was just sit there!"

I shook my head. "I prayed to God to help me to forgive you two but if both hadn't been fucking each other, my daughter would still be alive!"

"I even told myself I could forgive you if I had gotten an apology, but I got nothing! Neither one of you apologized to me. Hell Kristal, you left me and didn't even help me bury your own daughter! Deacon, you kept seeing me at church smiling in my fucking face like it was all good. I had to leave because of you."

They both dropped their heads. I didn't feel sorry for either of them.

They both looked at me then said, "I'm sorry, Elliott."

I laughed; they were fucking kidding me, right! Now they thought they could apologize! Nah, fuck that, it was too late.

"You want me to forgive you now?! Please tell me that you are not begging for forgiveness now!"

Kristal looked up. "Elliott, I couldn't handle it! I swear, I didn't just mean to leave you like that, but

I couldn't handle the fact that this was my entire fault!"

I rolled my eyes at her. "I don't care now! Do you both understand? I don't give a fuck now what you are saying, talking about nothing!"

He looked up at me. "Come on Elliott, the Lord would not allow this of a Christian man."

I laughed at him. "FUCK YOU, DEACON! You fucked my wife, and you are a married nigga, do I even look like I am going to forgive you! On top of that, I watched you kiss your daughter and son today! While my baby girl is buried six fucking feet underground! I don't get to kiss my little girl goodbye anymore! YOU STOLE THAT FROM ME YOU SON OF A BITCH!"

I punched him in the face again. This time I dislocated his jaw. He cried in agony. I looked at them. It was time; no more talking.

*

I yawned, looking at my watch. It was getting late, and I needed to sleep.

"Okay, you won't die tonight, but you will certainly."

Confessions in Whispers

I turned off the lights and left them in the dark. I went upstairs, fixed me some dinner, and went to bed. I could hear them yelling for help most of the night. I smiled to myself; I had sealed the house months before. No one would ever hear them. But I was awakened by the nightmare of my daughter's death during the night.

I wanted peace! All I wanted was peace of mind. She comes in my dreams every night begging for me to save her. I am in so much pain because I am unable to; there was nothing I could do. She died so quickly in my arms; I didn't even get to say goodbye to her.

I jumped up; I couldn't sleep anyway with all of that damn yelling! I stormed down the steps turning on the light.

I slapped them both.

"SHUT THE FUCK UP!"

I looked around the room for the duct tape. I found it.

Kristal cried. "No Elliott, not again, I'll be quiet.!"

I looked at him. "You won't though; she has been like that for days now."

I covered his mouth with tape, then went to turn off the lights when heard Kristal ask, "For tonight, just for tonight please Elliott, let me have the light on."

I look at her; I was so in love with her at one point. I left the light on and walked back upstairs. I paused as I closed the basement door. I could feel the tears falling down my cheeks.

I broke down as I prayed, "Please tell me what I should do. Somewhere I still love her."

I looked at the portrait of my family. For the first time, I noticed the distant look in Kristal's eyes. Her smile was as fake her hugs and kisses at night. I stood up in shock; she never loved me. God showed me clearly that this had to happen tomorrow. They had shed the blood of the innocent; this sin was punishable by death.

I had regained the strength to carry out this duty. I couldn't sleep. I sat in my living room looking over my daughter's photo album. Tears seem to

Confessions in Whispers

calm the fire of hate in my heart. I looked at my daughter's angelic face. She looks so much like me. My gaze fell on the calendar. It was her day.

I would not let this day mean nothing; I would get my revenge for their sins against my innocent child. Somehow, I fell asleep. When I woke up, I jumped as I saw a vision of my beautiful daughter standing in front of me. I cried out to her, and she hugged me, kissing my cheek. "Love is justice daddy, forgive them, and allow them to go to Him."

I blinked as the vision disappeared. I understand her words. I marched down to the basement. Kristal was awake, and Deacon was still sleeping. I slapped him awake.

"Wake up! It's time to be forgiven for your sins."

He spat at me. "You think the Lord would want this, Elliott? You are crazy and you will burn in hell for this."

I grabbed the urine that was killing the air in the room. "First, I have to bath you of your impurities."

Kristal's eyes grew wide. I threw the urine on the both of them. They both screamed.

"What the fuck, Elliott?!"

I laughed as I dropped the bucket. "I had to bathe you first, and then I have to forgive you."

Deacon laughed. "You're going to forgive us after throwing piss on us."

I nod, then pull out a set of gloves and the guns. I placed them on the table facing them.

I then pulled out a needle and a sleeping medication. I smiled manically as I filled the needle.

I took the large picture of my beloved daughter and placed it in the center of the table. I then picked up the needle and walked towards the Deacon.

"What the fuck is that man?!"

I looked at the needle. "Oh, it's your truth serum; I am going enjoy the truth babbling out of your unholy mouth." I stick him in the stomach with the needle. He shook and fell asleep.

I returned to the table to refill the needle. I could hear her speaking.

"Elliott, baby please you don't have to do this…"

Confessions in Whispers

I cut her off as I lift the needle to check the amount. "Kristal, why did you ever marry me, if you really didn't ever love me?"

Silence fills the room. "You never loved me at all?"

Kristal sighed. "I did love you Elliott, you were just so busy, and I felt you loved your job more than me."

I shook my head. "I loved my job more than you huh, is that's why I was home every night to hold you or why we made love every other night?"

Kristal cleared her throat.

"God knows my heart was in it for you Kristal, my whole life was you and Nyia."

Kristal laughed, which took me back. "I was your whole life huh Elliott? Once I had Nyia, you forgot who the hell I was to you. No, your whole life was Nyia, yes, your prefect precious daughter. You forgot the woman who carried her for nine months and who spent nine hours in labor with her!"

I wasn't going to stand there and allow her bad mouth my baby girl. I marched over to her, slapping her across the face. "Don't you dare talk about her that way! You were spoiled! Yes, I can admit it now. You were spoiled rotten, I did it. I made you too important in my life. Yes, she was prefect, she was the blessing God gave us, but you were so jealous of her. You hated the attention I gave to my daughter, that you went out to hurt me on purpose didn't you, Kristal?!"

Kristal's eyes focused on me, her green eyes flashing.

"YES! I fucked him to get back at you! I wanted you to hurt as much as me for loving her more than me! When she died, I thought it was a good thing, I could have my husband back, but her death became my curse. You wouldn't stop talking about her! You kept obsessively crying over her and it made me even madder that you still didn't see me!"

I stood back from her; she was a demon!

"So, I left you, thinking you would come after me, but you didn't. You didn't even care I didn't show up at the funeral, you had forgotten I even existed, Elliott!"

I felt my anger getting the best of me as I slapped her again. "You selfish bitch! You did all this to get

Confessions in Whispers

me to notice you! You ignored the fact I buried our daughter by my fucking self! All you cared about was getting your husband that spoiled you and loved only YOU!"

I stabbed her in the heart with the medicine. "You deserve to burn in hell."

I took them down and placed them on the floor. I checked the camera and went back upstairs. I grabbed the hammer and nailed the door shut. I then went into the living room and sat down in front of the T.V and turned on the camera.

I sat there and waited. Four hours they just slept; I got bored so fixed me some dinner. Around nine o'clock at night the Deacon stirred. I sat up to watch him as I ate. He looked around noticing he was unchained, he immediately looked at Kristal who was still asleep. He grabbed her shaking her awake. She touched her forehead, and she seemed dizzy as she opened her eyes looking around, then hugged the Deacon.

"Hmm...I wonder why she is so happy."

She looked around, "How did we get down, Melvin?"

He looked around shrugging his shoulders. "Maybe he took us down."

Kristal looked at the picture of Nyia, and then the guns. She laughed.

"He really is crazy to think we were going to commit suicide, bullshit!"

They both laughed. I did too because they didn't have a choice. It was sweet irony; they had both caused all the pain I was feeling; now they would give the peace my heart deserved. Kristal shook head. "She was a pretty little girl, Melvin, at one time she was my pride and joy."

He held her tightly. "I know Elliott abandoned your heart, but why are you still blaming your daughter, baby? I never got it myself."

Now this would be interesting to hear. Kristal started to cry. "He stopped loving me because of her!" She pointed at the picture of Nyia. She lowered her head down, wiping away her tears. "Even now after everything he still doesn't see me, he sees his dead daughter and he wants us to apologize for killing her when it was a fucking accident!"

Confessions in Whispers

Melvin looked at the picture, then cleared his throat.

"It wasn't an accident, Kristal."

Kristal jerked her head up. "What? What do you mean it wasn't an accident, Melvin?"

Melvin looked down. "When he caught us in bed together, I panicked, then we had that fight, and I really did think he would kill both of us. He was my friend at one point. I ran out of the house and hopped in the car. I saw Nyia in rear view mirror and I knew she was the real reason you were always so sad. I loved you so much that I thought…" He paused as he grabbed Kristal's hands. "So, I thought if I got rid of her, you would love me for it."

I sat back in my chair in total shock! He killed my daughter on purpose, all because he was in love with my fucking wife! Kristal's eyes widened as her eyes teared up. She broke down.

"You killed my daughter because you loved me, you took my child all because you wanted me!"

I had to laugh at the irony of it all. Her plan had backfired on her badly. Melvin's head fell as he laid on her knees.

"Yes! I was leaving my wife and kids to be with you, I was going to make you happier than Elliott ever could. I would do anything for you, Kristal."

Kristal nodded, smiled as she raised his head up to look into her eyes. She kissed his lips. As they parted, I heard her whisper, "Would you die for me, Melvin?"

Melvin opened his eyes. "Yes Kristal, I would die for you."

Kristal stood up and smiled, leaving Melvin kneeling. She walked over to the table and pick up the picture of Nyia. Tears streamed down her face as she hugged it, then smiled kissing it. "Mommy is so sorry Nyia, I'm sorry I was so selfish, but I'm gonna make it right."

Kristal placed the picture down and grabbed one of the guns. She held it up towards Melvin.

"Melvin, my love please turn around, won't you?"

Confessions in Whispers

He turned around to see the gun pointed directly at him. He stood up and stumbled towards her, then kneeled in front of her.

"Yes, Kristal baby?"

Kristal cried, "Baby, will you accompany me to hell?"

Melvin nods. "Elliott! I'm sorry man, Kristal I will go with you to hell."

He closed his eyes as Kristal pulled the trigger. I jumped as I watch the blood splatter on the basement wall. Kristal dropped the gun. Crying, she walked over to the table, then suddenly looked up at the camera. She smiled. "Elliott, come here please."

I suddenly stand, as I remove the nails from the door, then walk down the stairs. As I round the corner, I suddenly realize this may have been a dumb move as I stared down the barrel of the gun that Kristal was holding! She could kill me right now I thought.

Kristal puts the gun down, then ran into my arms.

"I love you, Elliott! I'm so sorry for everything baby, I now realize that it truly was my fault! I was selfish, but I never meant for Nyia to die. No matter what, I never intended for anyone to hurt my baby girl!"

I held her tightly in my arms as I looked down at my wife. I started to cry with her in my arms; I finally saw the woman I married.

In my heart I felt that God had even me the strength to finally forgive her for her selfishness. I was ready to rebuild a life together with her and I wanted her to know that. I was still very much in love with her, even after the affair, I wanted to make it work between us.

"I forgive you Kristal; we can work this out now, okay baby. I love you so much."

Suddenly Kristal pulled back from me, stepping backwards towards the table, shaking her head.

"No Elliott baby, I am not forgiven yet."

I watched, unable to move as she walked over to the gun and picked it up. I shouted at her as she stood there shaking with the gun in her hand.

Confessions in Whispers

"Kristal! You don't have to do this now baby, I understand now, why this all happened."

Kristal's green eyes softened as she smiles at me, then grabbed the picture of Nyia. "You're not the one who needs to forgive me now Elliott, Nyia is."

I am at a loss for words as her words hit me. I was still unable to move, and all of sudden I was unable to speak too. I watched Kristal. I watched as she held the gun firmly by her side.

She raised the gun. "I deserve to burn in hell, remember."

I jumped as she shot herself in the neck. I ran over to her, holding her as she bled to death still clinging to Nyia's picture.

Kristal looks up at me and smiled. "Nyia, do you forgive mommy, now?" Kristal laughed as she looked me in the eyes. "She forgives me, Elliott, I love you both."

I gasped as she started to cough up blood and died in my arms. I had lost both of the two most important women in my life the same way…In my arms. I cried uncontrollably as I held Kristal's lifeless body, telling her over and over, "And so do I baby, do you hear me Kristal, so do I."

I felt numb as I called the police and told them what happened. I show them the video tape as they questioned me.

The police cleared me of kidnapping charges I apologize to Melvin Drason's family for the kidnapping, his wife forgave me.

I buried my wife Kristal next to my daughter. As I stood there looking at the two graves, for the first time, I was finally at peace.

The emptiness and pain I felt was finally gone. I thanked God for this test and for this chance to heal my broken heart. My heart was full of peace knowing that in the end, Nyia forgave her mother. I could finally move forward and begin my life once again. I could return to work now; I had missed it.

I returned to church. As I walked in people were happy to see me there once again. I was happy to be back in the house of Lord, and I was happy to see everyone taking me back with open arms.

As I walked through the church, I saw a young girl walking towards me. I knelt to her.

Confessions in Whispers

"It's good to see you again, Pastor Elliott."

I smiled as I gave her a big hug. "It's good to see you again too little Cassandra Drason."

She hugged me tightly. "I've missed you Uncle; I miss Nyia too."

I smiled at her as I took a necklace out of my pocket, giving it her. It was a gold and diamond cross necklace that used to belong to my daughter.

"Now she will always be with you, just like she is always with me."

I looked up to see Drayia smile at me as her daughter runs back over to her. I nodded at her and continued to hug people of the congregation. It was almost time for the service to begin. Everyone took their seats.

I suddenly sensed the presence of my daughter and my wife as I walked over and stood at the purl pit thanking everyone for coming this Sunday.

I began, "I am happy to return the house of Lord and today's sermon is about Tangible Justice through Redemption."

Confession 9

Within Dreams

"Do you want more?"

I saw a blurred face in the dim light. I attempted to move but I couldn't. I could hear the raspy voice echoing around me.

"Did you hear me, Bitch! Do you want some more!"

I screamed as I felt the strap sting my bare thighs.

"No, I don't want anymore!"

Laugher was all I heard in response to my tear stained pleads for him to stop. Nothing helped; he continued to beat me with the strap. The pain seemed to last forever until… I gasped as I sat straight up in my bed, sweat pouring out of me.

"Shit! It was another nightmare."

My husband rolls over and looking at me. "Baby, are you okay?"

Confessions in Whispers

As I began to try to answer him, my airway felt tight; it was hard to breath. I dry heaved as I attempted to catch my breath. My husband turns quickly to the nightstand and grabbing my inhaler.

He shakes it for me. "Okay now, inhale in deep for me, Baby!"

I inhale and I feel myself open up. I cough once and take another puff. I cough again but I can breathe now.

He sighs. "Did you have another nightmare, Janika?"

I look down at the cotton sheets and nod.

"Oh baby, you know that is what causes your panic attacks." He gathers me in his arms, stroking my short auburn hair.

"I know but I can't help it, Shaun."

He kisses my forehead. "Do you want to tell what it was about?"

I shake my head; I rather not ruin the sweet mood we have going on right now with that hideous nightmare. I want to forget I even had it; I just want to stay here in his strong arms where I am safe.

I finally drift back to sleep and this time there are no nightmares, just pretty dreams of the day I married this amazing man, Shaun Blaircliff.

I wake up the next morning to a loud alarm clock. "Urgh, its five-forty five a.m. I have to get Kaidence up for school!" After hearing the alarm for the second time, I finally get out of bed. I stumble down the hall to my daughter's room and open the door to see my little angel still in the bed.

"Honey, it's time to get up for school."

She rolls onto one side and whines, "I don't want to go to the school today, Mommy."

I place both hands on my hips, and smirk. "And why not little lady?"

She looks up at me with puppy dog eyes, and then pokes her lip out. "Because it's going to be boring today; we have a coloring test."

I think for a moment I do not remember coloring tests in kindergarten.

"Well get up anyway, go brush your teeth and wash your face. If you do that and eat all your breakfast, we can talk about you staying home today."

Confessions in Whispers

Kaidence hops out of bed and runs to the bathroom.

I walk downstairs to start breakfast. I turn on the living room T.V. to see the traffic.

"Doesn't look too bad this morning, I will not have to fight the traffic so much to get her to school this morning, thank God."

As I am finishing up breakfast, as I hear the door open. I smile as I watch my husband walk in.

"Urgh! I so hate being on call!"

Shaun walks over to me and kisses my lips. "Hmmm blueberry pancakes this morning, yum."

I laugh as I give him a warm hug. "Yes, blueberry and you better eat all of it this morning, Dr. Blaircliff."

He bows as he removes his white lab coat and sits down at the table.

"Where, oh, where is my princess, oh, where, oh where can she be?"

I laugh as he calls for Kaidence. She runs down the stairs yelling, "DADDY! You're home!"

Kaidence jumps into Shaun's arms. He hugs her tightly, and then blows on her neck. She giggles and wiggles in his arms.

"Okay you two, it's time to eat."

Shaun pokes out his lip and Kaidence mimics him.

"We wanna play, Mommy!"

I sigh as I shake my head and laugh at them. "Kaidence doesn't want to go to school today."

Shaun looks over at Kaidence, who confirms it with a nod. "Okay Princess, why does my little angel want to stay home from school today?"

She clears her throat, then said, "Because Daddy we have a coloring test today. I don't want to fail it."

Shaun laughs and winks at me. "Oh, daddy's little princess, now why do you think that you will fail. You are great at coloring, honey."

Kaidence smiles big at her daddy, gives him a big hug, and then she runs upstairs.

"How do you always do that?"

Confessions in Whispers

Shaun winks at me, smiling slyly. "It's my undeniable charm. After all, that's how I charmed you into marrying me."

I laugh; he did have a dashing way about him.

"Fine, then since you have to head back to the hospital Dr. Charm, you can drop your adorable daughter off at school."

Shaun is about to say something when Kaidence runs into the kitchen with her backpack.

"Daddy! Daddy! We have to go; I am going to be late for school!"

"Alright! Alright, Princess, let's go."

Shaun picks her up and starts to walk out with her. As he walks pass me, he grabs me by my waist, pulling me in close. He nuzzles my ear.

"I'll charm you some more later."

My face feels hot. I smile at him, kissing his cheek. "I love you, Shaun."

"I love you too, Janika."

Kaidence is pouting, hanging on her daddy's shoulder. I caressed her face lightly, and then nuzzle her cute little nose. "I love you too, Mommy's Princess."

She laughs, hugging me, and then waves goodbye.

"BYE MOMMY!"

I watch my family leave from the window. I then decide to take a nap. As I drift off to sleep, I can hear someone calling me. "What do you want from me?"

The vision in front of me is hazy and dark, it looks like a woman. She tries to speak to me but as she reaches out, I see the chains tighten around her arm almost ripping through her flesh. I hear the muffled scream as she is dragged back into the darkness. I stand alone in the dark shutting my eyes wishing I were back at home.

As I beg and plead to go back, I hear him again. "NO! NO! NO!"

"Do you want more?"

I shake my head furiously; I just want him to stop taunting me but then I feel the hot steamy breath behind me. So close that it makes my body start to tremble. I begin to whimper as I hear him again. He says a name, but it was warped so I cannot understand it.

Confessions in Whispers

I blink as he tries to repeat it; I still couldn't understand what he is saying. He grabs my shoulders and I scream, fighting him off with all my might. He is shaking me; I smack him across the face.

As I attempt to get away, I trip and fall.

I scream again and I jerk my head up. I gasp for air; my heart felt like it would burst from my chest. I crawl to the desk drawer and grabbing my back up inhaler. I try to calm myself as I shake it. I take a puff.

"BREATHE JANIKA!"

I shake it again then take another puff.

"CALM DOWN AND JUST BREATHE!"

I keep telling myself to breathe, calm down and stay still. I am shaking on the floor, but I began to calm down. I start to cry, and I look up and see Shaun staring at me holding his face.

"OH MY GOD BABY, DID I DO THAT?"

Shaun shakes his head, and then looks down. "Another nightmare wasn't it."

I hold myself leaning against the side of the desk and begin to rock. I look up at Shaun, who runs over to me.

"I am gonna get you through this, Janika, I swear! You are not doing this alone, baby."

I grab him, hugging him tight. He embraces me, caressing my hair. "It's alright, I'm here, and no one is going to hurt you while I'm around, baby."

I know he is right; I know in my heart that Shaun would never let anything happen to me or Kaidence.

Shaun caresses my face, and then lifts my chin to look in his soft gray eyes. I get lost in those safe stares he gives me. I smile as he leans in to kiss me. Our lips touch and like every other time; he rejuvenated my soul.

As we part, I hear a soft whimper. I looked over to my left to see Kaidence standing by the couch rubbing her sleepy eyes.

Shaun leans in over me, then softly whispers, "Baby, you might want to go clean up your face, so she doesn't know you were upset."

Confessions in Whispers

I agree, she shouldn't see me like this. Shaun gets up first and picking Kaidence up. He takes her into the kitchen.

"Aww, my princess just woke up from her nap, how about a snack before dinner."

As they disappear, I hurry upstairs to clean my face. I walk into the bathroom, grab a washcloth off the shelf and stand in front of the sink. I start running the water trying to think why this is happening to me? Who was that woman and that man who scared me so much in my dreams?

I wash my face, then return downstairs to join Shaun and Kaidence in the kitchen. They were making jello and were laughing.

I have such a beautiful life, why are such ugly dreams haunting me? I can still see the chains wrapped around her arms, though I couldn't see her face or eyes, somehow, I could feel her pain. I shake away the image as I sit with my family to enjoy a snack before dinner.

Once dinner is over and I am putting Kaidence to bed, I try to get ready myself with a nice long bath. I walk into the bathroom to see lights dimmed, and a single white rose lying peaceful on the edge of the tub. I smile to myself. Suddenly I feel his embrace engulf me. In his arms I am always in heaven.

He whispers in my ear, "I was thinking it's been a while since I bathed you."

I giggle. I turn my head to the side and his eyes meet my mine.

"Not since I was your patient, Dr. Briarcliff."

He walks around me with ad raise eyebrow and looks me over. I playful turn to the side to give him a good look. I strip out of my clothes. His expression changes to both eyebrows raised.

"Mrs. I'm so sorry, what is your name again?"

I laugh coolly. "I'm Mrs. Shaun Briarcliff."

He smacks himself upside the head. "Oh yes, you are Dr. Briarcliff's wife. I'm Mr. Charming."

I burst out laughing and he raises a finger to silence me.

"Oh yes, I'm Prince Charming and I'm scheduled to give you a bath."

He leads me to the bathtub, helping me into the hot water. I love the steam! I get comfy and sit up leaning forward. I looked behind my shoulder at 'Charming', biting my lip.

"Now, now, Mrs. Blaircliff, I know that Dr. Blaircliff would be so jealous to know his beautiful wife is biting her tasty lips at another man."

All I can do is smile, and then nod my head. I turn back around, and Shaun begins to bathe me. I love it when he touches me. I feel so safe, and warm inside. I begin to feel sleepy and drift off to sleep for a second. I jerk myself awake, laughing at myself.

I turn to say sorry to Shaun. My eyes widened; tears well up in my eyes as I stare at his face. He has this dark smile; he was a white man with dirty blonde hair. He is not ugly but extremely attractive. His eyes are ice cold blue. He smiles, and then leans in whispering in a low, deep raspy voice.

"Do you want more?"

I begin to shake. I attempt to move, but I couldn't! I look to see chains wrap around my arms and legs. I looked up at him; he seemed pleased with his work. I look down at my arms again. I am stunned to see the scars, the cigarette burns, and the wounds covering my body.

I try to breathe; I want to scream but I couldn't. My head is spinning, my vision is blurry. I can still hear him asking me, "Do you want more! Bitch I know you want more!"

I shake my head, and as I black out.

*

I look around; I am in the dark. I scream but the sound echoes around me. I fall to my knees and call out for Shaun, for Kaidence. For a minute I think I just died. "OH GOD HELP ME! I CAN'T DIE YET; I HAVE TO BE THERE FOR KAIDENCE!"

I jump as I hear laughing behind me. I stand very still, but the laughing gets louder. I turn around to see the woman with chained arms laughing with her head down. Her dirty, matted long hair covering her face. I can't stop looking at her. Her head remains down, but she laughs.

"WHAT THE HELL IS SO FUNNY, HUH?!"

Confessions in Whispers

She goes silent. I shake my head; I need to get back home. I turn around to see if I can see a light anywhere, but it is just a grayish black mist.

I stand up and start to walk away when suddenly she grabs my shoulders from behind. I struggle to get away and push her back.

"WHAT IN THE HELL IS WRONG WITH YOU!"

She stands back up, head still down with her hair still covering her face. She turns to walk away from me. I stand there shaking. I look away for a minute when she knocks down. She is laughing, and I feel snake like fingers grip my neck. I try to get away, but she is so strong. She tightens her grip around my wrist...

I kick and twist trying to release myself. She laughs hysterically as she repeats, "YES, I WANT MORE! YES, YOUR BITCH WANTS MORE!"

I fight for breath.

"PLEASE GOD, LET ME GO!"

She is still laughing, humping me as she chokes me.

Finally, I give up. I can't fight anymore. I am too weak for her. And then I hear Shaun.

I started to fight, and I look around, stunned. I fight for breath; I cry because I realize I am at home.

Shaun grabs my shoulders and then forces the inhaler into my mouth. I breathe in deeply and relax a little bit. Then Shaun hits the inhaler again, I take another breath. I slowly feel my anxiety release. "BABY, WHAT HAPPENED? WHERE DID I GO?"

Shaun looks at me, rubbing his head. "Baby, I don't know. We were playing in the bathroom, and then you blacked out, I had to bring you back in here. He looks so scared as he continues, "You wouldn't snap out of it! I kept shaking you and calling you, but you wouldn't answer!"

He sits next to me on the bed. "Baby, don't ever scare me like that again, I thought I lost you!"

I hug him tightly; I didn't want to leave him either. He cries on my shoulder, and I pat his head.

"I don't know what I would do if something ever happened to you, Janika baby."

I kiss the side of his head. God, what in the hell is going on?

Confessions in Whispers

Somehow, we went to sleep. I didn't dream either. I was too damn exhausted to dream about anything.

*

Then next day after I take Kaidence off to school, I went to seek help from a therapist. I find a woman name Shayla Timkins. I ask if I can make an appointment with her.

A beautiful black woman comes out of an office. She is dark skin and wearing her makeup natural and her hair in locks with red tips. She looks up at me smiling as she extends her hand, "I'm Shayla Timkins, can I help you?"

I nod as I rise from my chair. "Please Ms. Timkins, I need your help, my dreams are trying to kill me!"

Shayla asks her assistant to hold her calls for the next hour. She asks me to follow her into her office. I look around the lovely, decorated office with marble and black furniture. I take a seat. "I know it sounds crazy, but I am having these terrible strange dreams about a woman with chains on her arms. She chokes me in one of my dreams and then there was this man. He is a white man asking me this sick question. What in the hell is wrong with me?"

Shayla seems to be thinking of what to say to the crazed woman who has come into her office.

"Okay, let's start with your name."

Oh my God, I cannot believe that I have been rambling for that long without even telling the woman my name!

"I'm so sorry, I'm Janika Blaircliff."

"Okay Janika, are you married?" I nod. "Okay do you have any children?"

I nod again. "I have a daughter, her name is Kaidence."

Shayla smiles deeply. "That is a beautiful name. Okay, when did these dreams start to occur?"

I had to think for a moment; I have been having bad dreams off and on for a while now. "I think they started about a year ago, around the time of my husband and I's anniversary." Shayla thinks a moment, and then starts writing. "And why would that day be sufficient?"

Confessions in Whispers

I had to think a moment. "Well, it is the date of my release from the hospital."

Shayla sits straight up in her chair. "Release from the hospital?"

I look back up at her nodding. "I was in a car accident, and I was badly hurt. They didn't think I would make it, but I did. My husband made sure of it. He told me that I had amnesia, because I couldn't even remember the love of my life's name. But with his love and help, I got through it. Besides, I was pregnant. I needed him more than ever. I consider myself one of the lucky ones."

She then asks, "What is your husband's first name?"

I smile, feeling that glow I get when I talk about him. "His name is Shaun, Dr. Shaun Blaircliff."

My smile fades as I look at Shayla's face. She just stares at me.

"I'm sorry Mrs. Blaircliff, but I cannot help you."

I stand up in disbelief. "You cannot be serious; I sat here and poured my soul to you, and you can't help me!"

She looks at me in a half ass sincere way.

"Yes, I know you did, but I can't help you. I simply can't. I'm sorry."

I am in total disbelief. I just leave. I am so lost now. What do I do now? I walk down the street, my life now seemed to be a big blur.

I got into my car and began to cry. "Why Lord is this happening to Me?"

I look at the time. Oh shit! I'm going to be late picking up Kaidence. I start looking for my phone and call her school to say I will be running late.

"Hello, Hopkins, Elementary."

I am telling the assistant at the front desk that I am running late, when I see Shayla leaving in a hurry. She looks determined and pissed off! I decide to follow her.

"Hello Mrs. Blaircliff?"

I blink, remembering I was on the phone.

"Oh, I am sorry Mrs. Hall, I am going to be late picking up Kaidence today, can you please allow her to attend the after-school program and I will be there shortly after."

She says she will, and I hang up. I have no idea why I am following Shayla, but when I see that she

Confessions in Whispers

is going to my husband's hospital, I knew I had to know.

I park a few cars back from Shayla's. She slams the door of her Mercedes. She makes a call, then paces back and forth in front of her car. It is like in slow motion as I watch Shaun come out of the hospital, running down the stairs. He marched over to Shayla.

"So, you're married now?! Oh, really now, and when in the hell did this happen, Shaun?!"

Shaun steps back from her with his hands up in defense. "We were over Shayla, and you knew it. We had not spoken to each other in over a year when I met Janika. Don't come to MY damn JOB talking to me about MY damn WIFE!"

Shayla stands there quietly a moment, looking at the ground. Shaun shakes his head, and then turns in confusion.

"How the hell do you know my wife anyway?" Shayla looks up at him in disbelief. "That's what you have to say to me?! How do I know her? She came marching into my office, begging for help for some bullshit dreams. That's how I find out MY ex-fiancée is married!"

I just sit there stunned. She knew him, that's why she couldn't help me all of a sudden. I just stare at the scene of them two standing out there. Shaun walks around in a circle, rubbing his head.

"Shayla, I'm sorry you found out that way, but I love Janika..."

Shayla slap him across the face. "FUCK YOU SHAUN! Oh, an on top of that you have a kid too! Damn you Shaun, you cheated on me?!"

Shaun is breathing hard, holding the side of his face. He then looks at Shayla, shaking his head.

"Hold on, I never cheated on you!"

Shayla looks at him with her hands on her hips.

"Really, how old is Kadence?"

He laughs "Her name is Kaidence, and she is ..." Shayla shakes her finger in his face. "Oh no, how old is she?" He refuses to answer, she keeps yelling in his face. "Tell me! Tell me the fucking truth, Shaun!"

Confessions in Whispers

Shaun seems to be at a breaking point. He finally blows up on Shyla, "SHE IS FIVE! OKAY, KAIDENCE ISN'T MINE!"

I jump out of the car running to him. Shaun's eyes widened and he grabs me.

"WHAT THE HELL ARE YOU TALKING ABOUT? WHY ARE YOU TELLING HER KAIDENCE ISN'T YOURS!"

I fight in his arms, and he just holds me tighter.

"BABY, I'M SORRY!"

Shayla just stands there. I finally get free from him, and then run to my car and leave. I cry all the way to pick up Kaidence.

What in the hell is going on here, was he having an affair with her? Why does he believe Kaidence isn't his?

I wipe my eyes as I pick up Kaidence and go home. As I pull up, I see that Shaun's car is there already. We go into the house, Kaidence runs over to hug Shaun, who is sitting on the couch.

"Hey Daddy's Angel, how was school today?"

Kaidence rambles off about her day; I am so heartbroken. I go upstairs to our room.

I sit there on the bed thinking, how in the hell did this happen to us? I sit there with my head in my hands. Silently crying to myself, I feel eyes on me.

I look up to see Shaun standing in the doorway. I don't want to look at him. I lie on the bed looking at our family photo.

"How could you tell her that?"

"I was trying to keep her out of our business baby, I'm so sorry it turned out like that."

I sit up to look at him; he is now sitting next to me.

"So, you told her that to get her off your back?"

Shaun tries to wrap his arms around me, but I push him off me. He looks in my eyes; I love those soft gray eyes. "Yes, I told her that to get her off my back. I dated her before we met baby. Yes, I was engaged to her at one point, but she didn't want the same life I did. She didn't want children; she didn't even really want to get married, just date."

"Exactly how long did you two date?"

"We didn't date long, about a year."

He is lying again, and I want to know why. "Shaun, you told me at the hospital that we have

Confessions in Whispers

been together for three years. You told Shayla that it had been a year since you spoke to each other. So, you were cheating on me and not her?" Shaun nods, and then wraps his arms around me.

"I'm so sorry baby, we were having issues and I needed time to think. Shayla was a fling that got out of control."

I hug him tightly. "Could I really be mad? If we had problems, I mean it's over now and we are married."

I decide to let the whole thing go. Shaun kisses me softly which ends in us making love. I am sleeping peacefully when I hear a crying sound. I sit up in bed thinking it is Kaidence, but it is HER.

This time I stay my distance; I just stare at her. She whimpers silently, and then she mumbles something. I couldn't hear her, so I step a little closer. She shies away from me, then screams something that comes out muffled.

"What are you trying to say to me? Why can't I understand you?"

Her head tilts to one side, and then she raises her head. Her dirty hair still covering her face, she looks down and tries to scream. She then looks up at me and shrugs her shoulders.

She backs away. I watch her arm rise and I stare at the chain wrapped around it. She then points at something. I turn to look right in his eyes. He smiles coolly, my body wouldn't move, and I feel her snake like fingers on my shoulders pushing me towards him.

His eyes are fixed on mine and I begged with all my heart, "PLEASE STOP HAUNTING ME!"

I can hear the echoes of her laughter, as she envelopes me from behind.

I struggle to get free; he grabs hold of my throat. His smile looks like a demon's as he tightens his grip. He begins to lift me in the air.

"Please!" I can barely get that out of my mouth.

"You belong to me! No one else!"

I slap at his hand, but he just laughs. Pulling me close to his face he screams, "YOU BELONG TO ME AND NO ONE ELSE!"

Confessions in Whispers

She is laughing and dancing around us. I fight him off, hitting the ground hard. I look up and find I am back at home.

I am on the floor, I can breathe, and then I start to cry. I roll up in a ball and begin to rock back and forth. Shaun jumps out of bed calling my name as I rock on the floor.

"Baby, what are you doing on the floor?"

I crawl to his feet and hold his legs tightly. He removed my hands as he kneels next to me. I wrap my arms around his neck and hold on to him. He rocks me back and forth in his arms.

"It was another nightmare huh, I wish you would tell me what these dreams are about?"

I look up at him. "I am having nightmares about a man who beats me and a woman with chains around her arms. She has dirty long hair so I can't see her face, but she laughs at me when he tries to choke me."

Shaun eyes widened as he listens to me tell him the twisted things this man puts me through. Shaun pulls me close to him and caresses my head.

"Baby, it's okay I'm here, you just be quite for now, no more talk of bad people. Shaun is going to take care of you baby. I will protect you, Janika."

Shaun rocks me back and forth in his arms. I hold on tightly, I want the nightmares to go away. I want to be safe in Shaun's arms forever. He helps me to my feet and back in bed, this time I go to sleep with no more nightmares.

*

The next morning, I wake to silence. I get up and head to Kaidence's room. I push the door open, but she is not there. I jogged downstairs to see if they are in the kitchen, but there is no one. I look at the dining room table and see that breakfast is made for me.

I sit to eat and picked up the note.

"Janika, baby you need to rest today. So, I called off work so you can do just that. I am taking and picking up Kaidence from school, so you have nothing to do but rest. Enjoy your day off mommy and wonderful wife, love Kaidence and Shaun."

I smile as I eat my breakfast; I will go out and shop. After I get dressed, I go to a few shops I have wanting to go to for a while. I buy a few things for the house, Kaidence, Shaun and of course myself. I am genuinely enjoying my day when my phone rang.

"Hello," I sing into the phone.

"Hi Janika, it's Ruth, how are you doing dear?"

It is Ruth Blaircliff, Shaun's Grandmother.

"I am fine, Mrs. Blaircliff, what can I do for you today?"

She goes right in complaining she has not seen her great granddaughter in a while and when Shaun and I are coming to North Carolina to visit.

"I assure you Mrs. Blaircliff, last I spoke to Shaun about it, he was planning a trip very soon."

"I do hope so. I did raise the little big head boy for Christ's sake, please have him call me, you will right dear?"

"Of course, I will Mrs. Blaircliff. I will talk to Shaun as soon as I get home, and he call you with the details."

We hang up and I sigh; it has been a while since Grandma Ruth has seen us, so a trip is in order. I am heading back to the car when I bump into someone coming out of the post office. I turn to apologize when my eyes lock on his. He smiles sweetly at me.

"Well, isn't this a surprise, it has been ages since I last saw your face, Nikolett."

I blink and then shake my head. It is him! Oh my God, it is man from my nightmares in the flesh. I pretended not to know him as I smile, "I'm sorry, but you must have me confused with someone else."

I excuse myself and quickly headed for my car, the thumping in my chest is so loud its echoes in my head. The sweat on my face and body seem to engulf me as I try to stay calm. I lean on the driver side door, trying to regain my composure. When I am finally calm, I laugh at myself, it is okay, Janika. He didn't even know your name, so it is fine, and you are fine.

I looked in my purse for my keys when I feel the hot breath of someone behind me. I didn't want to turn around; I didn't want to see his eyes or his face! Even though I couldn't see his face, I can clearly see his smile in my mind.

Confessions in Whispers

He sighs, "Oh my sweet Nikolett, it has been too long since we have seen each other, and you just leave me like that. Now that is not right."

I tremble with fear, I can't move or scream. Then I hear HER laughing at me, her laughter gets louder and louder.

He grabs my shoulders, and I jump. He pulls me close to him with his face touching my left cheek. "Tell me Nikolett, have you missed me at all?"

I plead to him. "I am not this Nikolett, my name is Janika. Please let me go."

He quickly released me, but I am still unable to move. I turn around to look at him. He is studying my face and body with his eyes. I am instantly uncomfortable, and now I can't breathe.

I ramble through my purse for my inhaler. I puff to regain my air. I hear him laughing at me. "Wow, you don't remember me huh, you have changed so much since the last time I saw you. You cut your hair; you have a new name and maybe even a new life."

I am confused to the point of a headache. Who is this Nikolett person? Why do I even know this man and why is he haunting my dreams? I then heard HER laughing at me again. I cover my ears and kneel down, but I am suddenly yanked to my feet by my hair. The intense pain runs through me. As I looked into his eyes, he grabs my throat. I shut my eyes, grabbing his hand. His grip tightens.

"So, tell me Nikolett, do you want some more?"

My body can't fight his strength. I begin to fade in and out. He runs his hand from my face down my body. I feel sick as he violates me.

His voice is calm and deep. "We used to have such fun until you wanted to stop. You may not remember now, but you will. You hear me, my little bitch! You will!"

He lets me go, then walks off. I sit on the ground holding myself. What is he talking about? My name was Janika Blaircliff not Nikolett! What in the hell is going on here?!

I finally get in the car and drive home. Shaun and Kaidence are already there when I reach the house. I run inside and straight upstairs. I didn't want Kaidence to see me upset. I collapse on my bed and cry with all my heart. Shaun comes inside the room, sitting me up. "BABY, WHAT IS WRONG?!"

I look at him with a tear-stained face, then at the door. I quickly run over to Kaidence who is silently crying in the doorway.

"Oh honey, Mommy isn't feeling well, okay, but I will be all better after a nap." She nods at me, then hugs me tightly. I fight, not to cry in her arms. She wipes her face on her shirt.

"I thought you were mad at me for not saying goodbye this morning, Mommy."

I shake my head, wiping her face with my hand. "Oh Princess, Mommy was not mad. I loved the breakfast you and daddy left for me."

She smiles, and then hugs me again.

"Princess, will you excuse mommy and daddy a minute?" Kaidence smiles, nods, and skips downstairs to watch T.V. Shaun looks at me, then sighs deeply.

"Baby, what is the matter...?"

I grab him, holding him tightly and trembling in his arms. Shaun jumps as he listens.

"HE FOUND ME SHAUN! THE MAN FROM MY NIGHTMARES FOUND ME!"

Shaun grabs my shoulders, shaking me, "Janika! What are you talking about?!"

"The man who hurts me in my nightmares, I saw him today when I was having my Mommy Day. Shaun, he kept calling me Nikolett, he kept telling me that I was his!"

Shaun hugs me tightly; he is trembling a little too, He soon lets me go.

"Where in the hell did you see him?"

Shaun's eyes become focused and determined as I watch him pace back and forth in front of me.

"No! Shaun, this man is dangerous, baby do not go out there looking for him, promise me!"

He kneels looking me in eyes, but his eyes were not soft like always, they are sharp and flashing. Shaun is not going to let this man get away with scaring his wife.

"I can't just sit back and do nothing, baby, this man has been haunting your dreams and I want to know why?!"

Confessions in Whispers

I just sit there shaking my head for the most part. "I don't know why he is haunting me or why he thinks I am this Nikolett character."

Shaun stands up, grabbing his keys, and heading for the door. I am right at his heels.

"You can't go! Shaun, leave it alone!"

Shaun halts, spins around looking at me. "Leave it alone! This bastard has you scared to death and YOU want me to leave it alone! Fuck that! I will leave it alone when I get some answers!"

He storms out of the door; there is nothing I could do. He wants to know why, and I can't blame him, I did too. The next thing I heard is the engine of Shaun's bike as he speeds off. I closed the door when I turn around to see Kaidence staring at me.

"Mommy, what's wrong with Daddy?'

I smile. "Daddy needs to go to find someone, princess."

She walks up to me with a confused look on her face.

"Is daddy mad at me not getting an A on my drawing final?" I laugh as I kneel down to her, kissing her forehead gently. "Oh no love, baby it's not that at all. I bet you did well though, huh?"

After reassuring Kaidence that she is not the reason Shaun went storming out, I fixed her dinner and put her to bed.

I need to lie down. I make sure the house is locked up as I collapse on the couch. It has been a tiring day and I just want Shaun to come home. I try to call him several times, but he would not answer.

Finally, after a dozen tries, I get him on the phone.

"Shaun! Come home!"

His voice is low, he wheezes and seems out of breath.

"Shaun? Shaun! Baby, are you okay?!"

He cleared his throat. "Yeah, I'm fine. I am on my way home."

I could breathe easy now, knowing he is safe and that he was coming home. I decide to take a nap.

I am sleeping peacefully till I hear HER laughing. I sit up, looking around the living room. I can't see her, but I can hear her laughing at me! I keep swirling my head and shaking it to stop hearing HER! Nothing was helping. She is there, I just knew she was in the house. I run upstairs to check on Kaidence. I push the door open. She looks to be sleeping peacefully. I feel relief, but not for long.

As I turn to leave, I hear a faint giggle. I shake my head as I walk over, sitting down next to her.

"Okay little girl, you are supposed to be asleep."

I smile as I lean down to kiss her goodnight once more. Then I scream realizing that my daughter is not in the bed, but HER! She sits up laughing at me. I jumped on her, grabbing her by her throat.

"STOP LAUGHING AT ME! WHO ARE YOU! WHAT DO YOU WANT! WHERE IS KAIDENCE!"

HER laughter is muffled, but she keeps laughing. She finally grabs my shoulders, pushing me down. I scream as the weight of the chains on her arms hold me down. She has me pinned and then leaned forward to show her face. I scream as I looked back at myself! Suddenly, she stops laughing. HER face looks me over, a smile curled across her lips, and she whispered in my ear.

"Yes, I want some more."

The sound of my own voice begging for more scares me more than anything else. I silently cry, "NO, I do not want anymore."

She sits up still pinning me down with her chained arms. She looks down at me as she throws her dirty hair over her shoulders.

"Now you don't but you did, Nikolett."

My eyes widened as I hear her call me that name. I cry shaking my head.

"MY NAME IS JANIKA BLAIRCLIFF! I AM NOT NICKOLETT!"

I look up at HER. She watches me with a disgusted look. Turning her head to the ceiling, she screams, and then smacks me in the face with one of the chains. I try to grab her, but I start to lose consciousness. I hear HER in a sad voice. "Remember Nikolett."

I try to say something, but everything faded to black.

My head is spinning as I wake up in an apartment. I stand up looking around.

"Where am I?"

Confessions in Whispers

I hear a man's voice. I try to hide. He walks in slapping a strap against his leg.

"How is Daddy's little bitch tonight."

I moved to see who he is talking to and as I rounded the corner, my eyes widened as I stare at MYSELF! I stared at myself smiling at the dark-skinned man with the bald head. I then notice it was HER! This is her memory!

I watch the scene. She sits there with long beautiful hair, her skin is flawless, and she smells sweet. I watch closely as the bald head man grabs her by the hair. I clench my fists as she whimpers. He pulls her up to her feet, dragging her towards the couch by her hair. He throws her over the couch. She cries a little as she falls against the edge hitting the ground. He laughs as he raises the strap in the air to hit her. She sudden sneezes then raises her hand. "Polka Dots!"

The bald head man instantly stops, looking down at her with concern.

"Hey Nick, you, okay?"

She nods as she stands up. "I hate it when I fuck up the scene with a damn sneeze. I thought you dusted this place, Don."

He laughs, rubbing his bald head.

"My bad. I was supposed to when I got home from the office, but I forgot. Do you want to start from the couch then?" She stands up; dusting herself off, and then smiles nodding. "Yeah, from the couch. And remember to pull harder, okay."

He nods. His demon like smile returns to his face. He grabs her by the roots of her hair and throws her over the couch, slightly knocking the wind out of her.

"You were late today to meet me my little bitch, and you know what happens to those who don't obey Daddy."

He began to whip her with the strap, she cries out of joy and pain as she screamed, "Thank You Daddy!" over and over.

I feel sick as I see the lashes being placed on her ass. I blink and it is over. She dresses and pays the bald head man. He kisses her on the cheek, and she

Confessions in Whispers

leaves. I walk out with her and watch her walk to her car. Her cell phone rings.

"Hello."

"Oh Trix, you are so crazy. Of course, I will be at the baby shower, see you there girl."

I stand in total disbelief. Triazane Miller, my best friend Trixy. She really is me!

I placed a hand over my mouth. I can't believe it; it really is me! I am really watching myself!

I feel a presence and see HIM watching me. I look at him, feeling uneasy. I am about to get in the car when HE grabs me, dragging me into a van.

Laughter is all I could hear. The van is dark inside. I hear laughter. In the near darkness, I see him ripping her clothes off, shoving himself inside of her, and raping her. I cry for her, until I see her face, she is loving it! He barks in her ear, "You are a dirty little black bitch huh? Yeah, you are a dirty black bitch!"

He looks down at the smiling face. "You like that my little bitch! You like being fucked by the white boy, huh?"

Then he slaps her across the face, she cries out a moan. She is fucking with him. He slaps her again and again till blood oozed from her nose.

He doesn't stop there. He takes a rope and wraps it around her throat, tightening it. She smiles, and moans as he tries to kill her!

I looked away; did I really do that? HE looks down at her and loosens the rope, allowing her to breathe.

"You like it too much, don't you?"

She nods as HE wipes the blood off her face. HE gets off her, and then hit the side of the van for the driver to stop. The other man emerges from the front.

"Is it my turn now?"

He shakes his head. "No, she is too into it, look at her. She is thirsty for more, she is no fun, Dale."

He looks pissed off as he kicked her, but HE grabbed him throwing him back to the front.

"Stop it Dale, let's take her back before you do something we didn't intend to do!"

They drive her back and dropped her off. She stands there naked, with just her keys. She quickly

Confessions in Whispers

gets into the car. I sit next to her; she is beaten pretty badly.

She drives home. I looked out of the window and realize this Michigan! I lived in Michigan, but I am in Chicago back at home! How in the hell did I end up in Chicago then?

When we pull up to the house, I recognized it immediately. I begin to cry again in disbelief. As we walk inside of the house, I see HIM sitting on the couch. She just stares at him, and he walked towards her.

I look at her; she is now scared. This bastard raped her and then shows up at her house! He pulls off his Polo shirt and before she can run, he wraps it around her. She looks at him; he looks down at her with a sincere face! Are you serious? What in the hell is going on here?

He hands her the purse he is holding. She sighs as she takes it, looking through it. Everything seemed to be there but her driver's license.

"My license, it's not in here."

He laughs, then pulls it from his back pocket.

"Sorry. I used it to find you, Nikolett Jamerson."

"Yes, that is me, and you are?"

He smiles deeply and sweetly. "I am Jeremy Daniels, your new boyfriend."

NO! I didn't date this rapist?! I couldn't have?! Everything flashed backwards. OH MY GOD, I DID DATE HIM! It looks like we dated for about six months, but something is different about me.

"NIKOLETT! Where are you, you little bitch!"

I look to see her run to him.

"Baby, what's wrong?"

He grabs her by the hair for real, and she cries out. "WHERE THE HELL HAVE YOU BEEN, HUH?"

He throws her to the floor, and then jumps on her punching her in the arm.

"OW! PLEASE STOP JEREMY, YOU ARE HURTING ME!"

He becomes madder and his face looks like the devil himself.

"OH, I'm hurting you huh? Let me show you what hurt is BITCH!"

Confessions in Whispers

"NO! Baby let me explain, I was downstairs in the basement washing clothes and I didn't hear you come home."

He looks at the clothes folded in the basket, then at her.

"Oh Baby, I'm sorry, I had too many drinks at the bar tonight. Football season just started, and I lost about fifty bucks."

He helps her up. She starts to walk towards the basket when he jumps on her again. He slams her down on the ground, feels between her legs.

"I WAS NOT DONE WITH YOU YET!"

She struggles to get free, crying out, "JEREMY! NO! NOT NOW!"

He ignores her cries; it raises excitement in him as he thrust her. She screams and cries as he grabs her by the throat, whispering in her ear, "Do you want more?"

I watch her face carefully as it changed from this frightened battered woman I see, to HER. She smiles, nodding and pushing back on him moaning loudly. "YES! I WANT MORE! TORTURE ME

BABY! I HAVE BEEN A BAD LITTLE BLACK BITCH!"

He squeezes her throat tighter. HER laughter echoes around the room. He is a mad man, and she is the addictive slave. I am disgusted as I stared at the scene.

*

Time flash forward once again, and I notice something that makes me ill. I am staring at HER some months later. The bump she is showing brings tears to my eyes. I can hardly see as the blurry image reveals the truth. I watch HER walk around trying not to make HIM mad. He slaps her a few times here and there. He rapes her at every turn. He is rougher than usual; I don't think he wants the baby.

I watch HER stumble to the bathroom, and she throw up. She sits on the toilet and then as she wipes ...I gasp to see blood. I watch her panic; she cries alone in the bathroom.

I shake my head. WHAT HAVE I DONE! OH GOD, WHAT HAPPENED TO ME?"

The next vision is of HER was talking to Trixy.

Confessions in Whispers

"Girl, what in the hell have you gotten yourself into?"

I watched her try to defend him. "He is just really into it is all, and I was too until…"

Trixy cut her off. "UNTIL YOU BECAME PREGNANT! THIS HAS TO STOP, NIKCOLETT!

I look at her; I am so ashamed that I allowed that shit to go on.

I watch her return home and pack. I am proud. Good, you are leaving that son of a bitch!"

I watched HER pack up the car, get in, and drive away from the house. I ride with HER till I see where she is driving to….MY MOM'S HOUSE! I remember this place. I watch as my mom comes out to meet HER. She cries in my mom's arms, and then goes into the house. She doesn't explain everything, but my mom didn't care, she is simply happy she is there.

They enjoyed four days together. My mom helps to attend to the bruises left by HIS playtime.

I am standing in the room. It is nighttime. I watch HER sleep. When I turned my head, I see HIM! HE FOUND HER!

He stares down at her sleeping, and then caresses her face gently. She stirs and she silently called his name. HE smiles, and then grabs her by the hair. I watch, her gasp! She looks up at him and begins to fight him. He laughs as he drags her by her hair to the mirror in the room.

"YOU THOUGHT YOU COULD JUST LEAVE ME NICK! NO, YOU CAN'T LEAVE ME! I OWN YOU BITCH!"

She spins around, kicks him in the groin, and runs... He falls to one knee but manages to stand, chasing after HER. She runs into my mom's room where she finds my mom tied up to a chair.

She locks the door behind her and unties my mom. "Momma, get out of here before he kills you! GO! I will be right behind you!"

My mom runs out the back and climbing out of the window. SHE throws my mom's purse to her and begins to climb out when she hears the door being broken down. He is coming towards her.

SHE looks down at the ground. It is a bit too high for her to jump. He finally breaks through and grabs HER by the throat. "WHERE YOU THINK

Confessions in Whispers

YOU ARE GOING? I TOLD YOU NICK! YOU BELONG TO ME!"

She nods and caressing his face, and then kisses him. He lets go of her, and then hugs her tightly, silently crying.

"Baby, I was so scared you were leaving me, I promise I will do better. Come home to me, Nikolett."

She nods as she walks pass him. He sighs as he tries to collect himself. She then bolts for the door, locking it behind her and knocking the dresser in front. I watched HER run downstairs to the front door. She looks for her mom's car, but it is gone.

SHE LEFT ME!

SHE runs for her car, but it is blocked by HIM! He jumped out the window! She tries to run but he grabs her by her night shirt and throws her to the ground. She is knocked unconscious. He drags her to his van and threw her in.

I ride with him to the city limits and out of the state. He stops on a dirt road where he wraps chains around HER arms and ties her mouth with a rag.

When she wakes up, she can't move, and she is in a metal tub. He smiles as he approaches her with a hot poker. SHE screams as he burned her skin, cutting into her flesh. Then, he beats her and rapes her for hours. I cannot look, I cry for HER.

That is how she ended up in chains and with all the scars. I want to say something to HER, but I am wakened by the sound of knocking on the door.

I sit up and look around. I am at home! I try to compose myself as I get up to answer the door. Before I get there, I look to see Kaidence walking towards me. "Aww honey, did the door wake you?"

She nods, and then jumps as the knock becomes louder and more urgent. I hear someone yelling on the other side.

"BITCH, OPEN THIS DOOR! NIKOLETT! OPEN THIS FUCKING DOOR!"

I feel sick. I grab Kaidence who starts to cry.

"It's okay Baby, come on."

I pick her up and start to run upstairs. I was midway when the door is kicked opened.

I drop Kaidence. "RUN KAIDENCE! GET OUT OF HERE!"

Confessions in Whispers

Kaidence runs upstairs for my room. I run behind her. I turn to lock the door and I see HIM round the corner. I slam the door, lock it, and then push the dresser in front of it.

Kaidence is crying hard now, she is so scared. I hold her.

"Sweetheart, Mommy needs you to be a big girl right now, you must hide and do not come out till Mommy says so, okay."

She nods and hides. I lean against the dresser trying to keep HIM from getting inside.

"NIKOLETT, YOU THINK YOU CAN GET AWAY FROM ME THAT EASY!"

I scan the room for something to fight back with and see a hammer. I jump over the bed and grab it. As I looked it over, the door burst open.

I turn to look at HIM standing in my doorway! He is standing tall, pointing at me.

"Nikolett, Baby come on, you cannot run from me forever, YOU know I will ALWAYS catch you!"

I stare back at him I am thinking 'This is your entire fault! You did this to yourself, Nikolett! Now you have to finish it!'

Before I can move, I see Kaidence. She is hiding in the closet near HIM! He hears her whimpering, and then snatches open the door, staring at her. He gasps as he looks at me.

"You had her after all huh, Nikolett."

I step forward. "JEREMY STOP! THIS HAS NOTHING TO DO WITH MY DAUGHTER!"

He looks behind his back at me, and then back at Kaidence. He extended his hand out to her, to help her out of the closet.

She shakes her head and screams, "MOMMY, HELP ME!"

I jump on HIS back before he can grab her. He is NOT going to hurt my little girl! He swings left and right trying to knock me off, but I am holding on for dear life.

"KAIDENCE, RUN!"

She jumps out of the closet and runs downstairs. "HIDE BABY!" I yell as I am thrown on the bed. He jumps on top. I kick him in the groin and as he falls over. I get off the bed and run out the door. I make it to the stairs when he kicks me down them. I tumble; balling up tight, I hit my back on the wall.

Confessions in Whispers

I fight to stand but I could feel an attack coming on. I crawl towards my purse that is lying on the ground and grab my inhaler. I take a puff before it is kicked from my hand.

I turn around to stare up at him. He smacks me in the face, and I spit in his face and head butt him. He hollers as he grabs my throat and looks down at me with blood oozing from his nose.

He laughs at me as he tightens his grip.

"You have become a real fighter these last five years huh, Nick! I like it baby, come let me show you how much I have missed you!"

He tightens his grip; I am blacking in and out. The lights become hazy as I slipped in and out of consciousness. I reached up and scratch his eyes. He screams letting me go. I cough uncontrollably for air. I sit up as he looks at me with the face of a demon.

He jumps for me, but I kick him in the face.

I stand over him for the first time since I have known him. I kick him again and again.

"DO YOU WANT MORE? HUH, DO YOU WANT MORE, HUH JEREMY! THIS IS FOR EVERY NIGHT YOU RAPED ME! FOR EVERYTIME YOU MADE ME THROW UP FROM THE SICK SHIT YOU HAVE DONE TO ME!"

He cries out, then spits at me.

"FUCK YOU NIKOLETT! YOU LOVED IT, YOU BEGGED FOR MORE, YOU ARE NOTHING MORE THAN A DIRTY BITCH. YOU LIKE BEING BEATEN AND TREATED LIKE THE NASTY SLUT YOU ARE!"

The tears fall from my eyes; I have to take responsibility for my actions. I look at HIM, I had begged for more, I hungered for HIS sick twisted ways until I became pregnant.

"I did want your sick games then Jeremy, but I don't anymore! You cannot handle the fact that I don't want to be your sick slave any longer. ITS OVER! I DO NOT WANT IT ANYMORE!"

He looks at me, and then stands up. His face is fucked up. He turns like he is leaving. I sigh to myself a moment, then suddenly gasp as I stare in his eyes. I gasped for air. I can see the blood pouring on the floor.

I look in his eyes as he smiles and stepping back from me. I stumble, then fall as I see Shaun in the doorway. I hear shots fire as I hit the ground. The lights become blurry as I look to my side and see HIM lying next to me. He coughs blood as he caresses my face, and then his eyes become lifeless.

I closed my eyes and when I opened them, I see Shaun's face.

"JANIKA! BABY HOLD ON! HOLD ON!"

I hear him calling to me, but my world went black. I look around till I see HER! She is standing in a champagne gown.

"Nikolett, you finally remembered who you are! Thank you for finally freeing me from our past!"

I just stare at her; she is beautiful, with long ebony hair and all.

"I'm not dead, am I? I can't leave them!"

She shakes her head. "You can go back to them with all your memories. I am just the one you do not need anymore. Goodbye, Nikolett."

I feel dizzy as I open my eyes. I look around. I am in a hospital room. Shaun is holding my hand, sleeping. I look to my left, and I see my baby girl, Kaidence is sleeping on a pull-out bed. I hear Shaun stir. He opens his eyes to see me looking at him.

"Baby, you're awake, we didn't know if you would wake up this time. Janika, please tell me you know who I am?"

I smile at him. "You're Shaun Blaircliff, my husband."

He cries as he kisses my hand. I sigh as I hugged him tightly.

"Shaun, my name is not Janika, is it? It's Nikolett Jamerson."

Shaun sighs. "You were brought in by the police; you didn't have any identification on you. You were badly bruised, dirty, your hair was long but matted and there were chains wrapped around your arms. You were about six months pregnant with Kaidence at the time." Shaun sighs deeply wiping his face.

Confessions in Whispers

"You stayed in a coma for a month. I looked for your real identity, but since records here only looked in this state, you didn't turn up missing anywhere. I thought we would never know. Once we had you cleaned up, I had your hair cut and you were better. You were seven months, almost eight months pregnant." He caresses my face softly.

"I had fallen in love with you; I wanted to protect you from whatever you had gone through. So, I lied to you when you woke up. I told you we were engaged when I had just been engaged to Shayla not less than a year before. I am so sorry Baby; do you hate me?"

I could not hate him; he had protected me from my past. I shake my head at him.

"Thank you, Shaun, for loving me for real, and for saving my life twice. I know…"

Shaun cut me off. "Look Nikolett, do want your old life back or would you rather stay here with me?"

I laugh out loud. "Of course, I want to stay with you! How did you come up with name Janika, though?"

Shaun rubs his head, then looks at me with those soft gray eyes of his.

"Shayla was pregnant when we were together with a little girl, she didn't want children, so she aborted my child without telling me. That's why I could never marry her. Janika was the name I had intended for my daughter."

I almost cried; he had given me his daughter's name.

I stayed with Shaun. We explained to Kaidence that the bad man was gone, and he would never come back. Shaun told me never to tell her that he was not her daddy.

I changed my name officially over to Janika Nikolett Blaircliff. I got in touch with my mom. She never gave up that I wasn't alive. I told her that Jeremy was dead, and I was married.

My life was now back to the way it was before my dreams had brought me full circle to understand the error of my ways. I had run out looking to be used to the point where I didn't want it anymore. It

Confessions in Whispers

came hunting me down. I had escaped within an inch of my life.

    I had fallen down an embankment when I was brought in and rescued by this man, I now call my husband. My dreams were now calm; my anxiety finally under control, and my fears finally gone. I was finally at peace.

Confession 10

Torturous Addiction

This was not my fault! She was the one to blame; she trapped me in her honey eyes, red skin and fiery touch! I let the rain cleanse me as I stand, in the middle of a thunderstorm. I was crying but the rain washed my tears away. I wish it would wash away these memories too.

I don't want to remember all the shit that went down in a course of a year. I just wanted it all to just go away. I lowered my head as I gripped the shovel in my hand. It didn't help; it's the past now. Only, I could still see it.

If I had stopped it sooner, maybe I could have steered clear of this shit. It all started when I was in my twelfth grade of high school. I first met her in high school; yes, she was the sexiest female there. I was just this nobody, your average knuckle head teenager with no real future. I was from a

Confessions in Whispers

broken home as society would call it. Yep, that was how it was; my parents were not together so what?

I lived with my dad because my mom gave him some bullshit excuse. Anyway, I should have known from the day I laid eyes on her. I knew she was trouble but what I didn't know was just how much trouble she would be. I was barely passing my classes due to the fact that I hated school. The only reason I was passing was because I was fucking three of my teachers. How else was I going to pass...study? Hell no, I had other things on my mind. I needed money. My Pops had just lost his job and we were starving. I took up a little drug hustle, nothing major, but it was helping out with the bills.

Pops wasn't mad; he was on his own grind trying to get another job. One day as I was sitting in English class, she walked in. Redbone, just the right height, you know - model status. She had these hypnotic honey eyes; her hair was dyed almond color. She was fucking fine! Our teacher Mrs. Candice Humphrey, yeah, I was fucking her later that night smiled in my direction. I winked, giving her confirmation we would meet later.

I then checked shorty back out, she smiled at me. I gave her a head nod and let Candice introduce her.

"Class, we have a new student today, Reya Matthews."

Reya smiled shyly. "It's a pleasure to meet all of you."

Candice told Reya that she could take a seat. She sat right next to me. I wasn't surprised, all the new girls sat by me. Class went on and once it ended, I got up to go to the only real class I liked. GYM.

I walked down the hall when I heard, "Hey!"

I stopped and turned to Reya smiling at me.

"What."

She gave a crooked smile and looped her arm in mine.

"So, are you fucking that teacher?"

I raised an eyebrow. She wasn't jealous already, was she? I mean, she had just got here, but I had to give it to her for catching on that Candice and I were fucking. I had to ask though. So, I shrugged saying, 'What's it to you?"

Reya pulled herself closer to me, then unbuttoned her shirt just enough so I could see her red and black lace bra. I liked what I saw and gave her a smile that I approved. She then quickly buttoned up her shirt.

"Too bad, if you weren't fucking the teacher, you could be fucking me."

I laughed, she wanted to play mind games, huh, shit... Fuck that. I pushed her off of me.

"Go and mind fuck these lames around here, leave me out of it."

I walked away. At the time that could have been it; the end but it was only the beginning. I went to gym; everyone was already on the courts. So, I walked into the locker room to change. As I took off my shirt, I looked up and saw Reya leaning against one of the lockers.

I jumped, then shook my head. "Now what the fuck do you want?"

Her smile lit up her perfect face and made her eyes sparkle.

She walked over to me and grabbed my dick. "I want this."

I smiled, then grabbed hold of her shirt. I stripped her down and fucked her on the bench right there in the locker room. She was better than I thought; she loved every minute of it. She liked it rough and hard. Pulling her hair, scratching, biting, choking her, she liked it all. Once we finished and were dressed, she looked at me saying, "I want YOU all to myself."

I laughed at her, "Well, we will see Shorty."

She pulled me close to her; I leaned down to kiss her. Yeah, I liked her ass, that bad girl attitude was a turn on. Once she was gone, I played ball, and then handled some business.

After school I got a call from Candice, she wanted to know if I was still coming over. I sighed to myself.

"Bitches always want to rush shit when they are horny."

I asked her where her husband was, and she told me he was out of town on a business trip. Cool. I told her I would be there in an hour.

Confessions in Whispers

I went home, hopped in the shower, threw on some clothes, and headed over Candice's place. I fucked her for a few hours, then she cooked me dinner, we ate, and talked some bullshit for a while. I pretended to give a fuck about her marriage problems and shit.

Then she said, "Patrick, what should I wear to school tomorrow?"

I looked at her then said, "Here wear this tomorrow."

I handed her a choker.

"Oh Patrick, it's beautiful!"

The choker had butterflies on it, and it was blue and white. I knew that blue was her favorite color, so I got it for her. I gave it to her to symbolize that she was mine despite being married.

Candice tried it on, standing in front of me. She asked. "How do I look?"

Candice's medium length blonde hair bounced lightly over her shoulders. She looked nice for a white chick. Light blue eyes, somewhat of a shape; I nodded in approval. I looked at my cell, it was time to go before she got too emotional on me. I looked up to tell her but by the tears slowly building in her eyes, all I could say in my head was, FUCK, I'm too late.

She started crying. I comforted her for a few minutes, kissed her, and then left. I went home and fell asleep.

The next day in English, I saw we had a substitute. Candice didn't make it in. I shrugged my shoulders; maybe she was resting from last night. I was trying to drift off to sleep when I felt a sharp pain on my knee. I opened my eyes looking around, and then noticed Reya; she had kicked me. "What the fuck did you do that for?" I whispered.

She just smiled at me. I rolled my eyes until I looked at her neck and her choker.

"Nice, where did you get that?"

Reya's smile grew larger. "I got it from Mrs. Humphrey."

I looked again at the choker; it was the same one I had given Candice just last night! I looked back up at Reya and she was still fucking smiling. I didn't see what the fuck was so damn funny.

Confessions in Whispers

"How in the hell did you get it from her, did you steal it?" Reya just kept fucking smiling at me, and then opened her book bag. She pulled the knife out just enough so I could see the blade. I stared at the knife, then back at Reya.

Nah! Hell, nah this bitch didn't. I looked back over a Reya, that smile she had on her face was not one that said she was not fucking joking. Then she slowly started nodding to confirm to me that she had killed Candice!

I shook my head again.

Hell, nah man, it wasn't real, she hadn't killed the teacher man, just call Candice when you get out of class Pat, don't trip she is bullshitting you.

I looked over at Reya and smiled. Reya turned to her desk, scribbled a note, and then handed it to me. I looked down at the note. It read:

"I told you I wanted you all to myself!"

I swung in her direction; she was still smiling at me, those fucking juicy lips and her eyes had drawn me in. I was getting hard just looking at her. That sign of devotion had me hooked.

FUCK Patrick, this is not the fucking time for this shit! This is wrong dog, but would you dare tell on her?

The answer was HELL THE FUCK NO! Telling on her would mean the school would find out I was fucking her, and then would try to pin that bullshit on me! So, I chilled the rest of class.

When class was over, I headed straight for the bathroom and Reya followed me in. I checked all the stalls before I said, "What the fuck is your problem?! What the fuck did you do to Candice?!"

Reya looked hurt as she pushed me into one of the stalls, locking it behind her. I slipped as I fell on the toilet seat. She looked down at me as she lifted her skirt, showing me, she wasn't wearing any panties.

I tried to get a hold of myself. FUCK, I was losing control. I stood up; she pulled my head down making me kiss her. She hopped on the toilet seat, balancing herself with her ass up exactly right. She looked back at me whispering, "Take me baby; punish me for being a bad girl."

Confessions in Whispers

I smiled; I loved that shit! I got behind her, and we fucked for a while, then I heard someone walk in.

I stopped stroking, but Reya wasn't having it. She bounced back on me. I grabbed the back of her hair, whispering in her ear, "Stop it."

No use, she kept going. The more I pulled, the more she bounced. When the guys left, I let go off her. I finished and got dressed. Reya got down, turning towards me. "Patrick, baby you do know you can have it any way you want with me."

I pulled her closer to me, and then leaned down and kissed her. She was becoming my favorite pretty fast. I mean, Reya was open to do anything I wanted, but it was her endless devotion to me that had me fucked up. She showed her ass too much. Reya was always showing me what would happen to females who messed with HER Master. She broke this chick's arm for just touching my fucking hair! I was tripping; Reya had my nose WIDE open!

She would wear whatever I told her to, and she did whatever she was told too. It was crazy. I told her to come to school and flash all the male teachers and she did it! I had to admit I was drunk with power. Having all that power had its drawbacks too. I had to tell Reya too many times not to fight every female I dealt with. I mean she tried to fight my fucking cousin once for God's sake; it took me fifteen minutes to explain she was family!

Then I told her over and over that I was still fucking some of my teachers to pass my classes. Reya would become pissed off. "YOUR MINE! YOU DON'T NEED ANYBODY ELSE!"

I would just shake my head, march over to her, and grab her by the back of the head.

"SHUT UP! You already knew what the fuck this was. I told you this was about my grades! Don't fuck with them, you hear me!"

Reya would pout then reach up to kiss me. I couldn't help it, I leaned down to her. After I kissed her, she would smile at me.

"FINE! I will leave them alone, Master."

I would nod, but that smile she gave me always told me she would do some shit. It didn't take long

Confessions in Whispers

before she did either. Grace Leaf was my history teacher, another white woman. She was a brunette, she had short, styled hair with a little thug flavor. That's what had me interested in her; Grace had grown up around the hood. She was more of a white ghetto chick.

I was sitting in her class, and she was showing some bullshit movie about some shit that was none of my concern. I was drifting off to sleep again when I felt a tongue sliding down my ear. I turned my head to see Grace smiling at me as she whispered, "Follow me."

I got up and walked out of the class. She instructed the class to take notes. I waited in our favorite part of the school; it was this old classroom in front of hers. She was the advisor of a club and held her meetings there. Grace came inside and attacked me.

I laughed as she jumped in my arms, begging me to tie her up and take her! She was into that fantasy shit, she loved being handled. I loved these power trip games, so I tied her up, spanking her, calling her all types of dirty names, and then fucked her silly. Once we were done, I told her I needed a minute. When she left, I sat on one of the desks. I was chilling when the door opened. Reya was standing there in tears. I looked confused as she ran over to me.

"YOU like her more, don't you!"

I shook my head, not this shit again. I pushed her back saying, "What the fuck are you talking about!"

She is pointing at the wall. "HER! That bitch, Ms. Leaf."

I grabbed her, shaking her. "What the fuck is wrong with you? I don't like her more than I like you Reya!"

She smiled; she was satisfied but I knew she wanted proof. I grabbed the rope that I had just tied Grace up with and tied Reya with it. I fucked her up against the wall so she could feel that Grace could hear us. I already knew that you couldn't hear through that wall.

Once I was sure Reya was happy, I went back to class. All I could think about was Reya's attitude. That shit was becoming a problem for real now. I

Confessions in Whispers

knew that I had to tame her ass soon, but I gave her the benefit of the doubt.

A couple of days passed with no outburst from Reya, and I thought for a moment everything was going back to normal.

I went to Grace's class that week; we were learning about the civil war. Grace went to drink some of her coffee and suddenly she started to choke. A student tried to help her, but she passed out! I stood up, then felt someone staring at me.

I turned my head towards the window to see Reya standing there smiling. She winked at me, then walked away. I ran out of the classroom.

"YO! Someone get some help! Ms. Leaf passed out!"

As three teachers ran to Ms. Leaf's aid, I went to look for Reya. I looked for her for a long time; I couldn't find her crazy ass anywhere. I was pissed off! She had done it again. As I thought about what she had done, I became turned on.

I could still see Reya's devilish smile. I wanted to yell at her. I suddenly snapped; I knew where the hell she was. I ran towards the basement of the school. Sure enough, she was down there in her "Dungeon". I marched right over to her and grabbed her hair, dragging her to the floor. I was still pissed! "WHAT THE FUCK DID I TELL YOU ABOUT THE TEACHERS!"

I gripped tighter as I continued to yell, "I need those teachers to pass Dammit!"

Reya screamed, "I'm sorry Master! Please have mercy on me!"

Fuck all that, I was pissed off! But her voice and tone were making me horny. I lost my concentration as Reya grabbed my dick. I shook my head, but she pulled it out anyway. She sucked me off. After she was done and I had released and calmed down, I looked down at Reya. She smiled up at me saying, "I love you, Patrick."

I was a little taken back but I leaned down to kiss her. "I love you too."

From then on, we were in a real relationship. I just stopped caring. She would do anything I told her anyway. So, I dated her openly. Ms. Leaf got out of the hospital, and weeks later I got my report card back. I had passing grades in all my classes

Confessions in Whispers

but one. I sighed deeply thinking of Trisha Mayfield. I didn't even try to go to her class. I was obsessed with that five foot and seven inches, her chocolate skin, model shape woman.

I dodged her on purpose. I was actually in love with her! She was special and I didn't want Reya to even see her, yet alone touch one hair on her ebony black head. She was my favorite teacher hands down. Reya would ask me why I just didn't let her handle her. I would always tell her I could pull that grade up on my own.

I did know money after all. I wasn't failing that class because of the work which I actually did; I was failing the class because I never went to her class anymore! A phone call went to my dad to make me have to go! I sighed as I walked into her classroom. I took my seat that had been empty for weeks. I sat quietly during class; I didn't even make eye contact with her. She called for break and asked me to step outside.

"Damnit!"

I got up and walked out into the hallway. Once she closed the door, she dragged me into the boy's restroom and into one of the stalls! Trisha then went in on me, "Patrick Quincy Forest! Where in the hell have you been?"

I shook my head as I looked into those concerned brown eyes.

"I have a girlfriend."

She smiled as she pressed herself against me. "Patrick, you stopped coming to my class over a silly little girl."

I refrained from touching her; I knew all too well how weak I was around her! She grabbed for it! I jumped back, shaking my head. I knew better than to let those baby soft hands near my skin. Trisha grabbed me and as she was about to kiss me, the door was kicked opened.

We both gasped as we stared at Reya! I pushed Trisha off me, walking to Reya whose eyes never left mine. I wrapped my arms around her and kissed Reya's cheek. "Trish, this is my girlfriend, Reya Matthews."

Trisha rolled her eyes at Reya and stated boldly, "So YOU are the reason he hasn't shown up to my class."

Confessions in Whispers

Reya just kept staring at her, like she wanted to kill her right there. Trisha was not fazed. She laughed and walked out of the stall. She started to walk out of the bathroom when she turned around and looked at Reya. "If you want him to pass my class, you better not interfere with OUR private business."

She looked at me, blew me a kiss and left. I sighed, then looked down at Reya who looked at me like she was going to cry. I turned her around to face me.

"Baby, don't look at me that way."

Reya let one single tear fall from her eye, then wiped it away and asked me, "You love me right, Patrick?"

I hugged her tightly and kissed her cheek saying, "Of course I love you, believe me."

Reya held me tightly, then pushed me away from me. I looked at her from behind and she said coldly, "Patrick, I will kill her if you ever touch her again, do you understand me."

I yelled at her, "You better not…!"

She cut me off as she spun around to face me, she stared right dead in my eyes, and then stated again in the same dark tone, "SHE WILL DIE AND YOU HAVE NO ONE TO BLAME, BUT YOURSELF."

I was frozen; Reya was dead serious! This was no longer some fun Master/Slave game anymore. Reya really meant to own me, and I took her warning to kill Trisha very seriously.

I kept away from Trisha; it took some real patience and cleverness on my part. Trisha tried to tell me over and over she would fail me if I stopped seeing her. I just shrugged my shoulders telling her, as I looked around for Reya.

"LOOK, I can't see you anymore Trish. THIS is for your own safety. Please believe me."

Trisha looked at me with fear in her eyes. "What are you talking about Patrick? Do you really believe that girl would actually hurt me?"

I wanted to hug her and tell her how much I had always loved her. All I could do was look down at the tile on the hallway floor.

Confessions in Whispers

"Trisha, I do not want to see you get hurt over this. PLEASE stay away from me."

Trisha saw it; I didn't have to tell her anything, she knew. She started to cry silently. "I love you too, Patrick." The words caught me off guard. I didn't want her to cry. "I love you too, but Trish you have no idea what I have gotten myself into. I CAN'T drag you in the middle of this."

I looked up into her beautiful brown eyes and she nodded. I turned to walk away and felt her grab hold of my t-shirt. I froze, I knew I couldn't let her touch me; this was already hard enough for me. I tugged away from her, and then walked away.

Trisha called my name. I turned around and she grabbed me, kissing me. I pushed her off so hard she fell to the ground. I ran away from her; I didn't look back. I just ran. I reached the hall and heard my name being called.

I stopped. It was Reya, she smiled proudly at me as she ran into my arms. Somewhere in my heart I did love this insane girl. I leaned into her and kissed her. As I looked up from her, I caught a glimpse of Trisha staring at us.

I tried my damn hardest not to see the hurt in her eyes, as I buried my face in Reya's hair. I had to block out the pain I was feeling and the pain I saw on Trisha's face.

Weeks went by and I really felt like things had returned to normal again. I had my dad transfer me out of Trisha's class to a male teacher, Mr. Julian Hawkins.

Reya and I were still having a fairly good relationship. She was still overly devoted to me; she served me as long as no one else could. I was able to handle it until I got a phone call one night.

"Hello."

I heard whisper, and then a sniffle.

"Patrick, listen to me please."

"Trisha! What are you doing?! Why are you calling me?"

She sounded like she was going to cry.

"I need to talk to you right away."

I sat up in my bed looking around, and I just knew Reya was somewhere stalking me. When I thought the coast was clear, I said, "Okay talk, but make it quick, you know I don't trust being on the phone with anyone."

"I have to see you; I need to talk to you in person. Please."

I knew this could get me killed but she seemed like she really needed to see me. I agreed to meet her at her house. I got up and snuck over there. We sat on the couch and talked. Trisha was silent for a while, then said, "I'm sorry Patrick, but there is a reason why I was so upset that you had not been showing up to class."

Trisha reached over and grabbed my hand placing it on her stomach. I gasped. SHE WAS PREGNANT! I was so fucking happy I forgot about Reya. Trisha held me tight, crying. "You're not mad?"

I pulled back from her. "Hell no! You have no idea how happy this has made me!" We kissed and ended up making love. I told Trisha I would break up with Reya.

I left early in the morning and headed back to my house. I had to be careful with how I was going to end this relationship with Reya. I already knew the dire consequences for touching Trisha.

I looked for Reya at school, but she wasn't there. I tried calling her cell phone all day with no answer. I couldn't concentrate in class.

"Where in the fuck was, she?"

I decided to look for her later; I needed to talk to Trisha anyway. So, I skipped class to go to her classroom. As I opened the classroom door, I saw a substitute teacher. I gasped. Could Reya have followed me last night to Trisha's house?'

I ran out of the school, hopped in my car, and drove as fast as I could to Trisha's house. As I pulled up, I saw Trisha's car in the driveway!

I panicked as I jumped out of the car, and ran on the front door, banging hard. I screamed, "Trish! Trisha!"

I turned the handle, it was open. I ran inside shouting for Trisha. I rounded the corner to see her lying on the floor! I dropped to my knees, shaking her and calling her name. She stirred as she looked up at me. "Patrick? What happened? I must have fainted."

Confessions in Whispers

I was so relieved that she was okay. I held her for the longest time. She kept trying to tell me she was fine. She had no idea how scared I was. She then explained to me why she wasn't at school today. She had a check-up for the baby and they took blood from her.

"They must have had taken too much or something, because when I came home, I felt lightheaded, then I fainted."

I didn't leave her side for the rest of the night. I even spent the night to make sure she and the baby were safe.

The next day I went to school looking for Reya again. She wasn't there again. I became worried so I went to her house looking for her. To my surprise her brother met me outside. "Reya ran away from home a couple a days ago."

I was shocked.

"Did she leave a note or something saying why?"

He shrugged stating, "Look, Patrick, Reya has always had issues; she would say she needed her space and leave. No one worries about her because she always comes back. She is probably at our grandma's, that's where she goes when she runs away. Our grandmother lives in Chicago. Don't worry she will be back eventually."

I was really worried now, what the fuck happened that made her leave now! I tried to find her myself but after a while, left it alone.

*

Months went by without a word from Reya. By then I had put all of my focus on Trisha and our baby. By the time Trisha had the baby, we had decided to get married after my graduation. I was already eighteen but since I was still a student where she worked, we thought it best to wait till then.

My dad had landed himself a new job, so I moved in with Trisha. I started to become content in my new role as the soon to be husband and father. I landed me a job at a hardware store as an Assistant Manager. I was at work when I got the call that Trisha was having the baby.

I ran out of the store; I was in such a hurry I almost tripped. I hopped in the car and headed to the hospital. They got me dressed in scrubs and I joined Trisha in the labor room.

Trisha was in labor for almost eight hours before our son Nicholas Patrick Forest was born. I remembered being so happy as I held my beautiful son in my arms. Nothing in the world mattered more than him at that moment.

I smiled at Trisha. She was so tired, but still so beautiful. I kissed her forehead, she gave me a weak smile, and then drifted off to sleep. I rocked Nicholas back to sleep. I looked up at the door and saw Reya's face! I gasped, holding Nicholas tightly. I didn't want to wake Trisha, so I placed Nicholas back in his infant cradle.; then I ran out into the hallway. I looked left, and then right, there was no sign of Reya anywhere.

This bugged the fuck out of me big time. I could have sworn I saw her standing in the door window. I went back inside to play with my son and kiss my future wife.

*

A few months went by since we had brought Nick home. We decorated his room in blue and green;

there were footballs all over the place. I had to get used to the routine of changing diapers, giving baths, and dealing with his baby fits.

   Trisha finally returned back to work, so we had to take turns watching the baby because we could not afford daycare. We didn't just want just anyone watching him anyways. One Tuesday night while I was at work, I got a phone call from Trisha telling me to come home quickly. Thinking that something was wrong with Nick, I told my boss I had to go home and ran out the door.

   When I got to my car, I was shocked to notice a pink baby blanket on my hood. I thought maybe someone dropped it and thought it was mine. I took it off thinking I would give it to the boss later.

   As I was driving home, I tried to call Trisha to let her know I was on my way, but there was no answer. As I came near the house and up the driveway, I noticed that the house was dark. I got out slowly, and then ran up to the door.

   I put my keys in the door, but found the door was already unlocked. I got scared. I started calling for Trish but then was no answer.

Confessions in Whispers

I saw a dim light as I walked inside. My eyes widened as I saw Trisha being held at gun point by Reya! In front of them were two baby car seats, in one was Nick and in the other was a pretty little girl.

I looked up at Reya, who looked pretty much the same as the last time I saw her. She smiled at me.

"Hello Master."

"Reya, what are you doing?"

Reya's eyes flashed with anger as she held tight to Trisha's hair.

"YOU TOUCHED HER! I TOLD YOU WHAT WOULD HAPPEN IF YOU TOUCHED HER! DID YOU THINK I WAS PLAYING WITH YOU?"

I watched her put the gun on the back of Trisha's head. Trisha was sobbing,

"WHO IS THIS?" I pointed at the little girl in the car seat. Reya paused a moment, then smiled. "That's Raven, your daughter."

I was shocked to hear those words come out of her mouth. "That's why you ran away, because you were pregnant?"

Reya walked around Trisha still holding the gun. She stood next me and said in a teary voice.

"Yeah, I knew back then there was something funny going on between you and her." She pointed the gun at Trisha. "I just didn't understand why you just suddenly stopped going to her class, and then it came to me you actually cared for that bitch."

All I did was stand there with my head down; they had both gotten pregnant around the same time frame. Reya smiled at Raven, then said softly, "She is beautiful, isn't she?"

I couldn't deny she wasn't. I thought if I could play on her emotions, maybe I could get her to spare Trisha.

"So, what are you gonna do with her?"

I motioned at Trisha with a nod in her direction.

"Well, you did betray me; she doesn't have to die but... Her voice trailed off as she pointed the gun upwards. It all seemed like it went in slow motion as she pointed the gun at Nick and fired.

Trisha pushed the car seats out of the way and the bullet went through her chest! I was frozen in place; this was not real! Reya had not just tried to kill my son! I was completely numb as I looked at Trisha's face staring at me "Protect our baby Patrick, I love you."

I dropped to my knees, tears streaming down my face as I held her lifeless body in my arms.

"Trish! Trisha! BABY, DON'T LEAVE ME!"

I could not believe she was gone. I cried silently as I rocked her in my arms, kissing her face, telling her how much I loved her. Behind me, I heard Reya sighing. "She could have made another baby from someone else."

I turned to her.

"YOU WANTED TO KILL MY SON! NO...YOU TRIED TO KILL MY SON!"

Reya smiled at me. She walked over to her daughter and picked her up.

"I knew she would save him, so problem solved."

I let Trish go, then walked over and picked up Nick. I stood there and stared at Reya as she rocked Raven. "What are we gonna to do with the body, Reya?"

Reya turned towards me as she tossed the gun at me. I caught it with my free hand. "You mean what are YOU gonna do."

She then turned around and placed raven back in her car seat. She removed the gloves she was wearing.

I dropped the gun.

"YOU FRAMED ME!"

She frowned, then shrugged her shoulders with a smile on her face.

"I WARNED YOU, over and over to not let ANYONE else touch you. All those teachers just couldn't get enough of you, but YOU WERE MINE! I mean I did ANYTHING you wanted so WHY did you have to still TOUCH THEM!"

I was so pissed off, I snatched the gun and pointed it at Reya. She just smiled. "Look, you got like an hour before the police come and take you to jail. I told them you killed the first teacher, poisoned the second one, and was about to kill another. All the evidence is here…"

Confessions in Whispers

She picked up my book bag and held it upside down. All my shit fell out, piling on the floor. I pointed the gun at her.

"YOU WILL NOT GET AWAY WITH THIS SHIT!"

Reya ran for the door. I shot her twice in the back. I put Nick down, then stuffed all that shit back in my book bag. Dammit, my prints were all over this shit! I grabbed my keys and drove the car into the garage. I went back inside, and grabbed both of the car seats, and put the kids in the car. I went back into the house and wrapped Trisha's body in a rug with care, then put her and Reya in the trunk. I cleaned the house as much as I could, and then got in the car.

As I drove out of the driveway, I could hear police sirens in the distance. I jumped out, closed the garage and locked it, then drove off. I made sure not to bring any attention to myself as I causally drove around the corner.

I saw the police drive up to Trisha's house. I drove for miles; I had no fucking idea what I was going to do with the bodies. I then saw this beautiful field of flowers. I drove up the hill to get a better look. I drove to the back of the field; no one could see me out there.

I decided that would be the place. I drove to a hardware store, and bought huge bags of roses, a shovel, heavy duty lawn bags, and tape. The cashier flirted a little as she asked if the kids were twins. I looked down, nodded, and said "Yes, they are."

The 'twins' and I drove back to the field. I had to get to work fast. I knew I didn't have a lot of time before the police would come looking for me, and I needed to get the hell of the state or get to someone's house soon, so I could think.

I buried my baby Trisha first; I kissed her still warm lips, then said my goodbyes, and my apologies for getting her in this mess in the first place. I cried as I placed my wife in the ground. I then grabbed Reya's body. I kissed her goodbye as well and I told her I was sorry, then placed her in the ground. I was still crying when the rain began to fall.

I HATE HER!

Confessions in Whispers

I wiped the rain from my face as I grabbed the shovel and covered them both with dirt. I could have stopped this in the beginning if I had only come clean about Candice, but I didn't though. I was addicted to her tortuous devotion to me. I wanted to rule over her, not knowing in time she ruled over me. The mixture of the dirt and rain exposed her body. I dug deeper.

"THIS IS NOT MY FAULT! She is the one to blame; she trapped me in with her evil honey eyes, that intoxicating red skin and seductive touch of hers!"

I stood there looking at the place where I had buried them, the shovel still my hand. The rain kept falling, making it almost impossible to see clearly or maybe it was my tears that were making it hard for me to see.

I hoped, more or less prayed that God would let these raindrops cleanse me. I wiped the tears from my face trying to clear my head, but my anger was getting the best of me! I threw the shovel down.

I had loved Reya, but our love was different. It was dangerous and I knew it, somewhere I knew

Reya was thrown the fuck off. I didn't do a damn thing to change it, and this was the ending. I picked up the shovel and tossed it in the trunk.

I jumped when I witnessed lightning strike the area where they were buried! I saw the earth bubble. I grabbed the bag of roses and shook it on top the bubbling earth.

I ran back to the car. As I got in, I heard them crying. I calmed them down, telling them I know they are scared but they don't have be because daddy is here.

We drove to the nearest dumpster and threw everything from the lawn bag and then burned it. I never looked back at the flames. I was afraid of looking back at the past now. I went to a store and bought the kids a diaper bag, clothes; you know stuff to take care of them. I went to my dad's house telling him that Trisha had twins.

He was happy to see Nick and Raven. The police came to my dad's house to tell me that Trisha was missing and about the phone call they received about me.

Confessions in Whispers

They investigated me for two months. By that time, I had got Raven's stuff; Reya had left everything with her brother. I went to Trisha's house to collect Nick's stuff and helped clear out the house with her parents. The police closed the case and I tried to live a normal life.

It was a long time before I really started getting the hang of raising two kids on my own. Raven had her mother's temper. I was always telling her that she needed to cool it. Nicholas was calm and content. He was a bit of cry baby when he couldn't have his way but for the most part both of them were great kids. It was at night when they were sleeping that I worried if they dreamed of the horrible way their mothers died.

I forcefully lay awake in the middle of the night to check on them. I was happy to see they were sleeping peacefully in their beds. Maybe they were watching over them.

My dad let us stay with him; eventually I told him everything.

He just said, "I bet you now understand how addictive women can be and the error of betraying their hearts; it can be a killer son."

He was never more right. I understood it all too well now, it was a damn shame it took all of this drama for me to realize it.

*

It's now been a year since it all happened and I still couldn't forget the shit that went on between Trisha, Reya, and I. I still saw them in my dreams; some of the worst parts still played back in my mind. I now blamed most of this shit on myself, if I had just...DAMN, nothing could bring them back!

I went back to the field at times on my own; I talked to them and begged them to forgive me for being so damn stupid. Today, I am standing here with my children. We are having a picnic with their mothers. As they run over to me each carrying a different color rose in their hands, I remember the two women I loved so much in two vastly different ways. I thought back to Reya and Trisha, and how much I loved them, how much I put them both

Confessions in Whispers

through, and how my selfishness made them both my most torturous addiction.

About the Author

Chimia Y. Hill-Burton was born in Chattanooga, Tennessee in December of 1981. She was raised in Giessen, Germany. Chimia is the proud daughter of Arline Agwai and Eric Hill. She is the eldest child of four children, her brothers Henry, Lemuel, and sister Hadijah. Even as a child Chimia had a great imagination, that she used to entertain her friends, and family with.

Chimia's creative talents started at twelve years old and flourished then after. During her adolescent years, Chimia continued to write. Stories, poems, and figurative writings were all her favorites. Chimia graduated from John McEachern in June of 2000.

Chimia then attended Chattahoochee Technical College where she majored in Criminal Justice. After graduating in 2004, Chimia attended Mercer University receiving her bachelor's in Social Science in 2008. Chimia wrote the manuscript for Beautiful & Hero in 2008. Chimia currently resides in Atlanta, Georgia.

"My passion for writing is a testament of the thoughts, troubles, joy and happiness of the human heart."

Sincerely,

Chimia Hill-Burton

CapricornAngel Books Presents

From the New Suspense Series:

Confessions in Whispers

Book II:

Darker Endeavors

Endeavor 1
Confess

"Where shall we start?"
I looked at my newest client, Phil Motors. He was an average white man, heavy in weight with glasses...blah blah you know one of those computer geek types.
I leaned back in my chair, adjusting to get comfortable. I had a feeling this one was going to be boring. You know the type.
"I have always been fat; people have always alienated me... blah blah.... Sigh blah."
I snapped back to my reality.
"Mr. Laxton? Did you hear me?"
I blinked realizing I had not been paying him any attention. I'm terribly sorry Mr. Motors, I was thinking about something else."
His face suddenly reddened a little...
"Awe I've hurt his little feelings."

I contained myself, and then continued, "Mr. Motors, will you please start again."

I reached for the recorder and was about to press play. He looked down at the recorder trembling. "Are you going to record me?"

I raised an eyebrow then stated in my professional voice,

"Yes Mr. Motors, this is so we may reference back on your progress in future sessions."

He seemed to regain color back on his face. He collected himself. "I was worried you were going to do something horrible with that."

I became a little intrigued so I asked, "And just what might that be Mr. Motors? Have you been recorded before?"

I carefully watched his eyes, then his face as he bit his lower lip, eyes cast down at the carpeted floor of my office. Okay now I was interested. I adjusted myself in my chair and leaned forward. "Mr. Motors?"

He still kept his eyes on the floor. He was shutting down. Okay, time for a different approach. I reached out and patted his knee.

Then in my humble and sincere voice, I said, "Phil?"

He seemed about to cry. By his reaction, it looked like his pain ran deep, but he then smiled at me.

"No one calls me that. You must be the first person to ever do it."

As I watched him regain his composure, I shook my head, yeah, he had been invisible his entire life.

"Phil, why has no one ever called you by your first name?" He sat up, cleared his throat, and said, "Because she told everyone that my name was Demon."

I raised both eyebrows. "Demon, huh." I thought to myself, Phil may not be boring after all…

I sat back in my chair and crossed my leg. "Please continue."

I pressed they play button on the recorder. Phil began to tell me the story of his relationship with his overly Christian mother. She called him a Demon because he was born out of wedlock. She was seduced by the devil she said, and Phil was the product of her sin.

Phil continued with telling me that she tortured him daily. She over fed him on purpose hoping he would die. Wow! She was the Demon! Poor Phil was going through hell! I looked at him; he was about to cry again.

"Phil, do you need a minute?"

He nodded, so I let him take five minutes. Then I give him directions to the restroom. Once he is gone, I leaned back in my chair.

The thought of the guy's mom torturing him was a turn on. I could see her yelling at him, making him feel small. I loosened my tie a little as I fantasized the pain. I knew she must hit him.

Yes, this was her secret obsession. Poor Phil was just the outlet. She wasn't a Christian, that was just her cover for a dark nasty little secret. OH YES, I LOVED THIS! I accidently blurted it out loud. I laughed, then collected myself as Phil came back into the room.

"Are you okay now, Phil?" He nodded as he asks if he should continue. I was screaming in my head, "Yes! Confess! Tell Me Every Dirty Detail!"

I could feel my body grow hot as I excused myself a minute to sip a drink of water from my cup. Come on Troy don't blow your top. I motioned for him to continue as I continue to drink my water.

"I'm sorry, I got emotional but what I am going to say next just really gets to me."

He sighed, looked down, and then whispered, "She sexually tortured me."

I paused drinking.

"Okay. Are you comfortable telling me how?"

He took a deep breath. "She spanked my testicles with a paddle." Oh shit! I gotta hear this! I sat my cup down. "Okay. Is that all?"

He shook his head and explained. "She sat on my face and smothered me till I passed out, she wrapped my penis with shoestring, and smacked me!"

I smirked. "Phil, are you here because she tortured you or because you liked it?"

Phil bit his lower lip then blushes bright red.

"Yes Mr. Laxton, I loved it! I got so hard and came every time she tortured me. That's the reason she called me a demon. She said I was a dark sinner that would never be able to repent. But I wanted her to beat and torture me. I wanted to be her demon."

I nodded slightly, I kinda understood why he felt that way. She showed her affection and love for him that way and doing it this way she could have him with her forever.

"Well Phil, I say if you are happy with your mom then stay happy."

Phil smiled for the first time. He jumped out of his chair. "I will! Thank you, Mr. Laxton."

Phil left after that. Once he was gone, I locked the door to my office. I sat down, plugged my headphones to the recorder and replay the session. As I listened to the details again and unzipped my pants, reaching for my throbbing hard on. I couldn't contain myself as I stroke myself, thinking of Phil's mom. Though he never gave any details of what she looked like, I could imagine a woman brutally torturing her son for hours. I lost concentration as I pleasured myself, letting my imagination run wild. I could see her standing there beating the hell out of him. Oh yes! Beat that fat fuck baby. I finally felt a tingle, telling me I was coming. I sighed as I felt the relief of my addiction being satisfied.

After a while, I got myself together and finished my report. I looked at my schedule; I had another new client. Aww, a female this time. I looked at the name on the file, Danielle Heart.

I skimmed through the file a minute, trying to guess if anything would be interesting about her.

Hmmm, now let me see here/ We have an obvious abusive childhood, boring. Inability to maintain relationships, even more boring. Damn it, she didn't have anything that would make her even remotely attractive.

I tossed the file back on my desk, and then rubbed my temples. I had nothing to calm myself with.

I opened my desk drawer and pulled out one of my old favorites. Kissing it lightly, I heard the buzzing from my phone. I put the tape down then, answered the phone.

"Yes., Patrice."

Patrice Manners was a sweet forty-five-year-old Caucasian woman. She had worked in my practice for the last six years. She was dependable and codependent. Her husband was killed in a car accident right before she accepted this job.

"I'm sorry to disturb you but your two-thirty is here, Mr. Laxton." I cleared my throat before answering, "Thank you, Patrice." Okay she was early; this would be over before it even began …. sigh, how boring.

I took my place in my soft chair. "You can show her in, Patrice."

I grabbed my pen and pad, then started writing down a quick note. I heard the door and looked up. I gasped a little as I saw the stunning creature taking a seat in front of me. She smiled. I looked around for her file. It was still on my desk, damn it!

I start to get out of the chair, explaining, "I'm sorry, I left your file on my desk, just a moment…

She got up. "I'll get it for you."

She retrieved the file, returned to her seat and smiled openly as she handed it to me. Oh my! This may not be boring after all; she was clearly trying to flirt with me, and it was working well. Bravo young lady. I nod as I took the file.

"So, what brings you to my office, Ms. Heart."

She sat up straight, crossed her ebony thighs together and said, "You can call me Danielle. I'm here because I have a problem. I am suicidal."

I tried to concentrate on her words, but they were fuzzy. I was into her body. Damn, why did I not have a picture of her first? I could have prepared myself for her earlier.

"And why do you feel this way, Danielle?"

She shrugged her shoulders. She was not suicidal; she wanted attention. Okay, I could play this game with her.

"Okay, have you attempted to kill yourself, Danielle?"

She shook her head, then made a gun with her fingers, placing it to her temple and pretended to pull the trigger.

"Does that count?"

I half smiled; she knew what she was doing. She liked my reaction.

"It counts. Should I place you on a treatment, Danielle?"

Her eyes sparkled as she smiled. "What treatment are you recommending me to take, doctor?"

I looked at her, she was a piece a work. She was either a sex addict or bipolar, either way I was turned on right now.

"There are various treatments you can undergo...." She interrupted me, "Would you be taking care of me personally, doctor?"

I smirked, she wanted me to treat her personally, huh?

"Well, if you would like me to monitor your progress, then yes."

She shook her head. "No, I mean YOU take care of me personally, Doctor?"

She flicked her fresh weave to her back and leaned forward. I could see down her loose-fitting blouse. Her luscious breasts looked back at me hungrily.

She reached out and touched my knee softly. I tried to keep cool but then leaned forward and stared into her eyes. Normally, I would not condone a patient's behavior but for some reason she just made me want to know more. She was still a mystery and I liked that. She was not even half open and right now she was craving a fix. I will oblige her for now.

    I grabbed her hand and pulled her towards me. She didn't pull back as I she straddled me. I could feel her full and thick thighs grazing my pants. Her ass rested comfortably in my lap.

    I placed my hands on her well arched back and stared up at her. She smiled down at me as she slowly began to rock on me. I smiled, but then looked over at the door. She turned and looked too. Without a word, she got up and locked the door for me, and then returned to my lap. Our kiss was not a passionate one, but a deliberate one. Nothing was sexy but more of an animal lust. She didn't wait for an answer, and just pulled off her blouse over her head. Her hair framed her face beautifully. I could only admire it a minute as I dived between her D-cup breasts and inhaled her soft scent. I snapped her bra off and sucked her nipples violently. The moans that escaped her mouth made the action that more intense. I clawed at her body, and she grabbed me tightly between my thighs.

Kicking the coffee table, to the side, I picked her up and placed her on the floor. She ripped my shirt.... Fuck, I just bought this! She better be damn glad she was fucking sexy as she was. I snatched off her pants and thong. I wasted no time entering her walls.

Danielle's actions were not of romance; she looking to get fucked. I could handle that. We fucked for about two hours. Our kisses were more optional during the entire act. She liked to be dominated but was dominate herself.

Once it was all over, I just got up and looked in my closet for another shirt. She stood up, got dressed and then sat on my desk. I also got dressed, then looked at her rocking back and forth on my desk. Yes, she was sexy, and now that I had satisfied myself with her, I could back to my job.

I watched her looking over my desk, and I saw it. Damn it, I forgot to put it back in my desk drawer.

She picked up the tape. "Is this a recording of a patient?"

I walked over and attempted to take it from her. She leaned back, shaking her head.

"Don't be like that, I wanna hear it."

I walked in between her legs and then leaned over, snatching the tape. As I got ready to move, she wrapped her legs around my waist. I shook my head. She was not buying it and pulled me closer to her. She wrapped her arms around my neck.

"Danielle, our session is over for today."

She laughed softly as she kisses my neck, then the fire is lit again.

"Is it Doctor?"

I grabbed her and began to take off her pants. She lifted her soft ass so they could slip off. I fucked her right on my desk. She was going to be hard to break I saw, oh well, as long as I could get my fill who cared. Once we finished for the second time, we left together. Patrice had already left.

She strutted to her car, got in and drove off. I locked up my office and get into my car. My phone rang. It was my boy, Tyler Worth. "Sup Ty."

"Where the hell are you, we are supposed to meet everybody at seven, Troy."

I sighed; going to my sister's engagement party was not at all thrilling for me, even when she is marrying my best friend. "Troy! Troy!"

I could hear him calling my name, but I was ignoring him because I didn't want to do this right now.

"I was working late tonight with a new patient. That's why I was running late."

I hear him sigh. "How sexy is she, Troy?"

I laughed because only my best friend would know I never stay late at work unless it was sexual.

"On a scale from one-ten, her sex was twenty."

"Troy, you are a dog. You took advantage of that broken woman for your own sick reasons."

I sighed; Ty has become such a boy scout since he decided to marry my sister.

"Yes, I did but it was amazing."

I could hear her voice in the background.

"Are you seriously blowing out of your best friend and sister's engagement for meaningless sex with another disturbed patient?"

I pause a moment to process my sister's question. Did I really continue that second round with Danielle because I didn't want to be there? Maybe, but since I was now sitting in front of my parent's house, I didn't go long enough to miss it.

I hung up the phone and walked up the steps to my parents' house. I didn't want to do this right now. I started to turn around and head down the steps when I heard the door open.

"You can't leave now Troy."

It was Tyler. "I don't want to be here Ty. You know why I don't want be here either."

He shook his head, and then marched down the stairs and grabbed my arm, dragging me up the stairs. I struggled to get free from him, but he didn't let go until I was in the house and the door was locked behind him. He then looked at me whispering, "This is not the time for your bullshit, okay Troy? I love Nikki okay, get over it. I am your friend, but I thought you would be happy for me since I was serious about your sister."

I snatched away from him. "What! Do you want my blessings now? Fuck you Tyler, you fucked my sister and got her pregnant."

He wiped his face. "What is the big deal?"

I grabbed his shirt slamming him into the door.

"It's not a big deal to you! Nikki is only seventeen, you asshole! Your thirty-five-year-old ass should be in jail, but because my family loves you, so it's okay! Well, I am still having a hard-fucking time accepting the fact you have been sleeping with my baby sister since she was thirteen."

I was about to say something else when I heard from behind me, "Leave me him alone T, just let him go okay?"

I turned to look into Nikki's eyes. I released Ty's shirt. He walked over to Nikki and hugged her.

"Go and sit-down baby, you are going to make the baby upset."

Nikki shook her head and walked over to me. She smiled sweetly, and said, "You can't protect me forever Troy, I have to grow up someday."

I hugged her tightly, I had no real reason to hate my sister, and she was so grown up that you would have never guessed she was seventeen. I nodded and kept my mouth shut for the rest of the night. I saw no point in it. I watched my family enjoy the party with a pedophile. Now I saw why I craved the lives of others to get me by, I had no life of my own.

I left early because what was the point of pretending, I was happy for them when I clearly was not. Oh well, back to my own void of a life. Walking into my four- bedroom house was almost an oxymoron. Why did I have all this space when it was just me? Well, that was the beginning of the void.

I was once happy and married. Funny when I stared that these walls, I still got a sense of calm even after what happened. Betrayal ran deep in my life. No wonder I had issues trusting anyone. I came home one beautiful evening to find my wife in bed with her own sister. Yes, not another man, or woman...her own flesh and blood. I admit, because of this unique arrangement, I was immediately turned on. Oh yes, walking in on them gave me a live action movie I would never forget. At first, I was surprised, then instantly as if someone lit my fire, I was hot, boiling hot! It didn't take my time and I jumped in bed with them. She protested of course, but it was far too late for that.

I grabbed her sister by the hair, pulling her to my lips, kissing her forcefully. My wife tried to fight me, but I slammed her face first into the covers. I mounted her like a raging beast and violently had my way with both of them. No seduction, pure revenge for my pain.

It lasted a blissful three days, yes, because I refused to let them leave my bedroom. You wanted to cheat on me, then you should know I was not the forgiving type. I fucked them blindly and violently for hours at a time. Oh yes, one would try to run but stayed at the thought of me breaking the others neck. They had no choice but to stay with me. Yes, even now it still made me smile. I dare not speak her filthy name any longer. My actions relieved my heart break for a woman I had actually tried to love in my life. How naive of me to ever believe that I could love so happily.

On the last day I gave them both a choice. They could stay in the room with me, and I would make them either my sex slaves or they could each brand themselves with a tattoo for my pain and leave.

Both didn't have agreeable futures, but funny enough they went for the second option for my silence about their relationship. My wife pleaded, "Please just get it over with Troy, we do not want our family finding out about this, so please."

The grin that came across my face was priceless because the fear in their eyes enticed my every move. I told them to stay at the house and I would be back. I went to my favorite tattoo artist Kyle and told him I needed a private session done at my house tonight.

"Private session huh, sounds kinky...Okay, I'll be there."

I drove back to the house. Surprisingly, they were both still there in bed getting it on again. I just stood in the doorway, shaking my head as I watched them caress and embrace each other. They each had a sickening addiction with one another. I tapped lightly on the door to get their attention. I laughed as they both gasped at my presence.

"I'm having a déjà vu right now, but didn't I catch you doing this like three days ago?"

Made in the USA
Columbia, SC
13 July 2021